THE DOLDRUMS

AND THE
HELMSLEY CURSE

Written and illustrated by

NICHOLAS GANNON

GREENWILLOW BOOKS
An Imprint of HarperCollins*Publishers*

The Doldrums and the Helmsley Curse
Text and illustrations copyright © 2017 by Nicholas Gannon
First published in hardcover in 2017, first Greenwillow paperback, 2018.

The text of this book is set in Joanna.
Book design by Christy Hale

Library of Congress Cataloging-in-Publication Data

Names: Gannon, Nicholas, author, illustrator.
Title: The Doldrums and the Helmsley curse /
written and illustrated by Nicholas Gannon.
Description: First edition. | New York : Greenwillow Books, an
imprint of HarperCollinsPublishers, [2017] |
Summary: "Archer Helmsley's grandparents have finally returned
home, but there are rumors they've brought a curse with them"
—Provided by publisher.
Identifiers: LCCN 2017026259 | ISBN 9780062320988 (paperback)
Subjects: | CYAC: Eccentrics and eccentricities—Fiction. |
Family life—Fiction. | Friendship—Fiction. | Explorers—Fiction. |
Humorous stories. |
BISAC: JUVENILE FICTION / Social Issues / Friendship. |
JUVENILE FICTION / Family / Multigenerational. |
JUVENILE FICTION / Humorous Stories.
Classification: LCC PZ7.1.G36 Dor 2017 | DDC [Fic]—
dc23 LC record available at https://lccn.loc.gov/2017026259

18 19 20 21 22 PC/LSCH 10 9 8 7 6 5 4 3 2 1

 Greenwillow Books

PRAISE FOR

THE
DOLDRUMS

Indies Next Pick   **Indies Introduce Pick**   **ABA Best Book of 2015**

Junior Library Guild Selection   **Amazon Best Book of the Month**

"A dreamy charmer of a book, full
of clever wordplay that practically
demands it be read out loud."
                    —*New York Times*

"Amusing, heartwarming, and zany."
        —*Kirkus Reviews* (STARRED REVIEW)

"Gannon reveals himself as a skilled
storyteller, both in his writing and
artwork. . . . It's a tender tale of
friendship, untapped courage, and
accidental adventure, filled with
the spirit of exploration."
        —*Publishers Weekly* (STARRED REVIEW)

THE
DOLDRUMS
AND THE
HELMSLEY CURSE

Indies Next Pick

"In this wildly whimsical stand-alone
sequel to *The Doldrums*, Nicholas
Gannon once again thrills and chills
his readers with the adventures of
characters who could have stepped
out of A Series of Unfortunate Events,
The Invention of Hugo Cabret, or
Withering-by-Sea."—*Shelf Awareness*

"Irresistible for fans of Brian
Selznick's multimedia stories or
Lemony Snicket's series about
similarly clever children outwitting
misguided adults."—*Booklist*

"[A] fast-paced and quirky
adventure. . . . Eccentric
characters, exciting action,
eye-catching spot art, and full-
page illustrations throughout."
                    —*School Library Journal*

THE

DOLDRUMS

AND THE
HELMSLEY CURSE

To Patrick and Gannon,
and Staple Guns and Dump Trucks

✦ TABLE OF CONTENTS ✦

✦ Snowflakes and Rumors ✦

The city of Rosewood was humming with rumors. They swirled every which way, across snowy rooftops and down narrow streets.

"How is it possible? It's been two years!"

They were exchanged in shops along Howling Bloom Street and slurped in Belmont Café.

"Are you saying you think we've been duped?"
"What would they have eaten?"

They were laughed about in student rooms at the Willow Academy and gulped in handfuls at DuttonLick's sweetshop.

"Weren't there penguins on the iceberg?"
"You think they survived by eating penguins?"

It was a blizzard of rumors. They piled as high as the snow. There were hundreds of answers to one single question:

ROSEWOOD CHRONICLE

HOW DID RALPH AND RACHEL HELMSLEY SURVIVE STRANDED ATOP AN ICEBERG?

Ralph and Rachel Helmsley were two of the city's most famed residents—explorers, once presumed dead, soon to return to their tall, skinny house on crooked, narrow Willow Street. And there wasn't a single person anticipating the explorers' return home more than their grandson, Archer B. Helmsley.

"Archer's dangerous. He set tigers loose in a museum just to see if he could outrun them!"

"I heard he can make acorns explode simply by looking at them."

"No, that's impossible. But he can turn a flamingo into a glass of pink lemonade when he's thirsty."

In truth, Archer couldn't make acorns explode or turn a flamingo into a glass of pink lemonade. But with the help of two friends and a life raft, Archer *had* outrun a pack of tigers. It had happened two months ago, during a botched rescue attempt to find his grandparents—who'd been missing from Archer's life since he was a mere two days old. As a result, for the past two months, Archer had been living at Raven Wood

Boarding School. His parents had insisted it was for his own good. And to make matters worse, just before he'd boarded the train north, Archer had discovered his grandparents were not only very much still alive—they were also finally coming home.

So Archer had missed the first rumor spread through Rosewood and the first snowflake fall on Willow Street. And he'd missed the countless others that followed. It had been a particularly cold start to winter—the kind of cold where if you wrinkled your nose, it could remain wrinkled forever. The whole of Rosewood had become a white sea, and the snow only got deeper with each passing day.

✦ CLANKING RADIATORS ✦

On North Willow Street, in the cellar of house number 376, a boiler was hard at work, forcing steam into pipes that traveled up four stories to a top-floor bedroom, where a radiator was hissing and clanking and Adélaïde Belmont sat at her desk, writing a letter.

> *. . . I haven't seen your grandparents yet.*
> *But everyone in Rosewood is talking about them . . .*

Adélaïde paused and glanced over her shoulder. Her friend and neighbor Oliver Glub stood a few feet from her desk.

"I might be able to sled over to your bedroom soon," he said, his face pressed to her balcony window.

Adélaïde joined him, both watching as snowflakes piled the secret Willow Street gardens high.

"I've never seen so much snow," Adélaïde said. "Those garden walls are seven feet tall, but I almost can't tell where one garden ends and the other begins."

Oliver lived diagonally across those snowy gardens. Next door to him was Helmsley House. Archer's house. But Archer's bedroom was dark. And had been ever since the tiger incident.

"Do you think he knows what they're saying about his grandparents?" Oliver asked.

"I can't tell," Adélaïde replied, returning to her desk. "He's never written about it. And even if we *were* allowed to tell him, I wouldn't know which rumor to begin with."

Oliver didn't know either. There were new rumors every day. And they were getting worse.

Adélaïde finished her letter, stuffed it into an envelope alongside Oliver's, and said, "I'm ready."

◆ THROW CARES AWAY ◆

At the front door, they pulled on their coats and wrapped their scarves. Adélaïde wedged a second scarf into her boot to fill the gap around her wooden leg. They trudged down the front steps and forged the sidewalk snow trenches. The sun was gone and the stars were out and the lampposts lit their way.

"If I didn't know any better," Oliver said, helping Adélaïde over a snowbank, "I'd think we actually made it to Antarctica."

On the corner, they passed a group of carolers.

Hark how the bells, sweet silver bells
All seem to say, "Throw cares away."
Christmas is here, bringing good cheer.

They turned onto Howling Bloom Street—a winding lane lined with small shops, including a corner café that belonged to Adélaïde's father. Bundled store owners stood high atop ladders, decking their windows with lights and garlands and festive displays while shoppers gathered to watch.

"Mind your heads!" Mr. Bray of Bray and Ink shouted as Oliver and Adélaïde dashed beneath his ladder. "That's bad luck!"

When they reached Belmont Café, their faces were red and stiff, but inside, it was crowded and warm, with steaming cups of coffee all around. Adélaïde scanned the overflowing bar. The barman caught her eye and shouted, "TWO HOT CHOCOLATES, ADIE?" Adélaïde nodded and led Oliver through the buzzing café to a table in the corner. Oliver unwrapped his scarf and tilted his head. Adélaïde did the same. A newspaper had been left on the table.

ROSEWOOD CHRONICLE
ICEBERG HOAX!

Another day, another rumor. Rosewood is perfectly drunk with them. And it's time you all stop drinking. But before you do, we ask that you stretch out your tankards one last time and allow *us* to refill them. We at the *Chronicle* have been informed that Ralph and Rachel Helmsley orchestrated their own disappearance. That's right, the iceberg was nothing more than a hoax!

Where does this information come from? A man whose name, while not as famous as Helmsley's, might be familiar to some: Herbert P. Birthwhistle—the sitting president of the Society.

"We're still gathering information," President Birthwhistle said via telephone from the Scotland Society. "But I can say without hesitation that the iceberg was no accident. We know the Helmsleys got onto an iceberg and that after an exhaustive search, the Helmsleys could not be found. We believe the Helmsleys did not *want* to be found."

For those unfamiliar, the Society is an organization of explorers and naturalists headquartered in Barrow's Bay.

"I hate to speak ill of a fellow explorer," President Birthwhistle elaborated, "so I will not go into the details, but while president, Ralph Helmsley had made increasingly bizarre decisions. Many of our members suspected the aging explorers had lost their minds. Many believed they were out to destroy our Society. An effort was taken up to unseat Ralph. When faced with this disgrace, the Helmsleys vanished.

"Vanishing in Antarctica has made legends of already-great explorers. I suspect the Helmsleys desired to join their numbers.

"I'm not sure how they survived. I'm not sure why they're suddenly coming home. But they are. Society members have been alerted. And I felt it my duty to extend a similar warning to the citizens of Rosewood. It's not with a light heart that I say the Helmsleys are a danger to everyone."

"This is *bad*," Adélaïde said, tearing the article from the paper as her father wove through the crowded café. He set two hot chocolates before them, and they scooped them up to warm their hands.

"It's good to see you again, Olrich," Mr. Belmont said.

"His name is *Oliver*," Adélaïde replied, grinning.

"That's nice."

A rush of cold air shot through the café as a short woman in a flowery coat dashed inside.

"Cold!" the woman cried, slamming the door behind her. "So terribly cold! So terribly cold indeed! Never in my life, never, not once have I experienced a winter so cold! It truly *must* be a curse! Yes, it's the Helmsley Curse!"

Many in the café echoed, "The Helmsley Curse!" The *Rosewood Chronicle* had coined that phrase to explain why the city was plunging into the harshest winter any of its residents could remember.

"The closer the Helmsleys get, the colder it gets," someone grumbled. "They're bringing their iceberg home."

"They should lock down the port. We shouldn't let them in."

The woman in the flowery coat bobbed her head in agreement and squeezed in at the bar. "A quadruple! Make it a quadruple! And make it *hot*!"

"The cold hasn't been a curse for business," Mr. Belmont mumbled, and returned to the bar.

Oliver wiped away his chocolate mustache. "I don't believe in curses," he whispered.

Adélaïde pointed out that Oliver also had something of a chocolate beard before responding. "I don't either. But you have to admit that all of this is *very* strange."

"My father says the *Chronicle* is tabloid trash," Oliver replied, reading the story once more. His father, Mr. Glub, owned a much smaller Rosewood newspaper called the *Doldrums Press.* "Archer's grandparents *lost their minds?* They *wanted* to vanish?"

"Who would make that up?" Adélaïde asked, swirling a finger through the steam rising from her mug. "Do you really not believe any of it?"

Oliver opened his mouth to respond, but filled it with hot chocolate instead.

✦ THREE HOURS BY TRAIN ✦

"We'd better go," Oliver said, gulping the last of his hot chocolate. "They'll be picking up the mail soon."

Adélaïde and Oliver left the café and crossed Foldink Street. The postbox was buried in the snow. Oliver wiped the door clean and pulled hard to open it. Adélaïde dropped the letter inside.

"How far away is Raven Wood, anyway?" she asked.

"Three hours by train," he replied.

And by train was exactly how their letter would travel. It was picked up later that evening, sorted at the post office, sent in a dirty bag to Rosewood Station, and tossed into a mail car. The train pushed north through Rosewood, clanked across a bridge spanning the frozen canal, and continued far outside the city. It snaked a rocky shoreline, billowing smoke high above snow-covered pines, till it arrived in the village of Stonewick. The letters were sorted once more and placed into the back of a mail truck. The truck puttered off into a thick pine forest, slid beneath a crooked wrought-iron gate, and entered a clearing where stood, at the edge of a cliff, Raven Wood Boarding School.

THE

DOLDRUMS

AND THE
HELMSLEY CURSE

PART ONE

AN ICEBERG IN ROSEWOOD

✦ RAVEN WOOD ✦

Archer couldn't sleep. He stretched a frozen hand out of bed and fiddled with the radiator knob, but it was no use. Like many things at Raven Wood, the heating was terrible.

Across the room, his roommate, Benjamin Birthwhistle, was snoring loudly.

Keeping his blanket pulled tight about him, Archer tiptoed to his desk and stared out his drafty window. Morning snow was falling onto the ocean waves, breaking against rocks. It wasn't exactly a cheery view, but Archer liked it. That ragged coastline connected him all the way back to Rosewood.

He grabbed a pen from his desk and put another X on his calendar. "One day left," he mumbled.

The train for Rosewood would leave tomorrow afternoon. Tomorrow he'd be reunited with Oliver and Adélaïde. But would anyone else be waiting for him? Archer's parents hadn't spoken to him since he'd left for Raven Wood, which didn't surprise him. But during his two and half months at the school, he hadn't heard from his grandparents either. He hadn't heard a word since they'd sent him a chunk of iceberg in the post. Were they already inside Helmsley House? Archer didn't know. And not knowing made him anxious.

Behind him, Benjamin stopped snoring. Archer glanced over his shoulder.

"Why are you up so early, Archer?" Benjamin asked, blinking at him sleepily.

"I was too cold. I couldn't sleep."

Benjamin stuck his feet out from beneath the blankets. They were twice the size they should have been.

"Your feet are swollen," Archer said, sitting down at his desk. "Did the spider come back? Did it bite you?"

Benjamin grinned and shook his head.

The night before, the two boys had gone to war against a large spider that had crawled into their room. Archer threw a lamp, three books, and to Benjamin's horror, a potted plant, but the eight-legged fiend had escaped unharmed.

"They're just socks," Benjamin said over a yawn. "I've got four pairs on." He rubbed his long, tousled hair. A leaf fell out. "But I wonder where that spider came from."

Archer thought it was obvious. Benjamin's side of the room was filled with plants, and Benjamin's desk was barely visible beneath them. They were strange plants—plants unlike any he'd seen growing in the Willow Street gardens.

Archer leaned over to poke at one on Benjamin's desk. "This one looks like it would sprout spiders."

"Is that my bog weed?" Benjamin asked. "Or the didactus that sprouted yesterday? If it has pink speckled leaves, then it's pugwort."

Archer had learned enough during his time as Benjamin's roommate to know the plant he was pointing to wasn't any of those. This one had long, spiraling stems covered in bumps, as though something inside was trying to get out.

"*Oh*," Benjamin said, stumbling stiffly to his desk. "That's my *Paria glavra*. Be careful with that one. It can be a bit hostile."

"*Hostile?*" Archer repeated, and quickly withdrew his hand.

Benjamin opened his notebook and inspected the plant more closely. "Like most *Parias*, the *glavras* starts off harmless," he explained. "But eventually it will become dangerous. Deadly, even."

Archer threw off his blanket and hurried to the corner sink to wash his hands. The last thing he wanted was to die before meeting his grandparents for the first time.

"The thorns haven't sprouted," Benjamin called, measuring the bumps with a pen. "The thorns are what you need to watch out for."

Thorns or not, Archer should have learned by now not to touch plants unless Benjamin said it was safe. He soaped his hands as Benjamin noted growths and observations in his notebook. It was almost like homework. Benjamin had once told him that if he knew what plants could do, he'd understand. But all Archer thought was that, in a funny way, Benjamin's long, leafy hair and tall, sticklike body made him resemble one of his seedlings.

"I want to go to the mail room after breakfast," Archer said, drying his hands and shoving his feet into his boots.

"*Again?*" Benjamin replied, struggling to pull a third sweater over his head. "That's why you couldn't sleep, isn't it? It's not the cold. It's your grandparents."

Benjamin was right. Archer hadn't slept for the past week.

"Maybe they finally wrote."

Benjamin sat on his bed to tie his shoelaces, staring as Archer pressed his ear to the door. Not many students attended Raven Wood, but when the few converged in the dusty, dimly lit corridors, they became something of a thundering horde.

"Let's wait a moment," Archer said. "You don't want to get trampled again."

"That was terrible," Benjamin replied, laughing. He pulled a collared shirt from his trunk. "Look. The footprint *still* won't wash out!"

Raven Wood students were kept to a very tight schedule, and there were steep consequences for being late. Archer was often late, but he never got into trouble.

Benjamin tossed the shirt back into his trunk. "You're lucky Mr. Churnick likes you."

· FORTUNATE CONSEQUENCES ·

Mr. Churnick was Raven's Wood's head of school, a somewhat crusty and thickset man whose overgrown teeth were often speckled with bits of cheesecake. Mr. Churnick was terribly fond of cheesecake. He was also quite fond of Archer, which was surprising considering his welcome when Archer had first arrived.

"I'm not in the habit of allowing *troubled* children into my school, Archer Helmsley. But as it is, Raven Wood has fallen on hard times. So against my better judgment, there you sit."

Archer's mother hadn't spared the slightest detail in listing every offense he'd ever committed. It had all been there in Mr.

Churnick's file, from talking to taxidermied animals to the tiger incident.

"Set tigers lose in a museum, did you?" he'd grumbled. "Nearly got *hundreds* killed! But your antics only claimed one victim. That's fortunate. Yes, it says here that you seriously damaged one Mrs. Murk—Mrs. *Murkley*? *You* took down Mrs. Murkley? But you're so . . . and she's so—you flattened her with A POLAR BEAR!"

Mrs. Murkley was a former Raven Wood instructor who'd ended up becoming Archer's instructor at the Willow Academy. Archer, Oliver, and Adélaïde hadn't been sure what had prompted Mrs. Murkley's departure from Raven Wood, but knowing her to be a brutish terror, they'd all agreed it must have been something bad—maybe as bad as crushing a teacher beneath a polar bear.

"De-tusked the ol' boar, did you, Archer?" Mr. Churnick had erupted into laughter and nearly fallen off his chair. "Justice has finally been served! By *you*! But how did I not hear about this sooner? Good news always travels slower than bad news, I suppose."

Archer hadn't understood Mr. Churnick's mirth at the time. And Benjamin had been no help in figuring it out. Benjamin was a temporary boarder. He only came to Raven Wood when his father, a travel guide, went away for long periods. (Benjamin never mentioned anything about his mother. Archer wasn't sure if he had one.) But eventually Archer pieced together the Murkley tale.

Though the exact details varied from source to source, all accounts followed the same basic premise: a boy named Phillip had fallen four stories from the Raven Wood rooftops and would have died had he not landed in a topiary shaped like a raven. It was *quite* a scandal. And Mrs. Murkley was at the center of it. Nothing could be proven, but most parents withdrew their children from the institution, leaving Raven Wood on the brink of bankruptcy. And Raven Wood looked it. The halls were filthy. Lights were always going out. The gardens were overgrown. And that's to say nothing of the food.

⋆ BENJAMIN'S LETTER ⋆

Archer and Benjamin scurried into the dining hall and took their usual spot in the corner. A miserable server plopped bowls before them with a surprising thud. Archer pried his spoon out and studied the white, clumpy slop.

"The oatmeal's getting worse," Benjamin groaned, staring despairingly at his bowl.

"I didn't think that was possible," Archer said, licking his spoon and quickly wishing he hadn't. "Now it tastes like cardboard and glue."

"And maybe a pound of lard?" Benjamin suggested.

Two large hands gripped Archer's shoulder.

"Morning, boys." Mr. Churnick was making his morning rounds. "Goodness, Archer! You're an ice cube! Sorry about the heating cuts. I'm doing the best I can. Must find ways to save money." Mr. Churnick leaned over Archer's shoulder to inspect their bowls. "At least the food has improved a bit."

"Would you mind if we skipped breakfast?" Archer asked, dropping his spoon into the bowl. "I want to go to the mailroom."

Mr. Churnick glanced around at the other students and nodded. "Quickly now. Don't make a show of it."

"I actually had a question for you, Archer," Mr. Churnick continued as they made for the mailroom. "It's about that Willow Academy. What's your opinion of it?"

Despite the fact that the school had expelled him, Archer had nothing against it. "It was fine before Mrs. Murkley showed up."

"That's what I'm curious about, Archer. I was discussing some important business with Mrs. Thimbleton, the head of school, but she wouldn't explain *why* she hired that festering oyster after I fired her. The decision was questionable at best, and I was hoping to get an opinion on the school from someone else."

"You could talk to Miss Whitewood," Archer suggested. "She's the librarian. She's very nice."

"Thanks for the tip, Archer. Now, try not to be late to class *again*. I think the teachers are catching on that your detention slips keep vanishing from my office."

Mr. Churnick slapped him on the back with a force that nearly sent him through a wall, and left the boys at the mailroom. Raven Wood's mailroom was a crevice of a space, dingy like everything else, and encircled with wooden slots. Benjamin rushed in before Archer and bumped into a small table. The stack of newspapers on top of it tumbled into an empty mail cart. Archer hurried to his slot, spotting a letter and two packages.

"Is that from your grandparents?" Benjamin asked, sounding almost nervous as he pulled a letter from his own slot.

"No, it's from Oliver and Adélaïde." Archer scratched a hot chocolate stain on the envelope. "But Mrs. Glub sent more pastries."

Benjamin pretended to swoon.

Oliver's mother was arguably the greatest pastry chef in Rosewood. And Archer was certain he'd have starved by now had it not been for her frequent care packages. Benjamin was equally grateful.

"Are *both* boxes for us?"

"One's a cheesecake for Mr. Churnick." Archer inspected the dampened box. "I hope it didn't get too smushed."

He slid it back into his slot and grabbed his letter and his other package, and they made for the school's front entrance. Archer pulled a coat from a hook and handed a second to Benjamin. They were adult coats that went well past their knees, but they didn't care. Benjamin followed him through a heavy oak door and down a stone walkway toward the sea.

"I don't understand why I haven't heard from my grandparents," Archer said, nearly slipping on an icy stone. "Or my parents. No one's saying anything."

"At least you're going home tomorrow." Benjamin sighed. "I'll be eating that slop on Christmas morning."

Archer grimaced. Benjamin's father was still traveling and he'd have to spend the entire winter holiday at Raven Wood. Archer didn't know much about Mr. Birthwhistle, but he couldn't shake the feeling he'd heard the name before. He'd told Benjamin as much, and Benjamin guessed he'd only imagined hearing it.

When they reached the seating area overlooking the sea, Archer used his extra-long coat sleeve to wipe snow off a bench, and they sat down. He opened the pastry box and handed Benjamin a walnut crumble muffin. Benjamin held it like a sacred object. Archer laughed and tore open his letter.

Dear Archer,

I hope you're doing well at Raven Wood. Things are still fine here. Well, Oliver has a black eye. He got into a fight with Charlie Brimble at the Button Factory. Charlie was making jokes about you and your family again so Oliver jumped in.

I think Oliver wanted to tell you about our new neighbor, a girl named Kana Misra, so I'll let him do that. But I think she likes him! (He gets angry every time I say that.)

I haven't seen your grandparents. But everyone in Rosewood is talking about them. Have you heard anything? I'm guessing they'll be home soon. And so will you.

We miss you,

Adélaïde

Dear Archer,

Charlie Brimble was making jokes about you at school. Adélaïde went after him, and she dragged me into it. I'm not sure what happened, but somehow I'm the one who got punched. Adélaïde's always had a death wish, but I think it's getting worse.

I forgot to tell you in my last letter—we have a new neighbor. She moved into Mrs. Murkley's old house. Diptikana Misra. I've never had a class with her, but she's that girl with dark hair and light blue fish eyes that never seem to see what they're looking at. Anyway, she's starting to creep me out. I've caught her staring at me a lot lately. She might even be spying on me. Adélaïde thinks something different, but I don't want to talk about that.

Safe travels,
Oliver
P.S. Our Christmas party is the night you get back.
Your father told mine you'd be there.
P.P.S. I have some news about DuttonLick's sweetshop.
But I've run out of room here, so I'll tell you when I
see you.

Archer could barely wait to see his friends again.

"I'll talk to Mrs. Glub when I get home," he said, folding the letters and tucking them back into the envelope. "I'll send you as many pastries as I can while I'm in Rosewood. And I was thinking, if I leave most of my things here and go home with an empty trunk, I could bring it back *filled* with—"

"I'm leaving tomorrow too," Benjamin said, lowering his letter. "My father cut his trip short. He's on his way back to Rosewood."

"Does that mean you won't be coming back to Raven Wood after the break?"

Benjamin nodded. He would return to his school in Rosewood, a small private institution called Drabblefort Academy. Archer was both upset and a little jealous. He secretly hoped his parents would let him stay in Rosewood after the winter holiday, but he felt certain his mother wouldn't hear of it. And now his only friend at Raven Wood was leaving for good? For Benjamin, at least, this should have been good news, but Benjamin didn't look pleased about it. He almost looked sick.

"Is something wrong?" Archer asked.

Benjamin took a bite of his walnut muffin and chewed slowly. "I've been thinking about your grandparents," he finally said. "You always speak very highly of them, but I was wondering, Archer, what if they're not what you think they are?" Benjamin took another bite. "There must be a reason your mother kept them away from you for nearly twelve years."

Archer plucked a walnut from his muffin. He had been only two days old when his parents struck an agreement with his grandparents that required the explorers to stay away from him until his twelfth birthday.

"My mother's disturbed by what they are," he explained, popping the walnut into his mouth. "She doesn't like that they're explorers. And she doesn't want me to end up like them."

"But what if she doesn't like *who* they are?" Benjamin asked. "What if they're not good people? What if they're *dangerous*?"

Archer almost laughed at the suggestion, but the laugh stayed inside his throat. Benjamin was perfectly serious. "Why would my grandparents be dangerous?" Archer asked.

"All I'm trying to say is you don't know your grandparents at all, Archer. And I think you should be ready for something you might not expect."

For the rest of that day, it seemed like Benjamin had lots

of other things he wanted to say, but though Archer prodded him, Benjamin stayed quiet. When they returned to their room that evening, Benjamin went straight to bed, despite it being their last night together. He even skipped his nightly plant inspection.

"Why won't you tell me what's wrong?" Archer asked.

Benjamin covered his head with a blanket.

"I'm just tired, is all. We have a long journey home tomorrow."

Archer tapped his fingers on his desk. Benjamin hadn't been this odd or quiet since their first week together. Did he not want to go home? Benjamin rarely spoke about his father. Maybe they didn't get on well. But what troubled Archer more was Benjamin's suggestion that his grandparents might be dangerous. Why would Benjamin say that?

Archer turned out the light and crawled into bed. When the hall clock chimed midnight, he was still wide awake. *Dangerous?* Archer peered across the oddly quiet room. Benjamin's head was still covered, but he wasn't snoring. Benjamin always snored.

CHAPTER

———◆———

TWO

◆ An Odd Farewell ◆

Archer's final hours at Raven Wood dragged, and Benjamin's continued silence only made them longer. When the final bell rang, Archer's scarlet trunk was already packed.

"Just go to the buses without me," Benjamin said, trying to make room inside his trunk for the *Paria glavra*.

Archer heaved his trunk out into the hall and went to Mr. Churnick's office. Mr. Churnick wasn't there, so Archer left the cheesecake on his desk alongside a thank-you note. On his way out, he bumped into Benjamin, who didn't look pleased about it. But together, they followed the shouts of teachers and a line of students boarding a rickety bus. After taking his seat, Archer spotted Mr. Churnick dashing out the school doors. The headmaster slid up to the bus windows and searched them till he and Archer were face-to-face. Mr. Churnick said something, but the engine roared and the bus pulled away and all Archer could do was wave, watching as Mr. Churnick grew smaller and smaller.

At Stonewick Station, excited students crowded into a train.

"Three weeks of no school!" someone shouted. Everyone cheered.

Benjamin sat down across from Archer, dug into his leather satchel, and set an emerald-green book on his lap. Benjamin was always poring over that book, filled with detailed plant drawings and descriptions.

"Did you know there's a place in Rosewood called the Society?" Archer asked. "I've never been there and I don't know much about it, but it's an organization of explorers and naturalists. My grandfather used to be its president. I'm hoping I'll get to see it while I'm home. You'd probably like it, too. I'm sure they have lots of great plant people."

Benjamin was still staring at his book, but Archer could tell he'd stopped reading.

"That sounds interesting," Benjamin said, turning a page. "They're called botanists, by the way."

Archer looked out the window.

The snowy pines gave way to more and more buildings as they pushed farther south. Three very long and very quiet hours later, the train crossed the frozen canal and entered Rosewood. Students crammed the windows to better see the darkened city dotted with lights. Benjamin pushed someone's elbow out of his face and grinned at Archer, but the grin vanished so quickly Archer thought he'd imagined it.

They arrived at Rosewood Station with a great rush. Train crew piled trunks and luggage on the platform. Archer and Benjamin wove through happy families greeting one another and found their trunks. Archer tried one last time to find out what was bothering Benjamin.

"We had a good time at Raven Wood, Archer," Benjamin said, searching the crowd. "But there's something I should have told you. I didn't want to. And even if I had, I don't think you'd have believed me. You'll understand soon enough. You're going to hate me." Benjamin grabbed one side of his trunk and nodded to a plump woman who was sprinting toward them. "That's Mrs. Fig. I'm staying with them until my father arrives."

"Welcome home, Benjamin!" Mrs. Fig cried, clamping the boy in a hug that could have split him in two. Her terribly festive bright green coat was blinding, and her jolly grin was almost frightening. "Digby was *so* thrilled to hear you'd be spending the holidays with us!"

Mrs. Fig's yuletide spirit melted the moment she noticed Archer.

"*You?*" She grabbed the other side of Benjamin's trunk and pulled him a safe distance. "You're Archer Helmsley, aren't you? Yes, I remember *you*. Nearly got my Digby eaten by tigers! And now all this about your grandparents—" Mrs. Fig shook a salami-like finger in his face. "You should all be ashamed of yourselves! Hurry now, Benjamin. You don't want to be anywhere near *that* one *or* his miserable family."

And just like that, Benjamin was gone.

Archer sat down on his trunk, thinking his friend had cracked. Had Benjamin eaten one too many bowls of Raven Wood oatmeal?

"Archer! Over here! Sorry I'm late!"

Archer's father was weaving his way through the crowd. Mr. Helmsley was a tall and skinny bifocaled lawyer—a fine and respectable profession, but a disappointing choice to Archer's grandparents.

"We heard the country air did wonders," Mr. Helmsley said, hugging Archer and then looking him over. "Mr. Churnick has been singing your praises ever since you left. Your mother wouldn't believe him at first. Have you lost weight? You didn't have much to lose!"

"The food at Raven Wood was terrible," Archer explained with a smile.

While Archer had always felt at odds with both his parents, he'd always been more comfortable around his father.

"Sounds like the same cuisine they served at my boarding school. I still have nightmares about it." Mr. Helmsley glanced at the clock. "But there will be plenty to eat at the Glubs' party tonight. And we'd best hurry, or your mother might add us to the soup!"

They hauled Archer's trunk out a station door and into a taxicab. Archer couldn't believe the snow as they set off. The mounds were almost as tall as the cab. Rosewood was completely buried.

"Have you heard anything about your grandparents?" Mr. Helmsley asked, cleaning his snow-speckled glasses with the end of his tie.

"No," Archer replied, watching snowflakes whirl past the window. "They never sent me a letter." He turned to his father, suddenly feeling more frightened than nervous. "Are they home?"

"Not yet. And you mustn't take it personally, Archer. They've been cryptic ever since news broke that they were still alive. From what little I've heard, they should arrive any day now."

◆ That Horrible Thing Is Back ◆

The taxi slid to a halt before Helmsley House. Archer and his father lugged the scarlet trunk up the icy front steps and heaved it into the foyer. It landed with a thud. Mrs. Helmsley poked her head from a door at the end of the hall. Archer's mother was usually quite poised and proper—a model for model citizens. But in that moment, she more resembled the frazzled Mrs. Glub.

"*Oh!* I thought you were *them*," she gasped.

"Any word?" Mr. Helmsley asked.

"No. And I know you don't think it necessary, but you *must* review the brochures. These *facilities* might be able to help them."

Mrs. Helmsley stepped down the hall, approaching Archer the way one might approach an old land mine, unsure if it was still active. She bent down, gave the land mine a kiss on the forehead, and proceeded to study it carefully.

"Mr. Churnick seems to have been *quite* the miracle worker," she said, her hands clasped behind her back. "He told me you were one of the finest students he's ever had. He even speculated your tendencies were a thing of the past."

Tendencies. That was the word Mrs. Helmsley gave to the many things Archer had done that she disapproved of, such as accidentally lighting a dinner party guest on fire. Archer suspected it also had something to do with a similarity between himself and his grandparents, but having never met them, he didn't know that for sure.

"Does that mean I don't have to go back to Raven Wood?" he said hopefully.

Archer knew in an instant that it was a silly thing to ask. It was clear his mother thought the land mine required further testing.

"Mr. Churnick has done *tremendous* work with you. You

must remain under his guidance. And *I'd* like to know his secrets," she mumbled.

"But we do have some news that might make you happy," Mr. Helmsley said, nudging Mrs. Helmsley.

"*Yes*. After careful thought, your father and I have agreed that it will only help to foster your progress if you spend more time outside the house while you're home."

Archer's jaw nearly hit the floor. Ever since his grandparents had vanished, he'd been kept a virtual prisoner inside Helmsley House.

"Now hurry upstairs and wash. You smell like a stale train car. The Glubs are expecting us any minute."

Mr. and Mrs. Helmsley disappeared down the hall. Archer stood frozen in the foyer, staring around at the familiar treasures and taxidermied animals collected by his grandparents. His old friend the badger, perched on a small table, was dressed in a Christmas sweater.

"Welcome home, Archer," the badger said miserably. "Would you mind helping me out of this thing? Why does she do this to me every year?"

"She thinks it makes you look like a gentleman," Archer said, pulling the tiny sweater over the badger's head.

The badger huffed as Archer smoothed its fur. "I was neither gentle nor a man in life, and I don't see why I should be made such things in death!" The badger lowered its voice.

"And while I'm glad you're back, Archer, I must say there's something strange going on. Why did Benjamin say you're going to hate him? Why haven't you heard a word from your grandparents? And why was that Mrs. Fig so furious at them? I'm not sure what it's all about, but I think it's bad."

Archer stared at the badger. "How do you know all that?"

"I know it because you know it."

"What's going on?" the ostrich shouted from the next room over. "I can't see with this lampshade on my head! Is that thing back? Don't tell me the thing with dirty hands is back!"

✦ JUST A CHRISTMAS PARTY ✦

Next door, the Glubs' house was filled with people and music and all sorts of delights. Everyone gathered in a room that, despite its chipping paint and loose floorboards, was called the great room. And it *was* great. Adélaïde was seated on a plaid couch before a crackling fire. Next to her were three tall windows overlooking the snowy gardens. Oliver scurried into the room and plopped himself beside her.

"I put more logs on," he said, sticking his shivering hands toward the fire. "It's freezing out there. You can go next time."

Adélaïde pointed to her wooden leg. Oliver rolled his eyes.

"How long are you going to milk that?"

Adélaïde smiled and got comfortable on the couch.

A few feet away, in the corner of the room, Oliver's

younger sister, Claire, was digging beneath a tree decked in tin ornaments and lights.

"What's she doing?" he asked slowly.

"She's moving her presents to the outside and yours to the inside."

Claire peeked over her shoulder at Adélaïde. Both started giggling.

"I don't like this at all," Oliver grumbled, and turned back to the fire. "The two of you are not becoming friends. I forbid it."

Lovely smells wafted from the other side of the room. Mrs. Glub was dashing between the kitchen and the great room, keeping a long table overflowing with food.

"Mind yourselves!" she called, setting a spiced pecan pie on the table. "Piping hot!"

Miss Whitewood, invited at Adélaïde's request, was also at that table, filling a plate and explaining her duties as the Willow Academy librarian to Belmont Café's barman, Amaury Guilbert. But Amaury was clearly more interested in the duties of Mrs. Glub's pastries, which, of course, were to be eaten.

"These strudels are delicious," he said, glancing over at Mr. Belmont. "We should be selling these at the café!"

Mr. Belmont wasn't paying attention. He had gifted an espresso machine to the Glubs and was showing Mr. Glub how to operate it by brewing a brand-new espresso blend he'd been working on and was finally quite pleased with.

"And then you simply pull this lever here."

A small cup filled with a dark, steamy brew.

"Most remarkable!" Mr. Glub said. He lifted the cup and took a sip. "And most delicious! But tell me, François . . . what am I tasting? Wait—it's hazelnut, isn't it? Yes, that's certainly hazelnut!"

"It should be *toffee*," Mr. Belmont said, frowning. "Hints of toffee?"

"Toffee?" Mr. Glub took another sip. "How fascinating! You're a genius, François! I had no idea toffee could taste just like hazelnut."

Mr. Belmont opened a notebook and crossed something out while muttering in French. Mrs. Glub returned from the kitchen, this time with a tray of cherry almond cookies, and shook her head at them.

"I like your family," Adélaïde said. "I wish mine was more like yours."

"Sure," said Oliver. "They're great. But when's Archer getting here?"

"The Helmsleys should be arriving any minute," Mrs. Glub said, stepping up behind the couch. "So I'll say it one last time: you two are not to tell Archer anything about the newspapers or his grandparents."

"But they're *his* grandparents," Adélaïde said, peering up

at her. "Don't you think he needs to know what everyone in Rosewood already does?"

"I very much do, dear," Mrs. Glub admitted somberly. "That boy's been awaiting this moment for as long as I've known him. It's all he's ever talked about. Unfortunately, it's not our decision. Mr. and Mrs. Helmsley made me promise it wouldn't be mentioned. I suspect, *and hope*, there's more to all of this than we know."

✦ SECRETS AND SNOWBALLS ✦

Oliver and Adélaïde left the couch and the great room and went to a window at the front of the house. Oliver forced the latch, slid open the window, and stuck his head out. Willow Street was deserted.

"We have to tell him," Adélaïde said, leaning next to Oliver.

"I know. I'm just worried he's going to hate us for not saying something sooner."

"He'll hate us even more if we don't do it now."

Oliver was about to agree when a snowball smacked him clean across the face. He jerked his head and clunked it on the window. *"Who did—?"*

"ARCHER!" yelled Adélaïde.

Oliver wiped the snow from his eyes. Archer was smiling at them from a snowdrift where the sidewalk should have been. Adélaïde and Oliver dashed to the door and, without bothering to grab their coats, jumped down the front steps and tackled him.

"It's about time!" Oliver said, pulling his arm from beneath Adélaïde. "But a hello would have worked just as well."

"*Hello*," Archer said, sitting up and inspecting Oliver's head. "Sorry about that."

"He's fine," Adélaïde assured him. "He's got a thick skull."

Oliver stood up grinning and offered them both a hand. They shook the snow from their clothes and stepped back inside the Glubs' house. Archer took a deep sniff. It smelled like gingerbread and caramel and pine. It smelled like home.

"Keep your coat," Oliver said, pulling his from a hook and handing Adélaïde hers. "We're going upstairs. But you should say hello first. Everyone's been waiting for you."

They crossed the hall and entered the great room, where Archer was greeted like royalty.

"Welcome home, Archer!" Mr. Glub cheered, popping him on the head with a closed fist. "This place hasn't been the same without you lurking around!" He pointed to Oliver and Adélaïde. "You should've seen them, Archer. They've been loafing about without you."

"Thank you for sending all those pastries and the cheese-cake," Archer said as Mrs. Glub wrapped him in a warm hug.

"It was my pleasure, dear. And there's plenty more for you tonight. Now where are your parents?"

"They'll be here soon."

Claire, still digging beneath the tree, jumped to her feet with one of Oliver's gifts in her hand. She tossed it over her shoulder and joined the merry crowd. It looked like she was going to give Archer a hug, but she shook his hand instead.

"That's awfully formal, Claire," Mr. Glub said, laughing.

Mr. Belmont smiled on from behind the Glubs while Amaury, who'd only recently arrived from France, seemed to be wondering who this Archer fellow was.

"And how was the Raven Wood library?" came a familiar voice.

Oliver whispered in Archer's ear as Miss Whitewood stepped forward. "Adélaïde invited her. I'm not sure how I feel about having a teacher in my home. I'd prefer to keep my worlds separated."

Archer hadn't seen Miss Whitewood since before the tiger incident, but he was pleased to discover she still smelled like books. "The Raven Wood head of school wanted to speak with you," he said. "Mr. Churnick. Did you ever talk to him?"

"I did," Miss Whitewood replied, handing him a small card. "I gave one to Oliver and Adélaïde, too. That'll get you into the library over the holiday if you'd like to come see me. Be discreet if you do. You mustn't let Mrs. Thimbleton catch you inside the Button Factory."

Oliver grabbed a tray of fudge crumble cookies from the

table. "We're going to my room," he announced.

"And why should you leave?" Mrs. Glub asked.

"You need coats to go into your room?" Mr. Glub added.

"It's cold up there," Oliver explained. "My radiator is dying. It clanks and clunks, but it's all lies. There's no heat."

Mr. Glub gave Archer a knowing smile. "It's not easy to be the son of a lowly newspaperman."

Mrs. Glub tapped her foot. "All right. I know you three have much to catch up on. But *please*, I don't want you getting any more *strange* ideas."

"And we don't need to be gossiping about things we're not supposed to gossip about," Mr. Glub warned. "We're a *Doldrums* family. Not a *Chronicle* family."

⋆ BAD TIDINGS TOWARD MAN ⋆

Oliver led the way up the stairs to his bedroom and then out onto his balcony, where they used a metal ladder to climb to the roof. When Archer's head poked over the ledge, he saw a shoveled pathway across the snowy flat rooftop and a roaring fire in a dented metal bowl.

"We wanted to talk without anyone else around," Adélaïde explained.

For a moment, Archer stood gazing down into the Willow Street gardens, and then at the Rosewood rooftops stretching in all directions, and finally at the Button Factory smokestacks, rising above all else. He truly *was* home. But something was different. The house next to Adélaïde's—Mrs. Murkley's former residence—was all lit up.

"That's where the girl I told you about lives," Oliver said. "She moved in two weeks after you left. Diptikana Misra."

"But everyone calls her Kana," Adélaïde added.

"No, everyone calls her *cuckoo*."

"She has a silver streak in her hair. That's usually the sign of a traumatic experience."

"And we know what that experience was, Archer." Oliver pointed to the metal bowl. "Do you remember the last time we had a rooftop fire—before the whole tiger disaster? We were tearing up a newspaper to get the fire going, and there was a story about a girl who'd vanished down a wishing well. According to everyone at the Button Factory, that girl was *Kana*."

"They said the water inside the well gave her psychic abilities," Adélaïde said, nodding.

"I don't believe that part," Oliver scoffed. "She was strange before that. And now she won't stop staring at me. I think she wants me to know she's doing it—like she's trying to tell me something without using words. It's creepy."

"Perhaps she's trying to say she likes you," Adélaïde suggested, batting her eyelashes.

Oliver scowled and moved closer to the fire. Archer and

Adélaïde followed. Archer told them all about Raven Wood and the rumors of what Mrs. Murkley had done. Their faces dropped when he told them he'd be going back after the holiday. Like Archer, they'd been secretly hoping his parents would let him stay.

"It's because my grandparents are coming home," he explained. "My parents even told me to spend more time outside. Something strange is going on. My roommate at Raven Wood, on our last day together, suggested my grandparents might be dangerous, but he wouldn't say any more. And then earlier today, at Rosewood Station, there was this . . ." Archer paused. Adélaïde and Oliver seemed to be having an argument with their eyes. "Do *you* know something?"

Oliver stopped rubbing his hands. "We're not supposed to tell you, Archer, but we've been hearing lots of things. None of it's good."

Archer sat perfectly still, staring at his friends. Adélaïde nudged Oliver. He sighed heavily, but continued.

"Everyone in Rosewood is saying the iceberg was a hoax— that your grandparents weren't actually on one for two years. And the only reason they were on one at all was because they wanted to vanish."

"We don't know the details," Adélaïde said. "But supposedly, before they vanished, your grandparents were doing strange things at the Society. The other members feared your grandparents had gone crazy and were out to destroy everything. There was even an effort to remove your grandfather from the presidency. That's when your grandparents vanished."

"Everyone thinks they're dangerous, Archer," Oliver continued, as Adélaïde dug into her pocket. "They think your grandparents have cursed the city. They're blaming all of this snow on *them*."

Adélaïde handed Archer a bundle of newspaper clippings. His head was reeling and his frown grew deeper as he skimmed headlines: HELMSLEYS' CURSE! ICEBERG HOAX! KEEP THEM OUT! THE ICEBERG COMES TO ROSEWOOD! He lowered the articles and stared blankly at the mounds of snow, flickering with the firelight.

"This has been going on ever since I left," he said, his fingers trembling. "Why didn't you tell me?"

"Your parents told us not to," Adélaïde explained. "Didn't they have newspapers at Raven Wood?"

Archer hadn't seen a newspaper since he'd left. Raven Wood kept some in the mailroom, but Benjamin always sat on them while waiting for him, or knocked them off the table, or took the last one.

"We don't understand—" Adélaïde continued, but Archer could no longer hear her.

He couldn't hear anything. The fire went blurry. His friends went blurry. Then everything started spinning. He'd spent two years hoping his grandparents weren't dead. *Two years.* If they weren't on an iceberg, where were they? Why would they let him think they were dead? This couldn't be right. His grandparents wouldn't do that. Archer shook himself.

"It's mostly the *Rosewood Chronicle* that's been printing these stories," Adélaïde was saying. "It's all they write about anymore."

"My father won't print anything until he hears from your grandparents," Oliver added. "He feels terrible that he got the story wrong the first time. He's not sure if it was a hoax."

"What do you mean, he's not sure?" Archer repeated, almost glaring at Oliver. "Of course it wasn't a hoax. They sent me a piece of the iceberg. You saw it. Don't tell me *you* believe this."

"Don't get angry at him," Adélaïde said. "No one's saying your grandparents *didn't* get onto an iceberg. They're just saying your grandparents *wanted* to vanish."

Archer's heart was thumping in his ears. Why would his grandparents *want* to vanish? To want something like that, you'd have to be out of your . . . His heart stopped.

Archer shot to his feet and shoved the articles into his pocket.

"My grandparents were lost," he said, moving to the ladder. "Now they're coming home. That's all there is to it. Everyone's going to feel very foolish when my grandparents set the record straight. So I'd suggest you two stop talking."

• A Pastry in a Glub Tree •

Archer hurried down the stairs. He poked his head into the Glubs' great room and saw his parents laughing with Miss Whitewood. Merry spirits danced all around, but they kept their distance from Archer. He continued to the Glubs' kitchen, which was a complete disaster. He opened the freezer, pushed aside a frozen fish and a pot roast, and there, at the back, saw a large chunk of ice—his piece of the iceberg. The one his grandparents had sent him. He'd left it with Oliver, fearing his mother might pitch it.

Archer pulled it out and went to the kitchen table, resting his head on his fists while his eyes flickered over the frozen hunk. This proved his grandparents were on an iceberg. It didn't prove it was an accident. And it didn't prove they were on one for two years. If they weren't, where had they been? Worse still, in all that time, why hadn't they sent him a message to let him know they were still alive? A letter. A secret gift. *Anything.* Were Oliver and Adélaïde right? Was everyone in Rosewood right? *Had* his grandparents gone round the bend?

Archer didn't want to return to the party, but the longer he stayed away, the more people might ask where he'd been. He stashed the iceberg back inside the freezer and slowly made his way to the great room. *Crazy?* Oliver and Adélaïde were sitting on the couch when Archer entered. He went straight to the table of delights, which seemed anything but.

"There you are," Mrs. Glub said, stepping to his side. "Oliver said you needed a bit of fresh air. Is everything all right?"

Archer's forced smile betrayed him, drooping into a terrible frown. Mrs. Glub didn't say a word, but it was clear she knew. She shot Oliver and Adélaïde a sharp eye and then grabbed a plate for Archer.

"You need to eat something, dear," she said, piling it as high as could be. "Everything seems worse on an empty stomach. Here, take this and have a seat near the windows."

Archer sat down. Claire immediately joined him. She didn't say a word, but smiled each time she took and ate a pastry from his plate. Archer could feel Mr. and Mrs. Glub staring at him. He wasn't sure if he felt more angry or foolish. He didn't notice that Oliver and Adélaïde had inched to his side.

"We didn't say we believe your grandparents are dangerous," Adélaïde whispered.

"Only that it's obvious something strange is going on," Oliver added.

Archer stood to flee, but tripped on the gift Claire had tossed over her shoulder earlier. Pastries took flight, and he went headlong into the Glubs' Christmas tree. The next thing he knew, he was sprawled across the couch with the tree on top of him. The party hushed as he untangled himself from the evergreen and its trimmings.

"I'm sorry!" he said, covered in tinsel, scrambling to gather ornaments and pastries from the floor.

"Don't you worry!" Mrs. Glub insisted. She swooped in alongside Mr. Glub to right the tree, and though they couldn't get it to stand straight again, she added, "Look! No harm done!"

Oliver and Adélaïde watched in silence as Archer brought the decorations and pastries back to the tree and began hanging pastries from the branches instead of ornaments.

"What's wrong, Archer?" Mr. Helmsley asked, stepping in to help him. "I don't believe the Glubs want pastries in their tree."

Archer was silent.

"Why don't you give those here, Richard?" Mrs. Glub said, taking the ornaments. "Yes, I'll take the pastries, too. Very good. Now, Archer's had a long day. Look at him. He's exhausted. Perhaps it's best he gets a good night's sleep."

The Glubs stood on the snowy front steps, watching as Archer followed his parents home. Mr. Helmsley paused outside the front door of Helmsley House. A note with a greasy thumbprint was taped to it. He read it aloud.

> *"Ralph and Rachel are arriving shortly. Expect them in Helmsley House later tonight or early tomorrow morning. —Cornelius"*

Mrs. Helmsley nearly collapsed on the spot. Mr. Helmsley helped her through the door. She fled down the hall. Archer made for the stairs, his head pulsing, but stopped and turned to his father.

"Why didn't you tell me what was going on?"

Mr. Helmsley removed his glasses and rubbed his closed eyelids. "I didn't want you to worry about something that might not be true, Archer. I'm not sure what the truth is, but let's hope it's not worse than the rumors."

Archer shook his head. *Worse?* "How could it be worse?"

His father didn't have an answer.

Archer went to his room and lay awake in bed. The moonlight was on his face as his ears searched the darkness, like many ears do on Christmas Eve. But it wasn't yet Christmas Eve, and Archer wasn't listening for sleigh bells. He was listening for footsteps. He was waiting for his grandparents.

"*Are* they crazy?" he mumbled, turning to the window, which glittered with moonlight.

◆ Brewing ◆

Outside Archer's moonlit window and down crooked Willow Street, across the barren treetops of Rosewood Park and beyond the winding canals that emptied into Rosewood Port, a man with a patch covering one of his eyes ran along a lamp-lit dock that dipped gently with the waves. The Eye Patch had a wooden case tucked under his arm, and his one visible eye searched the horizon. A darkened ship was entering Rosewood

Port. The ship didn't blow its horn, and its engine was low as it drifted past ice floes, sidled up to the dock, and dropped lines around bollards. Two silhouettes emerged on the deck. The Eye Patch called to them.

"You're a sight for a sore eye!" His smile faded as he unlatched the wooden case to reveal a bundle of newspapers. "Birthwhistle is brewing a storm."

CHAPTER

✦

THREE

✦ YEARS OF WONDER ✦

Archer awoke to a bustling and clanking of pots and pans.
He rubbed his droopy eyes and hurried down to the kitchen.
The stovetop was roaring, and Mrs. Helmsley was dashing this
way and that, cooking everything she could get her hands
on. Archer kept his distance, fearing she might fry him by
mistake. His father sat alone at the table.

"Are Grandma and Grandpa home?" he asked.

Mrs. Helmsley nearly toppled onto the stove.

"Not yet," Mr. Helmsley replied.

Archer wasn't hungry, but he didn't want to meet his
grandparents on an empty stomach. He took a plate and a fork
and went to the counter, buried beneath eggs and bacon and
toast and pancakes and waffles and oatmeal—and his mother
showed no sign of slowing.

"I can't take much more of this," she muttered, peering

over her shoulder as Mr. Helmsley refilled his coffee. "I was at Primble's Grocery yesterday, and when I got to the counter, they told me to take my business elsewhere! Where are we supposed to get food?"

"They'll sort out whatever is going on," Mr. Helmsley assured her. "In the meantime, I'd like them to have their room on the third floor."

"But we've been using it for storage! It's filled with boxes." Mrs. Helmsley clicked off the stove and frantically wiped her hands on her apron. "We mustn't upset them. They might get violent!"

Mrs. Helmsley hurried up the stairs. Mr. Helmsley sauntered after her.

Archer panicked, standing alone in the kitchen. He'd been waiting for this moment for as long as he could remember, but now he didn't think it'd be anything like he'd expected. Overcome with an urge to retreat to his room, he made for the hall, but froze at the sound of a knock at the door.

All throughout Helmsley House, the animals erupted in joyous furor. Archer had never once heard anything like it.

"It's time!" a porcupine bellowed. "It *is* time!"

"They're home!" cheered a zebra. "How do I look? The stripes, I mean. I should have had them pressed!"

"Shut it, you fool," the ostrich snapped. "And would someone take this blasted lampshade off my head?"

"Are you sick?" the badger asked Archer. "You look like you're going to be sick."

Archer was too fixated on the door to respond, and he was so flustered he didn't realize he was still clutching a fork as he inched his way toward it.

"We're gone for nearly twelve years and they change the locks?" came a voice on the other side.

"I'm sure they were changed the moment we left."

✦ Tea with Giants ✦

Archer took a deep breath and opened the door wide. He was immediately engulfed in the blinding whiteness of snow whirling into the foyer. He couldn't see anyone, but heard two voices, filled with laughter. Archer squinted. Two faces emerged. His eyes widened. Archer was staring at his grandparents.

"Why, hello there," they both said, with smiles so large they might crack lesser faces.

Those three words filled Archer all the way to the top.

"Hello," was his nervous and quiet reply. "I'm Archer Helmsley."

"How can *you* be Archer Helmsley?" Grandpa Helmsley asked. "The Archer *I* had a brief encounter with many years ago was dressed something like a Christmas tree. And if I'm not mistaken, he also had a *peculiar* fondness for cucumbers."

Grandpa Helmsley was as broad as he was tall. His beard, a

mix of white and gray, matched his hair, which was pushed back from his forehead. But it was Grandpa Helmsley's pale green eyes, sparkling with something wild, that held Archer entranced.

"I don't think he's that Archer anymore," Grandma Helmsley said.

Grandma Helmsley was smaller but no less brilliant. Her plump figure was hidden beneath a thick coat and a faded red dress. The warmth beaming from her smile could have thawed the whole of Rosewood.

"He certainly isn't," Grandpa Helmsley agreed. Then he pointed to the fork still clutched in Archer's hand. "You're not going to . . . what I mean to say is, that's a little . . ."

"*Hostile*," Grandma Helmsley finished. "I believe that's the word you're looking for?"

"*Quite.*"

Archer blushed and dropped the fork into his pocket.

"Much better." Grandpa Helmsley glanced over his shoulder as though they were being watched. "Now would you mind if we stepped inside? It's no iceberg out here, but it *is* quite chilly."

Archer's grandparents stepped over the threshold and into Helmsley House as though they'd only just returned from a very long walk.

"Best shut the door, dear," his grandmother said. "Rosewood has many prying eyes."

Archer closed the door and put his back to it. Stomps and thuds echoed down the stairs.

"Would that be your parents?" Grandma Helmsley asked, hanging her snow-laden coat on a caribou's antlers.

"They're fixing your room," Archer explained, his heart pounding.

"*Very* good. We did hope to have a moment alone with you."

"Forks out of the way!" his grandfather whispered, and with a firm hand on Archer's back, he ushered him down the hall and into the kitchen.

Grandma Helmsley inspected the countertop feast and poked a pancake. "*Tea,*" she said, shaking her head and taking a kettle to the sink. "Best to begin with tea. Builds an appetite for more."

"Splendid!" Grandpa Helmsley pulled a chair out from the kitchen table. "And while the water boils, I have a question for you, Archer. Come have a seat."

Archer wanted to pinch himself as he sat across the table from his grandfather. His grandparents were practically fictional characters to him. He'd read their journals. He knew their tales. They'd crashed planes in the desert and been lost in jungles. But now, here they were, two giants, stepping off the page and into the Helmsley House kitchen.

Grandpa Helmsley leaned forward and clasped his strong hands as though he was about to say something very important. "Tell me, Archer, are the stories *true?*"

Archer blinked a few times. *Stories?*

"He means the tigers," Grandma Helmsley clarified, pulling a tray from a cabinet and setting three cups on it.

Grandpa Helmsley slapped the table, his green eyes sparkling. "The tigers!"

"But more importantly," Grandma Helmsley said, "that you and two friends put together a plan in the hopes of finding us."

"We did," Archer replied. "But that's not a good story. We failed miserably."

"*Miserably?*" Grandpa Helmsley roared. "You mean it failed *gloriously!*"

"While it *was* a dangerous thing to have happened," his grandmother said, lifting the whistling kettle off the stove, "when we heard *why* it happened, well, we were tickled pink."

"I was tickled purple!" Grandpa Helmsley said, his eyes still twinkling. "Outrunning tigers? I've never heard of such a thing! You're a Helmsley all the way to the stars, Archer!"

"I can't imagine Helena was thrilled about it," Grandma Helmsley said, joining them at the table and pouring everyone a cup.

"No," Grandpa Helmsley agreed. "But don't give us this 'It's not a good story' nonsense, Archer. We want to hear all about it. And don't spare a single detail."

Archer had never imagined his grandparents would be eager to hear his story, especially with so many more important things to discuss. When he'd finished telling it, his grandparents were silent. Grandpa Helmsley's whole face had welled up. Grandma Helmsley patted his shoulder gently.

"Don't let your grandfather's scruffy outsides fool you, Archer. Inside, he's as soft and sweet as a caramel."

Grandpa Helmsley chuckled and cleared his throat. "Forget the caramel, Archer. It's only that, what I mean is—look at you! You're completely grown! And we missed it."

"Now *you're* talking nonsense," Grandma Helmsley said. "He still has *plenty* of growing up to do. That's not to say you're underdeveloped, Archer."

Grandpa Helmsley sized him up. "Tad short for your age. And skinny like your father. But with a bit of elbow grease, you'll sprout like an oak! The Society will help with that. Once you're a—"

"*Let's not* get ahead of ourselves," Grandma Helmsley urged.

Grandpa Helmsley sipped his tea. "Yes, lots to sort out first."

"Like the iceberg?" Archer asked hesitantly.

Grandpa Helmsley leaned back in his chair and folded his arms. "What have you heard, Archer?"

"Lots of things."

"People *do* love to talk." Grandma Helmsley shook her head in disgust. "Especially when they've not the slightest idea what they're talking about. Makes them feel clever."

"They're saying you *wanted* the iceberg to happen," Archer

explained. "They're saying you *wanted* to vanish. They're saying you went—" He stopped, not wanting to tell his grandparents the part about them being unhinged. But it was clear they already knew.

Grandpa Helmsley reddened liked a stubbed toe. "It's complete rubbish, Archer. You mustn't believe a word of it."

"So what happened? How did you survive the iceberg?"

"Well," Grandpa Helmsley said, running his fingers through his beard. "While I can promise we were on an iceberg, Archer, it wasn't for two years. It was more like, three days. Give or take."

"*Three days?* So where were you all this—"

Archer fell silent. His mother had suddenly appeared, standing frozen by the kitchen door, staring at his grandparents' backs the way one typically stares at ghosts. Grandma and Grandpa Helmsley spun around.

"HELENA!"

It was only one word, but even that seemed too much for her. She tried to respond, but instead glugged like a jug of water held upside down. And she went on glugging until eventually, she glugged, "You're *dead*!"

To be fair, it probably wasn't what she'd planned on saying.

"I'm dead?" Grandpa Helmsley repeated, winking at Archer as he glanced himself over. "Well, I do wish someone had told me sooner. That's the sort of thing people like to know. It's odd, though. I don't *feel* dead. Do *you* feel dead, Rachel?"

Mrs. Helmsley flushed. "That's not what I . . . I didn't mean to . . . I apologize if I—"

"Now, don't you apologize, Helena," Grandma Helmsley said, giving Grandpa Helmsley an eye that said many things. "Ralph's having a bit of fun with you, is all. It's as much a shock to us as it is to you."

Archer wasn't sure if that was possible. He'd never seen anyone look more shocked than his mother did. And he guessed her shock would not quickly vanish.

Everyone got to their feet when Mr. Helmsley entered. Archer's father looked like a toothpick next to his grandfather.

"Still as spindly as ever," Grandpa Helmsley said, clamping his giant hands on Mr. Helmsley's skinny shoulders. "I told you all that sitting around a law office was no good. It's never too late to change course! The order may have openings!"

"You might need a good lawyer," Mr. Helmsley replied with a smile.

"Isn't that what you'd call a conflict of interest?"

Mrs. Helmsley had been inching her way toward the dining room and finally escaped.

Grandma Helmsley smothered Archer's father in a hug and then fixed his hair. "It's been *quite* an ordeal, Richard."

"Icebergs often are," he replied, ushering them back to the table. "Why don't you tell me about it?"

"Archer!" Mrs. Helmsley called. "Please come here immediately. I need help . . . reorganizing the silverware drawers!"

Archer looked to his grandfather, wanting to join them at the table to find out what was going on.

"Don't you worry, Archer," Grandpa Helmsley assured him. "We're not going anywhere."

◆ DRIP, DRIP, DRIP ◆

"I'm going to repeat what I said yesterday," Mrs. Helmsley said when Archer stepped into the dining room. Her hands were trembling. "It's very important that you spend more time outside. You should know there are certain *accusations* against your grandparents. I'm not sure what to believe, but I'm worried they're not entirely . . . *sane*. Less so than usual, I mean."

Mrs. Helmsley shut the silverware drawer, which looked exactly as it had when she'd opened it, and led him to a closet filled with cleaning supplies. "I need to see for myself, and *you* need to keep yourself busy." She handed him a feather duster.

"What am I dusting?" Archer asked.

Mrs. Helmsley inspected the spotless dining room but, like Archer, saw nothing.

"The curtains! Dust the curtains!"

Archer grumbled as he went to the window. *Do people even dust curtains?* He raised the duster, but paused and peered through a slit between the fabric panels. A truck was idling outside his house. He squinted at the driver. *Is that the crooked man?*

Before the tiger incident, he, Oliver, and Adélaïde had visited a dilapidated expedition supply shop called Strait of Magellan. The crooked man was the nasty owner of the shop—a man who'd made lots of money betting that Archer's grandparents were dead.

"What's he doing outside my house?" Archer mumbled, and tilted his head to read the insignia on the side of the truck. "The Society . . . Barrow's Bay . . . Rosewood."

 *Was that the Society? The one his grandfather was once president of?*

Archer opened the curtain wide, hoping to get a better look, but the truck squealed off down Willow Street.

That was the first stranger to lurk outside Helmsley House, but it wasn't the last. No more than an hour later, reporters began incessantly knocking on the front door. It was like the constant drip of a leaky faucet.

"Only a moment of their time!" a reporter pleaded. "A glimpse of the insanity within—"

Mrs. Helmsley slammed the door in his face. That was the sixth knock of the morning.

"Do you have any idea where our trunks are, Archer?"

Grandpa Helmsley asked, straining to see behind a couch in the sitting room. "A friend said he'd brought them home."

"I used one when I went to Raven Wood," Archer answered. "The rest are down in the cellar. In a hole."

"In a *hole*! Who would put our—"

Mrs. Helmsley stormed into the room and shrieked. Two reporters had managed to climb the facade and were taking pictures through the windows. She nearly yanked the curtain from the rod as she wrenched it shut.

"It's a deluge!" she cried, eyeing Archer's grandparents as she marched off. "We're all going to drown unless you speak to someone!"

Archer couldn't believe it, but for what had to be the first time in his life, he actually agreed with his mother. His grandparents still hadn't explained the iceberg to him. And while he wasn't sure what they'd told his parents, it clearly wasn't enough to satisfy.

"Why won't you say something?" he asked.

"Telling the truth is not always easy," Grandma Helmsley replied. "Telling the truth can make you sound unhinged."

"And that's exactly what he wants," Grandpa Helmsley muttered, peeking through the curtain at the horde of reporters gathered outside. "I'll bet he's having a good laugh right now."

Mrs. Helmsley flew by clutching a sign.

DO NOT DISTURB
NO REPORTERS
NO INTERVIEWS
NO ANYONE

Archer heard the reporters booing his mother as she furiously nailed it to the front door.

"Follow me," he said to his grandparents, leading them into the cellar to retrieve their trunks.

✦ ANOTHER PIECE OF THE IMPOSSIBLE ✦

"Your grandfather's shirts go in the top drawer, dear."

Archer tucked them inside as his grandfather lifted a wooden crate from a trunk. Archer remembered that crate. Oliver had found it the day Adélaïde discovered that the trunks were hidden in the cellar hole. It was filled with corked jars of colorful powders and liquids.

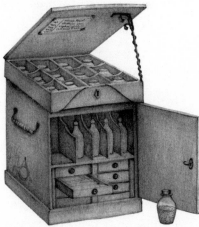

"What are those?" he asked, dragging an empty trunk to the closet and returning to his grandfather.

"Something we should have thrown overboard on our way to Antarctica," Grandma Helmsley said, glaring at the crate.

Grandpa Helmsley gave Archer an odd sort of smile. "I suppose you could say they were something of a parting gift. I'm surprised they're still here. Each of these bottles does something different." He set the crate on the floor and removed a jar that was filled with dark blue powder and pink specks.

"Take that one, for example," he continued, handing it to Archer. "That's Doxical Powder. One pinch of that, and you'll find yourself behaving the opposite of how you normally would. Temporarily, at least."

Archer brought the jar close to his eyes. "But that would be like magic."

"It's not magic, but it *is* powerful. Did you know there's a berry that grows in tropical West Africa called the miracle berry? When you eat it, the juices coat your tongue and, for a time, make sweet things taste sour."

Archer had never heard of such a thing.

"A botanist at the Society, a man named Wigstan Spinler—he told me Doxical Powder works from a similar principle, but with your brain's receptors instead of your tongue's taste buds."

Archer moved the jar from his face.

"It's strong, *yes*. But harmless."

"*Harmless?*" Grandma Helmsley questioned. "Honestly, Ralph, after everything that . . . What I mean is, in the wrong hands, Archer, that jar could do a great deal of harm."

Archer gently shook it and watched the fine powder shift. Could such a small thing really do so much?

"It's made from plants," his grandfather explained. "It should say on the back which ones."

"Slate leaf, yellow hotus, and pugwort." Archer lowered the jar. *"Pugwort?"* Benjamin had a plant of the same name.

"I believe pugwort gives it those pink specks," Grandpa Helmsley said, and stuck out his hand. Reluctantly, Archer passed it back.

"Curiosity is natural, Archer," his grandmother said. "But those jars are not to be played with. I'm not sure they should even exist."

"And best not talk about them publicly, Archer," his grandfather added. "Mr. Spinler's research is something of a secret."

"My roommate at Raven Wood would've liked that," Archer said, watching his grandfather set the crate next to a hedgehog high atop a wardrobe. "He loved plants and told me I would, too, if I knew what they could do."

"Is that so?" Grandma Helmsley said, digging in her trunk. "What was his name?"

"Benjamin Birthwhistle."

Grandma Helmsley stood straight up. Her arms were filled with sweaters, but from her expression, you'd think they were explosives. "Did you say *Birthwhistle*, Archer?"

Archer nodded. His grandfather's expression was the same. "Do you know Benjamin?"

"Mostly we know his father," Grandpa Helmsley explained, staring across the room at Grandma Helmsley. "A man named Herbert Birthwhistle. Or I suppose it's *President* Birthwhistle now. He took over at the Society after we vanished."

Archer shook his head. That couldn't be right. "Benjamin's father is a travel guide."

"*A travel guide?*" Grandpa Helmsley's laugh was filled with something bitter. "That's what he told you, is it? Well, I suppose at a certain point that was *almost* true. But he's one travel guide we'll never use again."

Archer was becoming uneasy. He had a vague idea where this was going. His grandfather stood before him and became very serious.

"You want to know more about the iceberg, Archer, and it's only right that you should. Above all things, a true explorer desires to make the unknown known."

"*Ralph.*"

"The first thing you need to know is that when I was president of the Society, I made decisions that Mr. Birthwhistle disagreed with. But there was one decision in particular that Mr. Birthwhistle hated me for—a decision he wanted to reverse. And sometimes, when you want something bad enough, you're willing to do something terrible to get it."

Archer's mouth fell open.

"Now that's quite enough of that," Grandma Helmsley said, dropping her sweaters into her trunk. "Your grandfather and I have a few *things* we need to discuss." She hurried Archer to the door and sent him out.

"We agreed he's not to be involved in any of this!"

"I'm not involving him! I only want him to know the truth!"

Archer pulled back from the closed door. Footsteps sounded on the stairs. Fearing his mother might ask him to dust more curtains, he hurried to his bedroom, his mind racing. *Benjamin's father is the president of the Society? He did something terrible?* Some thoughts are better left unspoken, so Archer said nothing as he passed the polar bear in the alcove.

"I know what you're thinking," the polar bear whispered. "And if you consider it more, you might find it's not as absurd as you think."

Archer shut his bedroom door. *It can't be true.* He went to his desk, grabbed the newspaper clippings, and there it was, right under his nose.

"We're still gathering information," President Birthwhistle said. "But I can say without hesitation that the iceberg was no accident."

The room began to spin. Archer took a breath. When he released it, out came the thought he didn't want to say. "Did Benjamin's father try to *kill* my grandparents?"

FOUR

✦ THE CENTER OF A MAZE ✦

On Christmas morning, joyful children all across Rosewood sat around trees, tearing into presents and gulping down more chocolate than their stomachs knew what to do with. In Helmsley House, Archer sat on his bed, encircled with newspaper clippings, tearing through his thoughts.

Did Benjamin know who Archer was? He had to. But did Benjamin know what his father had done? That had to be why Benjamin had said Archer would hate him. Didn't it?

"Merry Christmas, Archer! Come downstairs!"

Archer rolled off his bed and followed his father's voice.

It wasn't a completely cheerless Christmas morning. The Helmsleys gathered around the tree decked with metal ships and planes, exchanging and unwrapping gifts. Archer received his usual yearly planner from his parents, which he faked interest in and kindly thanked them for. Mrs. Helmsley received a tremendously colorful yak-hair sweater from Archer's grandparents, which she quickly averted her eyes from, perhaps fearing she might go blind. Mr. Helmsley received a paperweight, bearing a red crest: ORDER OF ORION. "It's never too late," Grandpa Helmsley said with a wink. Archer's gift from his grandparents was by far the greatest Christmas present he'd ever opened—a beautiful pair of binoculars, polished brass with leather grips.

"Finest they make," Grandpa Helmsley said, placing them around Archer's neck. "And you'll need a fine pair when you become a Green—"

Mrs. Helmsley coughed violently into her new sweater. Grandma Helmsley rushed her a cup of tea. By the time she recovered, Grandpa Helmsley had lost his train of thought.

After a sumptuous breakfast, Archer's grandparents went upstairs, Mr. Helmsley prodded a dwindling fire, and Archer helped his mother with the dishes. Aside from her coughing fit, she was in good spirits. Not a single person had knocked on the front door. Until someone did. Archer wasn't sure if his mother was startled and dropped the plate or if she was furious and threw it. The dish shattered regardless, and Archer narrowly dodged a ceramic shard. His mother tore down the hall, shouting before she'd even gotten the door open.

"It's Christmas morning! Don't you have a fam—"

Mrs. Helmsley hushed. It was no reporter. It was a tall man

in a greasy jumpsuit with an eye patch covering one of his eyes. The Eye Patch! Or at least, that's what Archer called him. He'd met the Eye Patch twice before, but all he knew was that the Eye Patch was the captain of a ship, a friend of his grandparents', and tremendously kind.

"Merry Christmas, Helena!" the Eye Patch cheered. "Hope I'm not disturbing you. I saw the sign. Was going to leave. But I'm here on *urgent* Society business. I was wondering if I might . . . *Helena?* You look a bit *queasy*. Don't you remember me? It was a long time ago, but I thought the grease might . . ."

Mrs. Helmsley's eyes narrowed and her forehead went splotchy. It was almost like she was trying to dig up a memory she'd killed off and buried deep in her mind.

"*Cornelius?*" she finally said, her voice quivering.

The Eye Patch smiled widely. Mrs. Helmsley didn't. He seemed to know why.

"I'll admit it wasn't the best way to introduce myself," he said, his smile waning. "Ralph and Rachel asked me to stay in the waiting room. And I did. But there was a pigeon, you see. It wandered into the viewing room—perched itself on his bassinet. Filthy creatures, pigeons." Cornelius paused and looked his greasy self over. "*Right*. But I was only trying to shoo it away. That's how I got the grease on his face. I tried to rub it off and, *well*, things sort of spiraled out of control.

To be fair, you did sic those nurses on me. They nearly ran me out of Rosewood."

Mrs. Helmsley had no response. Cornelius fished in his pockets and revealed a letter that would have been very pretty were it not spotted with grease. He handed it to Archer's mother, who held it at arm's length.

"For Ralph and Rachel," Cornelius explained, wiping his hands on his chest. "Sorry about the grease. Nature of the job."

Mrs. Helmsley glanced from the letter to Cornelius and back again. Archer wished she would say something. Cornelius was chewing his lip, his one eye looking left and right.

"I'll just be going now," he said, backing down the steps and nearly slipping on a patch of ice. "Sorry to disturb you. Again. And . . . Merry Christmas?"

Mrs. Helmsley slammed the door. "He will *not* become a regular visitor."

"Was that story about me?" Archer asked as he stepped to her side.

His mother nodded gravely. "One minute you were sleeping peacefully in your bassinet. The next you were in the arms of a greasy one-eyed man. I screamed so loud the nurses thought I'd been stabbed."

Archer suppressed his smile and stuck out his hand. "I'll give them the letter."

Mrs. Helmsley was all too pleased to get rid of it. "Wash up after you do." She sniffed her hand. "It might only be grease, but it's where that grease came from that disturbs me."

✦ URGENT BUSINESS ✦

Archer wanted to read the letter on his way up the stairs, but he presented it to his grandparents and waited patiently as they opened and read it. Well, not that patiently. While he was trying to see through the back of the letter, he realized something was scribbled there.

> *Please come. The order wants to help.*
> *Birthwhistle will not be there.*
> *You need to tell your side before he arrives.*
> *—Cornelius*

"There's something written on the back," Archer said.

His grandmother flipped the letter, and he finally saw the front.

RONALD H. SUPLARD

HEAD INQUIRER
SOCIETY CODES AND CONDUCT

DEPARTMENT OF INQUIRY

RALPH AND RACHEL HELMSLEY,

IT HAS BEEN BROUGHT TO MY ATTENTION THAT YOU'VE
BEEN IN ROSEWOOD FOR TWO DAYS, BUT HAVE YET COME TO
THE SOCIETY. I ASK THAT YOU NOT DELAY ANY FURTHER.
THERE WILL BE A BANQUET IN THE GRAND HALL THIS
EVENING FOR MEMBERS WHO ARE IN ROSEWOOD OVER THE
HOLIDAYS. CONSIDER THIS A PERSONAL INVITATION AND
STRONG SUGGESTION THAT YOU ATTEND.

REGARDS,

RONALD SUPLARD

Grandma Helmsley inspected both sides of the letter as
though she was looking for a clue. "Do we trust Suplard?" she
asked his grandfather.

"We have no reason not to."

"Then we'll go. I wish you could come, too, Archer, but
there are many—"

"Of course he's coming," Grandpa Helmsley interrupted.

"It's a banquet. He can bring his friends and see the Grand Hall while we attend to business."

Grandma Helmsley frowned, but she didn't argue.

His grandfather told him to invite his friends and then left to speak to his father. Archer hurried to his room but stopped outside the door. He couldn't imagine going to the Society without Oliver and Adélaïde. But he hadn't spoken to either of them since the Glubs' party. What if they were angry with him? They had every right to be. He slunk into his bedroom, not sure he wanted to face them. But there they were. Adélaïde froze, her hands poised to leave a brightly wrapped gift on his desk.

"Oh, *uh*, merry Christmas," she said. "We thought you were downstairs. We were just going to leave this."

"We still can," Oliver added. "If you'd prefer."

"Please don't," Archer said, shutting the door. "I'm sorry. For the other night. I didn't mean to ruin the party. I was—"

"We know you were upset," Adélaïde said, trying to give him the gift.

Archer was reluctant to take it. "I forgot to get you something."

"Don't worry about it," Oliver said as Adélaïde forced the present into Archer's hands. "My father was right. We've been loafing ever since you left. Go on. Open it."

Archer sat on his bed and unwrapped the gift. There

were two things inside. The first was a half-empty box of DuttonLick's chocolate caramel turtles.

"I might have eaten a few," Oliver said, blushing. "But I'll make you more. I wanted to tell you the other night—Mr. DuttonLick is having a *huge* party at the sweetshop, and he asked me to be his assistant. He's going to teach me how to make chocolate."

Oliver had gone from blushing to beaming. He'd even puffed out his chest a little. DuttonLick's sweetshop was Oliver's favorite store in Rosewood. And aside from Mr. DuttonLick himself, Oliver knew it better than anyone.

"You'll be a great assistant," Archer said, pouring the chocolates into his hand and offering his friends some.

Beneath the half-empty chocolate box was a brand-new leather-bound pocket journal.

"I thought you could use a new one," Adélaïde explained, licking a bit of caramel from her finger. "I hope you like it. It's from Bray and Ink on Howling Bloom Street. And look." She leaned in and lifted the cover. "This one even has a pen holder."

Many things in this world can rack you with guilt, but treating your good friends poorly and having those same friends acting as though it never happened at all takes the cake.

"It's perfect," Archer managed. "Thank you."

Adélaïde smiled and sat beside him, glancing over the

newspaper articles sprawled across his bed.

"We heard your grandparents are home," Oliver said hesitantly. "Have they said anything about the iceberg?"

"Not much," Archer sighed. "But it wasn't a hoax. My grandparents aren't dangerous. Mr. Birthwhistle is. He's the Society president, and I think I know what's really going on." He paused before adding, "I think Mr. Birthwhistle tried to kill my grandparents."

That was not quite in keeping with the spirit of Christmas morning. Oliver and Adélaïde needed a moment to digest it.

"Why do you think that?" Adélaïde finally asked.

"My grandfather basically said it." Archer searched the newspaper clippings for the Iceberg Hoax! article. "Think about it," he continued, handing it to Adélaïde. "Mr. Birthwhistle talked to the newspapers first. He got everyone to believe my grandparents wanted to vanish—that they went crazy. I'm sure he's doing the same thing at the Society. And now, if my grandparents tell the truth, if they say Mr. Birthwhistle tried to kill them, it will only reinforce the claim that they're insane. Who's going to believe them?"

"*Fait accompli*," Adélaïde mumbled, lowering the article.

"Stop using your fancy French words," Oliver insisted. "What does that even mean?"

"It means if Archer's right, Mr. Birthwhistle has trapped

his grandparents." She turned to Archer, frowning. "But why? Why would he want to kill your grandparents?"

"My grandfather said there was a disagreement about something."

Oliver wrinkled his forehead. "Adélaïde and I have disagreements all the time, but it's not like we would ever . . ." He paused. Adélaïde was grinning at him in an odd way. "Well, maybe *you* would leave *me* on an iceberg. But I wouldn't do that to you."

"My grandfather wouldn't tell me more," Archer explained. "But I know someone who will. My roommate at Raven Wood—I didn't know it, but his father is Mr. Birthwhistle! There's a banquet at the Society tonight. I'm going to find Benjamin there. And I'd like you two to come with me."

"You want us to come with you to the place where the president is someone who tried to kill your grandparents?" Oliver asked slowly.

At a knock on the door, Archer shoved the newspaper clippings behind his pillow. His grandparents stepped into the room with grins as wide as could be.

"Would this be the infamous trio?" Grandpa Helmsley asked. "Adélaïde and Oliver?"

"It's a pleasure to finally meet you," Grandma Helmsley said, shaking both their hands. "Archer has told us all about you. The life raft *and* your wooden leg. If you don't mind my asking, dear, how do you find getting around on that?"

"It changed everything," Adélaïde replied. "But I'm mostly used to it now."

"You'll fit right in at the Society," Grandpa Helmsley said. "Speaking of which, I can't say your mother is thrilled, Archer, but your father agreed. And will you two be joining us?"

"We'll talk to our parents," Adélaïde said, glancing at Oliver. "I'm sure *they* won't mind."

"Very good." Grandpa Helmsley looked at his watch. "Cornelius will be picking us up in a few hours, but we'd like to mention a few things now. Rachel and I have business to see to while we're at the Society. I don't expect you three to keep to our sides the whole time. In fact, I'd prefer that you don't."

"But we *do* expect you to stay nearby," Grandma Helmsley added. "There's a lot to see there, but no wandering off on your own. We'll be in the Grand Hall for the evening. And the Grand Hall is where we'd like you all to stay. I can assure you it will be filled with many characters."

Mr. Helmsley appeared in the doorway. "And when you return," he said to Archer's grandparents, "as promised, you begin to sort things out." He motioned for Archer to join him out in the hall.

"I know you're excited, Archer," his father said. "But while you're at the Society, you must follow your grandparents' rules. Your grandmother's right. The Society is filled with characters. But not everyone is good-natured. Use your head. Mind yourself."

◆ Bridges to Secrets ◆

That evening, Archer stood at the door pulling on his coat alongside his grandparents. Mrs. Helmsley was in the sitting room, peering through the curtain at a filthy black truck idling outside the house. "This will *not* become a regular thing." Next door, Oliver was also eyeing the truck from the Glubs' front steps. Adélaïde was with him, watching plumes of smoke dance around it.

"Isn't the mist pretty?" she said.

"That's exhaust," Oliver replied.

Archer and his grandparents climbed down the front steps. Oliver and Adélaïde joined them at the truck. Cornelius leaned out the window to greet them and spotted Adélaïde.

"The crocodile girl!"

Adélaïde curtsied.

"She's actually just the lamppost girl," Oliver clarified.

"Whatever you are, it's my pleasure to be your transport this evening."

The inside of the truck was every bit as a filthy as the outside.

"It smells like stale coffee and grease," Oliver noted,

climbing into the backseat alongside Archer and Adélaïde.

Grandma and Grandpa Helmsley joined Cornelius up front. Once their doors were shut, Cornelius slammed his foot on the gas, and they barreled off down the snowbound streets. Archer's grandparents didn't seem to notice the speed. But Archer, Oliver, and Adélaïde scrambled for something to brace themselves with as the truck swerved on the snow and ice.

"I think he's more used to steering ships," Archer whispered, taking holding of a strap dangling from the roof.

"And he does only have one eye," Adélaïde agreed, gripping the strap as well.

"Or maybe reckless is just his style?" Oliver suggested, prying his face off the front seat and reaching up.

The truck's sputtering tires spewed waves of snow as they careened along. Archer nearly cracked his head on the window as they fishtailed across a busy intersection. Lights flashed from all directions and horns blared. Cornelius casually spun the wheel. Down another street, they plowed through a huge drift, creating a gigantic tidal wave of snow that immersed a poor fellow struggling to walk his dog. The man shouted and began furiously digging with his hands. His dog had vanished. Cornelius sped on, oblivious to the havoc he and his truck were wreaking. Before the jostled trio knew it, they were crossing out of the Willows and into the warehouses of Barrow's Bay.

Barrow's Bay was Rosewood's easternmost point. And

while it was the sort of place you only went when you had to, in the dark of night, the glittering warehouse windows gave it a distinct air of magic. They flew across a bridge glowing beneath lampposts. Down below, wooden boats were stuck in the frozen canal. Then the main canal fractured into smaller waterways, and the truck roared over many smaller bridges. The warehouses became more condensed and the streets increasingly narrow.

"Cornelius should slow down," Oliver said, closing his eyes. "We're going to crash into a building."

But Cornelius didn't. With all the abrupt turns, Archer was convinced they were winding through an intricate maze. What would they find at the center? Benjamin, hopefully. But then what?

"Eyes wide, Archer!" Grandpa Helmsley announced. "It's around the next corner."

Archer's window had gone foggy, and he didn't dare release the strap to wipe it clean. When the truck finally slid to halt, he opened the door and hopped out.

They were in a massive, cobbled piazza enclosed by warehouses on all sides. And there, at the very center, rising before him, built from many different kinds of stone, was the Society. It was surrounded by a narrow canal, much like Strait of Magellan was, but this concrete island held only the Society. There wasn't room for anything else. The Society was enormous.

THE SOCIETY

5 THONET STREET · SOCIETY ISLE

He couldn't tell how high it reached because its towers and roofs and ornate intricacies disappeared into the starry sky.

Archer had never seen anything more magnificent.

Adélaïde pointed to marvelous footbridges, half buried with snow and lit by lampposts that stretched to the Society from all sides. "It's like a secret," she said. "Right in the middle of Rosewood."

"A *big* secret," Archer agreed.

Oliver stumbled out of the truck, looking disoriented from the wild ride. He steadied himself on Archer's shoulder and gazed up. "I have to admit, that is impressive."

"Isn't it?" Grandpa Helmsley said, stepping to their sides. "I'll never forget my first time seeing it. I was not much older than you three."

"We'll meet you inside, Cornelius," Grandma Helmsley said, shutting the door.

Cornelius sped off to return the vehicle, and Grandpa Helmsley led everyone to a footbridge.

"Now remember what we told you," Grandma Helmsley said. "You three are to remain inside the Grand Hall where we can see you."

The night air, sweeping up from the canal, was biting as they entered the front courtyard. The Society loomed high over their heads, glowing. Two stone narwhals with crossing tusks stood at the center of the snowy walkway. Grandpa

Helmsley stopped and instructed everyone to take hold of a tusk.

"It's for good luck and safe passage," he explained. "Before embarking on an expedition, all explorers take a moment here."

The courtyard ended with a set of stairs leading to three giant doors. Grandpa Helmsley opened the middle one and signaled for Archer to go first. Archer hesitated a moment. He was about to enter his grandparents' world—a place where greatness stood shoulder to shoulder with courage and daring. *And* a place where Mr. Birthwhistle plotted and schemed.

Archer exchanged an uncertain glance with Oliver and Adélaïde, and then he vanished inside.

✦ THE GREENHORN AND HIS FATHER ✦

The Society's entrance hall was every bit as majestic as the outside promised. An ornately tiled floor stretched before Archer. At the other end, two sweeping staircases leading to an arched balcony rose around more narwhals with crossing tusks. Oliver and Adélaïde joined him and watched a pale, gaunt man thumping a trunk down the steps. The man didn't notice them till he was halfway across the checkered floor.

"Who are . . . never before . . . new Greenhorns?" he stammered, his ghostly eyes peering over the trunk.

The man's confusion turned to shock when Archer's grandparents stepped through the Society doors. His trunk slammed against the floor. "So it's true . . . had hoped you . . . wasn't certain!" He turned excitedly to Archer. "And that makes . . . you must be—"

"My grandson!" Grandpa Helmsley said proudly. "It's

wonderful to see you, Harptree!" His grandfather shook Mr. Harptree's hand so fiercely that Archer thought he might launch him up to the balcony. "Harptree's the Society Archivist."

"Where are you going, Harptree?" Grandma Helmsley asked, pointing to the trunk.

"Scotland Society . . . archival emergency . . . ship sails . . . one hour . . . but so good to . . . welcome home!"

Mr. Harptree tapped a finger to his forehead, lifted his trunk, and was gone.

"Is there something wrong with him?" Oliver asked.

"You might not guess it," Grandpa Helmsley said, ushering them to the staircases. "But Harptree has a brilliant mind. The Archives are extensive. Not many go in without getting lost. But Harptree knows every inch of them. Unfortunately, such a mind often makes life's simple tasks more difficult."

"He's never been able to finish a sentence," Grandma Helmsley explained.

The staircases were lined with busts of former Society presidents. And the final bust, at the top stairs, was none other than Grandpa Helmsley himself.

"That's a bit chilling," Grandpa Helmsley said, staring himself in the face. "Your mother was right, Archer. I'm *dead*."

Straight ahead were the doors of the Grand Hall. It sounded like quite a gathering inside as they approached.

"Ralph, Rachel! You made it!" A man was rushing down the corridor toward them.

"This is Mr. Suplard," Grandma Helmsley told Archer. "Mr. Suplard is the Head Inquirer of Society Codes and Conduct."

Mr. Suplard was not much taller than Archer. He had round glasses, perched on the tip of his nose, and looked something like a walking file cabinet. His arms were overflowing with papers and folders.

"I would shake your hand, Master Helmsley," Mr. Suplard said in a nasal voice. "But as you can see, mine are full at the moment." He turned to Grandma Helmsley. "The department had a *bit* of an emergency. Oslo Grogger. Order of Hollander. Volcanic issue. He's no longer with us."

"*Volcanic issue?*" Oliver repeated.

Mr. Suplard nodded gravely. "Was told it was dormant. It wasn't."

"That's a cruel joke," Grandpa Helmsley said. "But I suppose humor is relative?"

"*Quite.* We're investigating." Mr. Suplard pointed to the

doors, doing his best to not drop anything. "It's a holiday banquet. Consider it a welcome home. And I do welcome you home. You're *all* the Society has been talking about."

Archer wasn't sure if he liked the way Mr. Suplard was now studying his grandparents.

"You both seem in good health, which is very good indeed. There's much to discuss. *Many* questions need answers. I'll join as soon as I can. But I'll warn you. While the Inquiry Department remains impartial, you know others do not do the same. Presidents included. President Birthwhistle is *very* displeased."

"*We're aware,*" Grandma Helmsley replied. "He's not in there, is he?"

"No. I'm told he will arrive tomorrow."

With that, Mr. Suplard waddled off down the corridor, and Archer's grandparents led the trio into the Grand Hall.

✦ Dazzling Sights and Strange Delights ✦

Archer caught his breath. Giant rafters wrapped in garlands lifted a cathedral ceiling, and a sapphire rug, embroidered with constellations, stretched across the vast floor. A peculiar assortment of individuals filled long rows of heavy oak tables lining the cavernous hall. Adélaïde wasn't the only one missing a limb, and Cornelius wasn't the only one missing an eye. All were drinking and eating and making a great stir, until someone shouted, *"HELMSLEYS?"*

The hall fell perfectly silent, and every face turned toward them. Many were scowling. Archer looked to his grandparents, whose grim expressions broke into smiles as a small group, seated at nearby table, jumped to their feet and swarmed them. What followed was many back slaps and handshakes and many a "Welcome back from the grave!" His grandmother introduced him to a slender woman with dark hair not much older than Miss Whitewood.

"Beatrice Lune," she said, sticking out her hand. "It's a real pleasure to finally meet you, Archer."

"Beatrice is the Society's finest pilot," Grandma Helmsley explained.

"Your grandmother exaggerates. But it's true I've never crashed a plane in the desert."

Grandma Helmsley laughed. "That was Ralph's fault!"

Beatrice released his hand when a second, larger group pressed in. Archer lost sight of his grandparents as he, Oliver, and Adélaïde were squeezed to the periphery. Oliver wrenched his foot from beneath a man's giant, weathered boot. Grandpa Helmsley's head emerged above the crowd. He pointed toward a banquet table.

"See if there's something you'd like to eat!"

Though they'd already eaten, something about cold weather gives one a bottomless appetite. When they reached the table, however, they all hesitated, inspecting the sprawling feast. Finally Oliver said what they were all thinking.

"This can't be real food."

"Maybe it doesn't taste as bad as it looks?" Adélaïde suggested hopefully.

The food couldn't taste worse than it looked.

"Deep-fried tarantula?" Oliver said, moving down the line. "I think I'll pass. Rice balls with . . . are those fried grasshoppers? *No thank you.* Let's see: broiled elk tongue, snake on a stick, pickled newts, and what is . . . that almost looks like—*did you see that? It sneezed!*"

"I'm not sure *what* that is," Adélaïde said, searching for the name card.

"Who cares? I don't eat things that sneeze."

The table went on and on, but they wished it didn't.

"Let's skip the food," Oliver said, moving toward the silver punch bowls at the end.

Adélaïde sniffed a few. "I think they're alcoholic."

"This one isn't." Oliver grabbed three cups and ladled them to their brims. "It's called Greenhorn Apple Cider."

"What's Greenhorn?" Archer wondered, lifting his cup.

"Maybe it's a spice?" Adélaïde guessed.

"I've never heard of it," Oliver said, taking a gulp. "But I do know what apple cider is, and I know it doesn't sneeze."

Archer nearly forgot about Mr. Birthwhistle and Benjamin

as he gazed around the Grand Hall, sipping his cider. There were more Christmas trees than he could count. To his left, at the head of the room, was an elevated platform where a pleasant fire crackled. Above the fireplace hung a crest with a giant B on it. Archer scowled. He turned to point it out to Oliver and Adélaïde, but stopped.

Across the hall sat a group of fifty boys and girls, all his age and older. They were in uniform. The boys had on dark brown pants and the girls had on dark brown skirts, and everyone wore thick blue sweaters over shirts with ties. The younger ones were whispering and pointing to Archer, Oliver, and Adélaïde. The older ones didn't seem to care.

"Are they talking about us?" Oliver asked, lowering his cider.

"They're laughing at us," Adélaïde replied. "Do you see Benjamin, Archer? Is he with them?"

Archer scanned the table and shook his head. "But maybe they know where we can find him."

The uniformed group quickly turned away as the trio approached. Archer, Oliver, and Adélaïde stood before them, but it was like they were invisible.

"Excuse me," Archer said. "I was just wondering if any of you might know a boy named Benjamin Birthwhistle?"

Everyone burst into laughter. Archer flushed in embarrassment.

"Of course we know Benjamin," snickered a large boy who

bore a strong resemblance to a cinder block. "What business is it of yours? Who are you? Are *you* anybody?"

A girl seated with her back to them spun around and studied Archer with bright brown eyes. She had dark hair, chopped to her chin, and a few light freckles on her cheeks.

"Ignore him," she advised. "He knows who you are. We all do. *You're* Archer Helmsley."

"How—how do you know me?"

"We know your grandparents, of course. Your family isn't *exactly* a secret here."

"Your grandparents are deranged!" the cinder block wailed, nearly knocking a plate off the table as he pounded his fist. Two boys seated next to him nodded and sneered. "Have they returned to finish their work? Who are they going to banish this time?"

"Can it, Fledger," the girl said, flashing the boy a sharp eye. "My parents said they had good reasons to do what they did." She turned back to Archer. "Anyway, if you're looking for Benjamin, you should check the Greenhouse. He snuck out as soon as you arrived. I'm certain that's where he went."

"How do we get to the Greenhouse?" Adélaïde asked.

The girl pinched her lips. "That's going to be difficult to explain." She stood up and searched the hall. "I'll take you, but we'll have to be quick." She aimed her gaze at Fledger.

"If Malmurna checks in before I'm back, tell her I'm in the lavatory. Do *not* rat on me. *Again.*"

The girl opened a small door behind the table and motioned for them to follow her.

"Are you sure this is a good idea?" Oliver whispered.

"Your grandparents *were* pretty serious about us staying in the Grand Hall," Adélaïde agreed.

"Do hurry!" the girl called.

Archer took one last look at his grandparents, who were still surrounded, before leading Oliver and Adélaïde out. He had to find Benjamin.

⋆ GREEN BEHIND THE EARS ⋆

The noise from the Grand Hall faded as the girl led them deeper and deeper into the Society. Archer lost all sense of direction. There were too many corridors, and the wood moldings and cold marble floors often changed.

"My name is Darby, by the way," the girl said as they clomped up a wooden staircase. "Sorry about Fledger. He's annoying, isn't he?"

"He doesn't like Archer's grandparents very much," Adélaïde said.

Darby shook her head. "But that's not surprising. Fledger's parents are in President Birthwhistle's order—the Order of Magellan."

"The order of what?" Oliver asked.

"Magellan. You know, Ferdinand Magellan—the first explorer to circumnavigate the earth? Anyway, my parents have a saying, 'Order of Magellans are all potential felons.'"

"But what's an order?" Archer asked.

"A group of explorers who work together. My parents are with your grandparents in the Order of Orion. You might have seen them in the crowd that greeted you." Darby glanced sideways at him. "They don't believe any of it, by the way. What's being said about your grandparents, I mean. I know there's more to it, but they won't tell me. Do you know what happened?"

While Archer was glad to hear this, he didn't think it was a good idea to tell Darby what he suspected. He shook his head

and pointed to a patch on her sweater. It was a crest—a leaping goat with striped horns that said SOCIETY GREENHORN.

"What does 'Greenhorn' mean?" he asked.

"You don't know very much about anything, do you?" Darby replied, blinking at him. "Greenhorn means you're new at something. I'm a Greenhorn. And everyone you saw at the table is one too. We're students of the Society. Our parents are explorers."

"What do you do?" Adélaïde asked. "Is it exciting?"

Darby smiled as though she thought the answer should be obvious. "If you're interested in learning how to sail ships and fly airplanes and survive in a jungle for ten days with no supplies, then yes, you might find being a Greenhorn exciting. But there are things like History of Exploration, which I find very boring. I'd rather my hands be covered in dirt than paper cuts."

Darby had been staring at Adélaïde's wooden leg while speaking.

"A lamppost fell on me," Adélaïde explained.

Darby pinched her lips in disappointment. "You should work on that story. Explorers always embellish their adventures."

"You could tell people a crocodile ate it," Oliver suggested with a smile.

"That's much better!" Darby said.

Archer and Adélaïde stifled their laughs and followed her around a corner.

"There are a few ways to get into the Greenhouse," Darby continued, leading them toward an elevator. "But this is my personal favorite. I'd come with you, but I can't get written up again." She opened the gate and watched them enter. "Go to the sixth floor. The Greenhouse doors will be straight ahead of you. I think you'll find Benjamin in the lab. It's his

second home. It's in the back right corner."

They thanked Darby, and she scurried back down the hall. Adélaïde shut the gate, and Archer pushed up on the lever.

"Did you know about Greenhorns?" she asked as they ascended.

Archer had no idea. Was that why his mother had wanted to keep his grandparents away? Had she wanted time to ensure he'd have no interest in being one?

"I wonder if my father was a Greenhorn," he said, but then remembered his father once telling him he'd never had much interest in such things.

Archer stopped the elevator on the sixth floor, and Oliver opened the gate. Straight ahead were two large doors. An ornate title above them read Greenhouse and Lab.

✦ WHAT ARE YOU TALKING ABOUT? ✦

The trio's eyes were as wide as could be. Ivy dripped from the ceiling, which was an arched network of steel beams and glass panes. The starry sky glittered through the glass, and they would have been able to see the canals of Barrow's Bay all around had the greenhouse not been teeming with twining plants and twisted trees. It was like Benjamin's desk at Raven Wood. Except bigger. Much bigger. It was a jungle. They stood on a metal platform overlooking it all.

"What kind of—" Oliver ducked as a bright blue bird swooped over his head. "What is this place?"

"It's a greenhouse," Adélaïde said.

Oliver eyed her. *"Thank you."*

"Darby said the lab was in the back right corner," Archer said, trying to swallow his astonishment.

They couldn't see the back, but they quietly spiraled down a metal stair to the humid Greenhouse floor and set off. Leaves and vines brushed their cheeks as they wove through rusted metal troughs until Archer glimpsed a sparkle of copper through the green. He signaled to Oliver and Adélaïde. They crouched behind a trough, pushed aside leaves, and just as Darby had guessed, there was Benjamin, not even twenty feet away, standing on a stool in a cramped space filled with all sorts of equipment. Copper vats with tubes leading to dispensers, a giant orb set atop three stubby legs, and cabinets all around. Archer couldn't tell if it resembled the Button Factory's science lab or a place a madman tinkers.

"What do we do now?" Adélaïde whispered as they watched Benjamin happily scrub the insides of a copper vat.

Archer wasn't sure exactly. It would have to be something along the lines of "Merry Christmas, Benjamin. Now tell me why your father tried to kill my grandparents."

"*Archer.* There's . . . *uh.*"

Oliver had backed away from the trough and was pointing a shaky finger at it. Something was moving inside. It wasn't plants. In the dirt just below Adélaïde, insects were pouring out of a hole. Archer vaulted back as one shot into the air and latched onto Adélaïde's neck.

"GET IT OFF ME!" she shrieked, reeling.

Archer swatted, and the bug flew off toward the ceiling.

"*Who's there?*"

Insects were suddenly everywhere, springing from the hole like popping popcorn. Archer brushed three off his face. Oliver plucked one out of his ear. Adélaïde tripped, rushing to get away, and they all tumbled into the lab. Benjamin lost his balance and fell backward off the stool, smacking his head on the cool tiled floor.

"Well, that was discreet," Adélaïde said, flicking an insect from her dress.

Oliver pulled another from her hair as they rushed to

where Benjamin's twiggy body lay sprawled like a tree that had been chopped down. They jostled his shoulders and called his name with no success. Oliver was about to dump a bucket of water on his head when Benjamin's eyes shot open and immediately locked with Archer's. Archer felt like he was seeing Benjamin for the first time.

"You lied to me. Your father's not a *travel guide*."

Benjamin sighed heavily as he sat up. "I'm sorry, Archer. But it wasn't a complete lie. My father used to be Director of Transport."

"You *knew* my grandparents," Archer continued, barely listening. "You knew *me*."

"I knew who you were the moment you walked into my room," Benjamin admitted, rubbing the back of his head. "And I've been told my whole life to stay away from Helmsleys. But after our first week together, I knew you weren't dangerous. And I liked you."

"But why didn't you tell me who *you* were?" Archer asked. "You had to know I'd find out everything eventually."

"I didn't want to be the one to tell you what had happened to your grandparents. I knew it would make you miserable."

Archer frowned. "Yes, knowing your father tried to kill my grandparents has made things a little miserable."

Benjamin stared at him as though he'd just stuck a firework in his mouth and lit it.

"Kill your grandparents?" he repeated, stumbling to his feet. "Who said my father tried to *kill* your grandparents?"

"My grandfather. Isn't that what you didn't want to tell me? Isn't that why you thought I'd hate you?"

Benjamin shook his head slowly. Oliver and Adélaïde backed away.

"Your grandfather told you my father tried to *kill* them?" Benjamin continued. "I mean, I suppose I shouldn't be surprised. They were and probably still are completely paranoid." He glanced over his shoulder after a loud clang. "Careful!"

Oliver had brushed against a plant that dripped thick yellow goo and then bumped into a copper vat as he rubbed the goo from his sweater.

"Sorry," he said, steadying the vat. "But that plant, it's not poisonous, is it?"

Benjamin shook his head and pointed through the back windows. Across an outdoor courtyard, buried in snow, stood a much smaller greenhouse.

"Poisonous plants are kept in Greenhouse Four."

"I'm confused," Archer said, grabbing Benjamin's arm. "What were you talking about then? What didn't you want to tell me?"

There was another clang. The door to the metal platform had opened and slammed shut, but they couldn't see who had entered. Benjamin flashed Archer a panicked look as footsteps clanked down the metal steps.

"How did you know I was here? How did you find me?"

"A girl named Darby brought us," Adélaïde explained. "She was with the other Greenhorns."

"Those rats! I'll bet they told on me."

"Do you know who that is?" Oliver asked. "Are we in trouble?"

"I think it's Malmurna," Benjamin said. "She's in charge of Greenhorns. She'll write me up if she finds me here by myself. Follow me. I know somewhere she won't find us."

⋆ OBSERVATORY INSIGHTS ⋆

They ducked through a door at the back of the lab, which led to a narrow passageway crammed with pipes that were spitting steam. There were so many stairs that Archer guessed Benjamin was leading them near the roof. He was right. Benjamin opened another door, and they stepped out onto a causeway overlooking the entire Society.

"That's the Observatory," Benjamin said, pointing to a round stone structure set apart from the main building.

"And that's a long way to fall," Oliver added, staring over the side of the causeway at the frozen canal far below.

As they crossed and wound their way up icy steps to the top of the Observatory, Benjamin explained that it was one of the largest in the world, but aside from teaching basic astronomy to Greenhorns, it wasn't used anymore.

"Rosewood got too big. It gives off too much light."

The whole of Rosewood, shrouded in snow, spread out below them. The Button Factory smokestacks; ships docking and departing Rosewood Port; the maze of canals and warehouses. But Archer would have enjoyed the view more under different circumstances.

"Someone's down there," Adélaïde said, pointing to the poisonous Greenhouse Four, which lit up like a lantern.

"Malmurna knows I love the Greenhouses." Benjamin sighed, peering down. "I'm in trouble. But I have to set the record straight." He put his back to the railing and stared at Archer. "My father didn't try to kill anyone. You're not going to like it, but I'll tell you what's really going on."

Adélaïde and Oliver moved closer to Archer.

"Your grandparents and my father have never liked each other, Archer. Their orders have always been at odds. Did your grandparents tell you what was happening *before* they disappeared?"

Archer didn't respond.

"I didn't think so," Benjamin said. "It was terrible. Your grandfather tried to banish the Society's *greatest* botanist—a man named Wigstan Spinler. He's in my father's order. My father thinks I could become as talented a botanist as him. Mr. Spinler thinks so, too."

"Why did my grandfather try to banish him?" Archer asked warily.

"That's just it," Benjamin said. "Your grandfather wouldn't say *why*. Mr. Spinler had done his research in private for many years. When he revealed it to the Society, everyone marveled. He's famous here, and he should be. Mr. Spinler uses plants to do the impossible."

Archer thought of the crate of jars his grandfather had showed him. Using Doxical Powder to change someone's personality sounded impossible. What could the other jars do?

"Your grandfather was jealous," Benjamin continued. "And my father got worried—especially for his order. Mr. Spinler was only the beginning. Your grandparents had a *list*, Archer. They were planning to purge the Society of any member who got more attention than they did. They completely lost it."

"But they *didn't* banish Mr. Spinler?" Adélaïde asked, her head tilted.

"No. Thanks to my father," Benjamin said. "He led an effort to oust Archer's grandfather from the presidency before anything could happen. And he had a lot of support. Your grandparents knew it, Archer. That's when they vanished. We think your grandfather didn't want the shame of being thrown out of office. It's only ever happened once before."

Archer was certain this couldn't be right. No one had told him any of this. Had his father known? Or his mother?

"*That's* what I didn't want to tell you," Benjamin said. "I'm sorry, Archer, but your grandparents are nothing like what you hoped they'd be."

"But at Rosewood Station," Archer said, shaking his head, "you told me I was going to hate you. Why?"

Benjamin's eyes fell to his boots. "It's my father. He can't allow your grandparents to return to the Society. They'll put everyone in danger. They almost killed themselves, Archer. My father has to banish them, like your grandfather tried to do to Mr. Spinler. I found out in that letter I received. That's why my father cut his trip short. That's why he returned. There's going to be a vote. Tonight."

"But your father's not in Rosewood," Archer said, turning to Oliver and Adélaïde, who were staring straight back at him. "Mr. Suplard said . . ."

Benjamin peered up from his boots, shaking his head, genuinely sorry.

"My father's coming, Archer. Or maybe he's already here."

✦ BITE BY BITE AND PIECE BY PIECE ✦

Archer, Oliver, and Adélaïde dashed from the Observatory with reckless speed, not thinking of the frozen canal, which was only a quick stumble away. When they slid back inside the Society, they slowed almost to a crawl, wandering the top floors of the building without the slightest idea how to find their way back to the Grand Hall.

"We need Darby," Oliver said, peering down corridors for anything that looked familiar.

Archer was trying to make sense of what Benjamin had told him.

"If my grandparents tried to banish Wigstan Spinler, I'm sure they had a good reason," he said, following Oliver past arched windows overlooking a lit courtyard.

"And don't you think it's odd?" Adélaïde agreed. "The

timing of everything? They disappeared before anything happened at all."

Archer hadn't thought about that. "Mr. Birthwhistle was trying to stop my grandfather from banishing Mr. Spinler. That's why the iceberg happened. How can Benjamin not see that?"

"Others must know," Oliver said, stomping down a wooden staircase lined with animal paintings. "Mr. Birthwhistle couldn't have arranged the iceberg by himself, could he?" At the bottom, he pointed to a door. "That's the one Darby led us through!"

Archer rushed toward it, wanting desperately to get back to his grandparents. They shoved through and stumbled into a smartly furnished, fire-lit office. Definitely not the Grand Hall. Archer slumped and was about to turn, but froze. The office wasn't empty. A man stood hunched over a desk in the corner—a man now glaring at them. The same man Archer had seen lurking outside his house. The crooked man.

"What are *you* three doing in here?" he asked, stepping around the desk, the firelight casting deep shadows on his sunken face.

"We're looking for—" Archer stopped. The desk was in complete disarray, with all of the drawers hanging open. The crooked man had clearly been searching for something.

"We're looking for the Grand Hall," Adélaïde explained.

Oliver was silent. During their previous encounter at Strait of Magellan, the crooked man had threatened to cut out his tongue if he didn't watch it in the future.

The trio made for the door, but the crooked man threw himself in front of it.

"What's the hurry?" he asked, slamming it shut and forcing them back farther into the office. "It's *so lovely* to see you again. Much has transpired since our last visit! I must tell you, I nearly laughed myself silly reading all about your failed expedition. I knew you wouldn't make it to the port, of course. But I must say—not being able to get out of a museum?" The crooked man clicked his tongue. "Not the wunderkind your grandparents had hoped you'd be, are you?"

"There were tigers," Adélaïde said. "That made it a *little* difficult."

"Yes, you did have some luck with the tigers, didn't you? And considering your grandparents are not what they once were, perhaps your antics impressed them? It's a shame, but too much salty air drives even the best of them loopy."

"They're not loopy," Archer said, clenching his teeth. "Mr. Birthwhistle is lying."

The crooked man's mocking grin disappeared.

"That's *quite* the accusation. Is *that* why you're in here?" He stepped to the fireplace mantel, which was adorned with piranhas, and ran his silvery finger down the spine of one. "Do you know what this creature is?"

"It's a piranha," Archer said.

"*Very* good. And piranhas are nothing like tigers, are they? You see, a tiger you can spot hunting you. You can't do that with piranhas. With piranhas, you won't know you're being hunted. You won't even know you're in trouble. You'll just be swimming merrily along until you unwittingly enter their territory.

"You'll feel a pinch on your toe, but you'll try to think positive. Perhaps you struck it against a sunken branch? *No.* You'll know something *bit* you. And in a panic, you'll make for the shore, but that's pointless. It's already over."

Oliver and Adélaïde stared at each other.

"Once that piranha discovers you're edible, it's going to want all of you—and not just that *one* piranha. The entire school will swarm you with such vigor that the water will look like it's boiling. Then, bite by bite and piece by piece, they'll greedily devour you until there's *nothing* left. And they'll do such a *fine* job of it that when they're finished, it will be like you never existed in the first place."

They all took a few steps away from the crooked man.

"That sounded like a threat," Oliver whispered.

"It *was* a threat," Adélaïde replied.

"You had something to do with the iceberg, too," Archer said. "That's why you were spying on my house. That's why you made bets my grandparents were dead."

"*Another* accusation." The crooked man left the mantel

and circled the trio. "Let's assume you're right. Let's say there *was* a plot. Let's say someone wanted your grandparents to *vanish*. If all of that is true, do you *really* think it wise to get involved?"

Adélaïde shivered. The crooked man stopped directly behind her and wrapped his long fingers around her shoulders. He lowered his head, and his voice became little more than a whisper. "Do you *really* want to swim into waters you know *nothing* about?"

The crooked man yanked Adélaïde toward the fire.

"Let her go!" Oliver shouted, taking hold of her arm. Archer lunged for her other one.

Adélaïde kicked her wooden leg at the crooked man's shin. "Get your hands off me!"

"I didn't think so," the crooked man said, releasing her. "Now run along, children. The excitement has already begun. You don't want to miss it."

They tore from the office and collided with Cornelius, who'd been running the opposite way.

"There you are!" he cried, his one visible eye showing great relief. "Your grandparents were . . . What were you doing in the President's Office?"

"We got lost trying to find the Grand Hall," Archer explained, breathing heavily.

"That's where I'm supposed to bring you. Hurry now. Follow me."

The trio had to take three steps for each of Cornelius's great strides. As they neared the Grand Hall, Greenhorns were being led out by a tall woman in a taut, high-collared dress. Fledger grinned nastily, while Darby's eyes seemed to say, "You do *not* want to go in there."

Cornelius nodded at the tall woman. "Evening, Malmurna."

"You're not taking them into the Grand Hall, are you, Cornelius? It's getting a bit *rough*. And have you seen Benjamin? He snuck away from the banquet, and I haven't been able to find him."

"Can't say I have. Sorry."

Cornelius paused at the doors to the hall. Hysterical shouting echoed from the other side. "Maybe Malmurna's right. Perhaps it's best we all wait in the commons."

"We have to go in," Archer said, almost pleading.

"Very well. But I'll warn you, Archer, it might not be pleasant. Stay by my side. All of you."

◆

• THE THING WITH DIRTY HANDS •

The banquet guests had turned into an angry mob. Most everyone was on their feet, shouting. Cornelius led them to the banquet table, where they stood with their backs to the wall. At the head of the room, before a roaring fire, stood a man with dark hair and a beard as thick as moss.

"Is that Mr. Birthwhistle?" Archer asked.

"That's him, all right," Cornelius replied, his lip curling. "The sleazy pelican."

Archer didn't see much of a resemblance to Benjamin. Mr. Birthwhistle was a very proud-looking man. Or perhaps vain—like a peacock. He wore the finest suit Archer had ever seen. Benjamin was a bit sloppy and disheveled. His father was meticulous. Even with his emotions. Mr. Birthwhistle was the calmest person in the hall.

"Now let's not lose our heads," he called from a podium, gazing down his sharp nose.

The hall remained in chaos. Oliver was struck with a grasshopper rice ball. Beatrice Lune shot to her feet when someone lobbed a broiled elk tongue at her. Archer spotted his grandparents next to her, encircled by the crowd, his grandfather standing tall. When Grandpa Helmsley spoke, his voice rang with authority.

"This is madness, Birthwhistle! We were promised a banquet. Not a trap!"

"Forgive me, Ralph, but I do not believe you're in any position to be calling others *mad*." The hall shook with laughter. "And it's *President* Birthwhistle, if you please."

"What's going on?" Oliver asked Cornelius while shaking rice from his hair.

Cornelius crouched so they could better hear him over the noise.

"Birthwhistle wants a vote," he explained, fetching a tattered book from his jumpsuit pocket. "He can't banish your grandparents outright, but as president, he can have them ostracized. I'm no expert on the Society's Code, but an Ostracization is rare—only taken up when a member is deemed a danger to others."

"Is that what's happening now?" Adélaïde asked.

Cornelius nodded and motioned to the mob. "But the

vote won't be fair. See those purple pins many are wearing? The few armbands and crests with Ms on them? Those are Birthwhistle's flock—the Order of Magellan."

"That's almost everyone," Archer said.

Cornelius flipped open his book and read to them.

CODE AND CONDUCT

162. ON SAFETY

1.5. ANY MEMBER(S) WHO IS THOUGHT TO BE OF UNSOUND MIND AND A DANGER TO OTHERS CAN BE, AT THE DISCRETION OF THE PRESIDENT, TEMPORARILY BANISHED VIA AN OSTRACIZATION VOTE. OSTRACIZED MEMBERS ARE PROHIBITED FROM ANY AND ALL ACTIVITIES OF THE SOCIETY.

"If I had to guess," Cornelius said, "Birthwhistle doesn't want Ralph and Rachel speaking to the other members. That will make what he wants to do next easier."

IF OSTRACIZATION PASSES, A FORMAL INQUIRY WILL BE ARRANGED, AND A SECOND VOTE WILL TAKE PLACE ON WHETHER OR NOT TO MAKE THE TEMPORARY BANISHMENT PERMANENT.

Beatrice Lune's voice rose above the others. "What proof

do you have that the Helmsleys wanted to vanish?"

Mr. Birthwhistle lifted a paper from the podium and dangled it a moment before responding. "Captain Lemurn will soon be in port, but he *graciously* provided written testimony." He started to read. "'The iceberg was thoroughly searched. The Helmsleys were not found. I'm certain they did not want to be found. My crew of five will attest to this.'"

"That's a lie," Grandpa Helmsley insisted. "And you *know it*."

That statement caused a lot of murmuring.

"How exactly would I *know* this is a lie?" Mr. Birthwhistle asked. "And please be clear, Ralph, because it almost sounds like you're suggesting *I* knew something about the iceberg." The murmurs turned to chuckles. "Are you saying you believe *I* had arranged for you to vanish?"

"Ralph's as paranoid as the day he disappeared!"

Mr. Birthwhistle raised a hand to hush the shouter. Grandpa Helmsley was silent. Grandma Helmsley didn't say anything either. She hadn't spoken a word since Archer had entered the hall. But her expression, directed at Mr. Birthwhistle, said a great deal. If his grandmother had the ability to conjure objects out of thin air, Mr. Birthwhistle would, at that very moment, have had a rhinoceros fall on his head.

"Why won't they say anything?" Archer asked, turning back to Cornelius.

"It wouldn't matter with this crowd, Archer," Cornelius

said. "Even if it did, they're in a difficult position. Birthwhistle poisoned many minds against your grandparents—even before they vanished. Without proof, there's not much they can do."

"I'll assume your silence means you've misspoken?" Mr. Birthwhistle continued. "Not to worry. The mind *does* have a tendency to slip with age. Now, I strongly encourage anyone who disagrees with my assessment to vote against the Ostracization. I'm only doing what I feel is in the best interest of our Society. And with that, I give the floor to Mr. Suplard."

Mr. Suplard waddled up to the stage. Archer couldn't believe it. "Is he with Mr. Birthwhistle?"

"Suplard?" Cornelius asked. "I wouldn't think so. He's a bit stuffy—likes to triple starch that collar. But he's just doing his job."

Mr. Suplard stepped behind the podium, but he wasn't tall enough to see over it. "Oh for the love of . . . Where's my stool?" A Society attendant rushed a wooden crate across the stage for him to stand on. When Mr. Suplard's head finally emerged, his expression was perfectly blank.

"What is his job exactly?" Adélaïde asked. "Why does the Society need an Inquiry Department?"

"There's a lot of foul play between the orders," Cornelius explained. "Suplard and his Deputies investigate misconduct, enforce the Code, and oversee all official decisions and votes."

"Quiet, now—I'll ask for quiet, please!" Mr. Suplard adjusted his glasses. "Thirty hands are required to initiate an Ostracization. Do we have thirty hands?"

Far more than thirty hands went up, and among them was the crooked man, who Archer spotted lurking and grinning at the back of the hall.

"Very well." Mr. Suplard motioned, and his Deputies began handing out slips of paper. "Time did not allow for a formal motion to be provided. Mark yea if you believe the Helmsleys *ought* to be ostracized. Nay if you do not."

THE SOCIETY

OSTRACIZATION

☐ YEA

☐ NAY

"Should the vote pass, my department will immediately arrange for a formal Inquiry requiring the attendance of at least eighty percent of our members."

"*Eighty percent?*" Cornelius repeated, nearly shouting. "That's going to be . . . Rosewood will be overrun!"

"I asked for *quiet*," Mr. Suplard insisted, squinting in their direction.

Mr. Birthwhistle, seated at the side of the stage, also turned in their direction. He locked Archer in his gaze, and Archer went prickly all over. Did Mr. Birthwhistle know who he was? The man wasn't smiling—his face was like a statue's—but Archer had the distinct impression that inside, Mr. Birthwhistle was laughing like a madman. Archer shook himself and watched as members marked their ballots and brought them to a wooden box next to the podium.

Archer was overcome with an urge to shout something in his grandparents' defense. This wasn't right. But what could he say? And who would listen? Archer had never felt more insignificant than he did at that moment.

"Chin up, Archer," Cornelius said. "Don't hang your head unless you've done something wrong. Even if the vote passes, and it probably will, this isn't the end."

When the final vote was cast, Mr. Suplard and the Deputies tallied them. After much bickering, the results were in. Mr. Suplard marched to the podium as a Deputy whispered in Mr. Birthwhistle's ear. Mr. Birthwhistle allowed himself a very discreet smile. It vanished a second later, but Archer saw it. So did Cornelius.

"Let's not act surprised," Cornelius said, ushering the trio through the silent crowd to Archer's grandparents. "Don't give that pelican the satisfaction."

"By one hundred and twenty-seven votes," Mr. Suplard announced, "and effective immediately, Ralph and Rachel

Helmsley are hereby ostracized from the Society."

The crowd erupted.

"It sounds like fireworks," Oliver said, shouting so Archer and Adélaïde could hear him.

"As such," Mr. Suplard continued, raising his nasal voice above the crowd, "the Helmsleys are to be excluded from any and all involvement with the Society, its members, and activities. As is stated, should anyone have contact with the Helmsleys after this evening, they too will face Ostracization. My department will begin notifying all members local and abroad and appoint a date for the Inquiry." Mr. Suplard motioned to Society attendants and hesitated before saying, "Escort the Helmsleys out."

Beatrice Lune was fuming. "That Birthwhistle's got a silver tongue. I'd love to slice . . . There they are!"

Grandma and Grandpa Helmsley looked greatly relieved to see them with Cornelius. Grandpa Helmsley placed a firm hand on Archer's shoulder and spoke as though no chaos was encircling them.

"I do believe that's enough excitement for one evening, yes? This was not *quite* the introduction to the Society I was hoping you'd have, Archer."

"We'll see ourselves out, thank you very much!" Grandma Helmsley insisted, shooing the attendants away. She led the group through crowd, her head held high despite the jeers and cries and boos.

◆ The Truth About the Iceberg ◆

Outside, they crossed a footbridge and waited for Cornelius to retrieve the truck. Grandpa Helmsley leaned against the metal railing alongside the canal and gazed somberly at the glowing Society. Grandma Helmsley was more angry than anything.

"We never should have brought them tonight," she said, pacing the snowy cobblestones. "I knew it was a mistake."

"Birthwhistle wasn't supposed to be here." Grandpa Helmsley sighed.

"Speaking of supposed to." Grandma Helmsley turned her sharp eyes to Archer and his friends. "Where were you three? We told you to—" She stopped, seeing their sorry eyes, and put a hand to Archer's cheek. "Forgive me, dear. I'm not angry at you."

"Why didn't you tell them Mr. Birthwhistle was responsible?" Archer asked. "Why didn't you say he wanted you dead? We figured it out. We were with Benjamin. He told us you tried to get rid of a botanist named Wigstan Spinler. He said you had lots of members you want to banish."

"You could start with whoever threw the rice ball grasshopper at me," Oliver suggested.

"Benjamin thinks you wanted to destroy the Society," Archer continued, watching his grandfather, who didn't turn around. "He doesn't think his father had anything to do with the iceberg."

"I don't think anyone in there would believe that," Adélaïde said.

"You should talk to my father," Oliver suggested. "He wants to put your story in his paper. At least the readers of the *Doldrums Press* want to hear what you have to say."

"They want to hear *a* story," Grandma Helmsley replied. "Not necessarily the *true* story. Remember, Oliver, these are the same people who think we brought a curse to Rosewood. That's a difficult audience to work with."

Truck brakes squealed as Cornelius pulled up next to them. Oliver and Adélaïde climbed into the backseat. Grandma Helmsley climbed into the front. Grandpa Helmsley remained at the railing. Archer leaned next to him, feeling a

pang of guilt, and stared down at the frozen canal. He didn't want to look at the Society. The magic had all but vanished.

"Come now, Archer," Grandpa Helmsley said, placing an arm around him. "You mustn't judge the Society based on what you witnessed inside the Grand Hall. I promise you, it's a marvelous place."

"I should have said something," Archer replied. "I wanted to. I almost did."

"I'm glad you didn't," Grandpa Helmsley said. "We must be careful, Archer. What Benjamin told you isn't entirely true. We weren't out to destroy the Society. We were trying to protect it."

"Protect it from what?"

"I can't tell you everything," his grandfather replied. "But you should know there are many discoveries within the Society that are still unknown to the outside world. Wigstan Spinler's work is one of them. We call such work 'Society Restricted.' And we have good reasons for doing that. The problem was, for a long time, no one *inside* the Society knew about Wigstan Spinler's research either—at least, no member outside the Order of Magellan. Mr. Birthwhistle wanted to keep it a secret. When I found out about it, I made Mr. Spinler's work known to all. Mr. Birthwhistle hated me for that."

"Why would he want to keep it a secret?" Archer asked.

"We feared Mr. Birthwhistle intended to use Mr. Spinler's

work to manipulate Society members. You remember what I told you about Doxical Powder? Making someone behave differently would have raised eyebrows, but no one would've known *why* it was happening."

"Why would he want to do that?"

"We have a few guesses, but that's a question we wanted Mr. Birthwhistle to answer. That's why we arranged for Mr. Suplard to be ostracized. We hoped an Inquiry would shed light on the Order of Magellan. We hoped it would get Mr. Birthwhistle to talk. And he did talk. That's when things got bad."

"He told everyone you were jealous of Wigstan Spinler," Archer said. "He told everyone you had a list and were planning to purge the Society. He told everyone you were unfit to be president."

"That's exactly it, Archer. He knew we couldn't defend the decision. All we had were suspicions. And ostracizing Wigstan Spinler was tremendously unpopular. Members sneered at us wherever we went. Threats were even made. It was recommended that your grandmother and I make ourselves scarce until the Inquiry. We boarded a ship for Antarctica . . . and sailed right into Mr. Birthwhistle's trap."

"But if ostracizing Mr. Spinler was so unpopular," Archer said, "would the vote to banish him pass? Mr. Birthwhistle must have been worried it would. Why else would he make the iceberg happen?"

"Mr. Birthwhistle wasn't worried about Mr. Spinler, Archer. He was worried about having the Inquiry Department poking around his Order of Magellan. I'm not sure what else he's hiding, but I am sure he's too careful and meticulous to do something like he did with the iceberg without a good reason. His order is keeping many secrets. And while Mr. Spinler's work is no longer one of them, Mr. Birthwhistle can still use it in subtle ways. He already has."

Archer stared at his grandfather. "The jars inside your trunks."

His grandfather nodded. "During the journey south, your grandmother discovered that crate aboard our ship. She hid the jars inside her trunk, not realizing a jar of Doxical Powder was missing. It's one thing for Mr. Birthwhistle to buy Captain Lemurn. It's another to buy his entire crew. Their job is to get you somewhere safely. Can you imagine Cornelius harming anyone?"

Archer couldn't imagine that. "The captain used Doxical Powder on them?"

"I'm certain he did. I don't know if the crew is aware of that, but they know what they did. And now, fearing punishment, they're lying."

Archer gripped the cold metal railing. "Do you think Benjamin knows any of this?" he asked. "Do you think he knows what his father did?"

"I can't see any reason Mr. Birthwhistle would have told

him about the iceberg," Grandpa Helmsley replied. "And you mustn't hold it against him if he doesn't believe you. In situations like these, the best we can do is what we think's right, and hope others will do the same."

Archer kicked a bit of snow and watched it cascade onto the frozen canal. "What happens now?" he asked.

Grandpa Helmsley smiled wryly, pointing a finger into the air. "The Helmsley Inquiry begins! We have lots to figure out. And I'll let you in on a well-known secret: your grandmother is *far* wiser in these matters. For my own part, I've always found, especially on an expedition, that difficult decisions are best put off till the morning, when everything is less dark. So let's get ourselves back to Willow Street."

Archer released the railing and followed his grandfather into the truck. Few things might be fair, but he couldn't swallow this one. His grandparents didn't *want* to banish Wigstan Spinler. They were trying to protect the Society from Mr. Birthwhistle. They ended up on an iceberg for asking a question he didn't want answered.

Archer watched from the window as they left the cobbled piazza. He could just make out a thin sliver of glass sparkling with moonlight—the greenhouse. And for the entire ride home, all he could do was think about Benjamin, happily poking away at his plants, while in the Grand Hall, Mr. Birthwhistle feasted with delight.

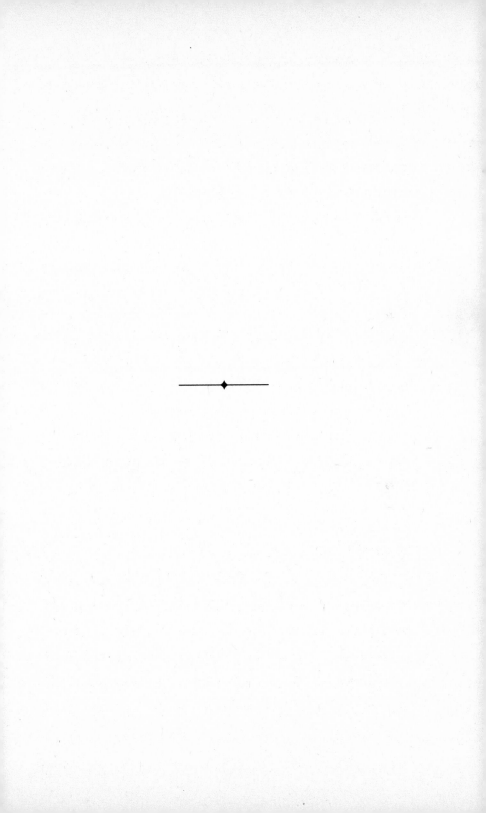

✦ Part Two ✦

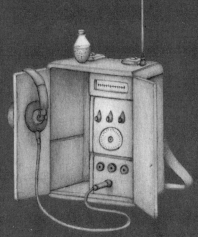

JUST AND UNJUST DESSERTS

CHAPTER
———✦———
SEVEN

✦ Murder Is Kind of Serious ✦

Letters had been sent out. Phone calls had been made. The Society gathering had begun. And life inside Helmsley House had become terribly tense. The day after the disastrous night at the Society, Archer's grandparents told his parents the whole truth of the iceberg. Archer was sent upstairs, so he wasn't sure exactly what they said, but if he hadn't known any better, he'd have thought the house had caught fire.

After a great deal of shouting, there was a meeting at the Glubs'. Archer was under strict instructions to remain home, but that didn't happen. As soon as his parents shut the front door, he bolted to his room, climbed the ladder to the snowy rooftop, carefully hopped over the crack between the houses, and slid down the icy ladder to Oliver's balcony. Oliver was punching his radiator knob when Archer ducked inside.

"Do you know what's happening?" Oliver asked, rubbing

his shivering hands. "Everyone's downstairs. My parents told me to stay up here."

"My grandparents are finally talking," Archer explained. "They told my parents everything. I want to hear what my mother has to say."

They crept down the stairs, which creaked loudly, as stairs always do when you're trying to be quiet, and continued down a narrow hall to where all that separated them from the adults was a double-hinged door.

"Your parents sound calm," Archer whispered, setting his ear against it.

"Your mother doesn't. She might sprain her tongue."

"Richard always suspected there was more to this iceberg story, *but this?*" Mrs. Helmsley said, nearly shouting. "Are you honestly telling us there's someone at that Society who wanted you both *dead?*"

"It's complicated," Grandma Helmsley said. "But that's the gist of it."

A heavy silence followed. Archer and Oliver backed away from the door, thinking it might blow off its hinges with whatever came next.

"There's a crazed iceberg lunatic out there and you'd not thought of telling us *sooner?* Are we in danger? Is Archer in danger?"

"I've already told you, Helena," Grandpa Helmsley said

mildly. "No one is in danger."

"Now let's all calm down a moment," Mr. Glub urged. "Why haven't you involved the authorities?"

"Shouldn't there be an investigation?" Mr. Helmsley agreed.

"The Society handles its own investigations," Grandpa Helmsley explained. "You know that, Richard. We don't allow outsiders to meddle in our affairs."

"So why did that President Birthwhistle speak to the *Chronicle?*" Mrs. Glub asked.

"The effort is not only to banish us from Society but, if possible, from Rosewood itself."

"Let's fight paper with paper," Mr. Glub said. "Come to the *Doldrums Press.* You know the address—just off Howling Bloom on Tullery. Let me write your story."

"Breathe, Helena!" Mrs. Glub cried. "You're going to explode. Here, have another cup of tea. Now take a big sip."

"How much does Archer know?" Mr. Helmsley asked.

"He knows enough, Richard," Grandma Helmsley said. "But he *won't* be told any more."

Archer had a feeling this was said more to his grandfather than his father.

"Finally, some sense has been spoken!" Mrs. Helmsley exclaimed. "Now let me make myself very clear. You two *must* sort this mess out. Archer will be on a train for Raven Wood in two and half weeks. In the meantime, if I have even the *slightest* reason to think he's in danger, I'm taking him out of Rosewood. *For good.*"

Chairs slid backward and footsteps sounded. Archer and Oliver dashed up the stairs. Oliver shut his bedroom door and stared at Archer, not saying a word.

"I think they need help," Archer said, pacing the floor. "What can I do?"

"You can't do anything," Oliver replied. "Mr. Birthwhistle tried to kill your grandparents, Archer. If you get yourself involved, he wouldn't think twice about coming after you."

⋆ Pressing Matters ⋆

Early the following morning, Archer woke to a knock at the front door. From the alcove window above it, he saw a Society truck parked outside. He unlatched the window and leaned out. Beatrice Lune and Cornelius were on the front steps with his grandparents.

"The Inquiry will happen in two weeks," Beatrice was saying as she handed his grandfather a note. "Birthwhistle pressured Suplard. He wants it over as quickly as possible. Suplard's been frantic. The other Orions wanted to come and lend their support too, but it's difficult. Don't take it personally."

"We don't," Grandpa Helmsley assured her. "And I don't want you two getting yourselves into trouble either."

"We're here for more than that." Beatrice lowered her voice. Cornelius looked concerned. "The ostricization vote passed because the hall was stacked with Magellans. Banishment won't be that easy. The other orders are not so against you as Birthwhistle would like to believe."

"Why aren't you saying that like it's a good thing?"

"It's not, Ralph." Grandma Helmsley sighed. "Birthwhistle doesn't want us back. And he's going to do whatever he needs to do to ensure a reinstatement doesn't happen."

Cornelius scratched his eye patch and nodded. "Right now it's your word against Captain Lemurn's. Birthwhistle needs something more. I don't know what that something is, but I'll keep my eye out."

"We're telling our story to the *Doldrums Press*," Grandpa Helmsley said.

"We'll make sure it circulates throughout the Society," Beatrice promised.

Archer shut the window as Beatrice Lune and Cornelius sped off.

Late that evening, when shop owners on Howling Bloom Street turned off their lights and locked their doors, the *Doldrums Press* was still aglow. Mr. Glub gulped his coffee, and throughout the night, his press spat out hundreds of papers. The following morning, they were flung onto every single doorstep in Rosewood, whether they were subscribers or not. The only doorstep without one was Archer's. Mrs. Helmsley must have crept down in the early morning hours and fed it to the garbage disposal. But her efforts were in vain. That same morning, Oliver and Adélaïde stepped through Archer's balcony door with a copy in hand. Archer sat on his bed alongside Adélaïde, listening intently as Oliver read the front page aloud.

THE DOLDRUMS PRESS
HIDDEN PARTS OF THE ICEBERG

Once upon a time, everyone thought the earth was flat. It's not. Once upon a time, everyone thought the sun revolved around the earth. It doesn't. Once upon a time, two explorers were called deranged frauds. They're not. Truth does not stop being true because you believe something different. So what really happened on that iceberg? This is the story you're not supposed to believe.

Ralph and Rachel Helmsley embarked on an expedition to Antarctica with the intention of documenting the relational habits of penguins. During their voyage south, Ralph spotted an iceberg hosting two separate colonies of penguins.

"We must get close," he said. "I'm getting on that iceberg."

After an hour observing the penguins, Ralph and Rachel returned to their dinghy—only to discover that their ship had left without them. They shouted and waved. The ship vanished over the horizon.

"That was no accident," Rachel said as Ralph secured their dinghy to the iceberg.

They dug into the ice to make a shelter. Penguins joined them for the evening.

"It was cramped," Ralph said. "Warm. But cramped."

Ralph and Rachel spent the following day hoping to spot a ship. But that second day quickly turned into a second night, and they returned to their shelter. Day three. Seeing no other option, Ralph and Rachel got into their dinghy and pushed off from the iceberg with the hope of finding rescue. Ralph chiseled a piece of iceberg to take with them, and the penguins saw them off.

The Helmsleys took turns rowing through the frigid waters. The air grew cold. Day became night and hope became desolation.

"Well, my dear," Ralph said. "No one can say we haven't had a lovely go at it all these—"

Ralph's speech was interrupted by a horn. A ship's horn. Not their ship, but a French ship. It was members of the French Société. The Helmsleys were rescued and remained alongside the French explorers for what became a yearlong expedition around Antarctica.

Upon returning to France, the Helmsleys went into hiding. Suspecting that what had happened to them on the iceberg was no accident, they took their time plotting a path home, fearing that a misstep or betrayal could lead to another incident. It was to be a winding journey. It was to be a secret journey. Their first message home came in the form of a package. That package arrived in Rosewood and was sorted at the post office, where someone noticed the names of the senders.

"Ralph and Rachel Helmsley are *alive?*"

What happened on that iceberg was not an accident. It was not a hoax. It was an attempt to dispose of the Helmsleys. That's the truth, whether you believe it or not.

Aubrey Glub
Editor-in-Chief

"I think that'll do a lot of good," Adélaïde said.

"In Rosewood, maybe," Oliver replied, lowering the paper. "I'm not so sure it will at the Society."

Archer agreed with Oliver. His grandfather had never

directly accused Mr. Birthwhistle. His grandmother had probably advised against it. Like Cornelius had said, his grandparents had no evidence, and without evidence, who would believe them?

"Beatrice Lune and Cornelius were here yesterday. The Inquiry is in two weeks," Archer said.

"And there are only two and half weeks until you have to return to Raven Wood." Oliver nudged Adélaïde. "We were talking about something before you got here."

"Do you remember Oliver telling you about that holiday party at DuttonLick's?" Adélaïde asked. "We wanted to see if Mr. DuttonLick would let all of us be assistants."

"Learning how to make chocolates will be fun," Oliver added, nodding. "It'd be nice to have some fun together before you have to leave again."

Under normal circumstances, Archer would have enjoyed that. But with everything going on, it didn't seem right. How would making chocolate help his grandparents?

"We're going to DuttonLick's tonight after dinner," Oliver explained, leaving the paper with Archer and following Adélaïde to the balcony door. "Mr. DuttonLick has a form he wants my parents to sign. I thought we could go together. I'll wait for you if you decide you'd like to come."

◆

✦ UNSPEAKABLE ✦

Archer spent the rest of the afternoon on his bed, and he was still there when dinnertime neared. He'd pasted every newspaper article about his grandparents into his journal and was flipping through the pages. When he heard his grandfather out in the hall, he stashed it beneath a pillow.

"We'll sort it out. We have to."

Archer went to the door and poked his head out. His grandfather was alone, standing before the polar bear.

"*Oh*, Archer. I was just coming to fetch you for dinner."

Archer stared from his grandfather to the polar bear and back again. "Who were you talking to?"

Grandpa Helmsley twinkled. "You might think it a *bit* strange, Archer."

He knew it! "You were speaking with the polar bear, weren't you? He speaks to me too. All of the animals do."

Grandpa Helmsley's laugh filled the hall. "Does your mother know? She does? She must have been horrified when she found out!"

Grandpa Helmsley was still chuckling as he stepped into Archer's bedroom.

"Many years ago, before your mother married your father, they came to Helmsley House for a visit. She overheard me speaking to the zebra downstairs. She's never looked at me the same way since. But I've always had a particular fondness for your mother, Archer. I know she can be a bit *strong*—but I admire her conviction."

Archer thought the word *strong* was a bit weak. His mother had kept his grandparents out of their own home for nearly twelve years.

Grandpa Helmsley approached the dresser. Scattered atop it were many of the gifts his grandparents had secretly sent him when he was little.

"There's something I don't understand," Archer said, watching his grandfather closely. "You were gone for two years. But you were only on the iceberg for three days. Why didn't you let us know you were alive? Why didn't you let us know you'd eventually come home?"

"I wanted to, Archer," his grandfather assured him. "But we were in hiding. We didn't know who we could trust. And we were afraid our letters might be intercepted. We couldn't risk that until we decided what to do."

Grandpa Helmsley began fidgeting with the jade elephant house.

"In a sense, we *did* want to vanish. We learned Birthwhistle had become president of the Society, and we knew the moment he discovered we were still alive, any attempt to return home would cause a storm. I'm not proud to say it, Archer, but I didn't want to face that storm."

"What changed your minds?" Archer asked. "Why did you come home?"

"I had this piece of ice that wouldn't stop nagging me. Every day it told me I needed to return." Grandpa Helmsley turned to face him. "There are a great many things I've been waiting to show you, Archer. I've been waiting nearly twelve years! We'll have to wait a little longer, but it's my hope you'll become a Greenhorn soon. There's nothing that would give me more pleasure. I think you'd become First Greenhorn in no time. And when you're a bit older, we'll embark on an expedition together. Would you like that, Archer?"

Archer swallowed hard. He'd been thinking about Greenhorns ever since he had discovered there was such a thing. Being a Greenhorn sounded like what he'd always dreamed about. And to go on an *actual* expedition with his grandparents?

"But what will happen if the Society banishes you?" he asked.

"Let's not play that game, Archer. We must always hope. Once Dalligold arrives, we'll put something together."

"Dalligold?"

"Mr. Dalligold. He's a dear friend—once head of the Order of Orion. Mr. Dalligold left the Society shortly after we vanished. He knew the iceberg was no accident and searched for us until he found us in France. Your grandmother asked him to represent us during the Inquiry. And let's not forget that we have the truth, Archer. Mr. Birthwhistle must prove a lie. But I suspect, at this very moment, he's hard at work doing just that."

During dinner, Mrs. Helmsley wouldn't even look at Archer's grandparents. She didn't say a word. No one said a word. But the silence said a great deal. Archer ate as fast as he could, eager to get out of there.

"I'm supposed to go to Oliver's," he explained, standing up, his mouth half full of mashed potatoes.

"But it's home by eight at the *very* latest," his mother replied, smiling happily.

It was still rather strange for him to see his mother so delighted about him leaving the house.

◆ WAS THAT WHO I THINK IT WAS? ◆

Oliver was standing on the Glubs' front steps, reading a newspaper, when Archer approached.

"I'm glad you came," he called, joining Archer on the sidewalk. "Adélaïde didn't think you would."

"Why are you reading the *Rosewood Chronicle?*" Archer asked.

"It's for my father. It's garbage, but he needs to keep up on what they're saying."

Adélaïde greeted them on the corner of North Willow Street, and she did look pleasantly surprised. Together, they set off for DuttonLick's sweetshop.

It was snowing less that evening, but it was still very cold, and the wind was swift. Oliver was having a difficult time keeping his newspaper open and steady as they made their way north on Foldink Street.

"Listen to this," he said, clutching it tight as they passed the Button Factory.

ROSEWOOD CHRONICLE
BUS STOPS AFTER LEMON DROPS

Lemon drops were left scattered in the snow after a Rosewood bus, barreling up Foldink Street, struck a patch of ice, lost control, blasted through a snowbank, slid onto Howling Bloom Street, and flattened a lady leaving DuttonLick's with a bag of them. That's right—the Helmsley Curse has claimed another victim.

This is the third freak bus incident in as many days. In response, the city has announced it will suspend all bus service until further notice. It's a decision leading many to wonder: *Could the Helmsley Curse get any worse?*

Oliver finished reading just as they turned onto Howling Bloom Street, which was lucky because a violent gust tore the paper from his hands and carried it far over Rosewood Park. But Oliver barely cared because they were standing before DuttonLick's sweetshop—three stories of pure confection. Through the paneled windows, Archer could see that it was crowded with many of his former Button Factory classmates—including the nasty ones. Alice P. Suggins was tossing jelly beans into Charlie H. Brimble's mouth, while Molly S. Mellings was trying to see how many lollipops she could lick and stick to Digby Fig's back without him noticing. Christmas was over, but Mr. DuttonLick was still celebrating the season with free chocolate days leading up to the big party. Posters were plastered all over the windows. Oliver pointed to one. Today's free sweet was a chocolate raspberry snurple.

"What's a snurple?" he asked.

"It sounds like a disease," Adélaïde replied.

"I hope they're not all gone. I want to try one."

"You mean contract one?"

A huge snowdrift stood between them and the sweetshop doors. And just as they began to scale it, a figure approached from behind and plowed right into them, knocking everyone face-first into the snow. Oliver lifted his head, ready to shout at the rude person, but Archer quickly put a hand over his mouth.

"Was that who I think that was?" Adélaïde whispered, wiping snow off her face.

"If you think it was the crooked man," Archer replied.

Archer had only glimpsed the side of the man's face, but that was enough. The crooked man continued down Howling Bloom Street, clapped his boots outside the door of Bray and Ink, and vanished inside. Archer, Oliver, and Adélaïde hurried after him, slid up to the shop windows, and pressed their faces to the cold glass.

✦ CROOKED EUSTACE MULLFORT ✦

Bray and Ink was narrow, like all the shops along Howling Bloom Street. Inside, it was crowded with tall shelves that leaned one way or the other. Archer, Oliver, and Adélaïde watched the crooked man hastily search those shelves, piled with journals and paper and stamps and ink, before delving deeper into the shop and banging a bell on the counter.

"Follow me," Archer said, pulling away from the glass.

The trio crept through the door and snuck across the aisles until they were at the far side of the shop. They inched to the edge of a shelf and peered around it. The crooked man was still banging the bell, staring over his shoulder at the door.

"*Ah*, Eustace Mullfort!" Mr. Bray called, waddling out from a back room. "Always a pleasure."

Oliver almost laughed. He turned to Adélaïde and mouthed, "His name is *Eustace Mullfort*?"

"Your shop's drafty," Mr. Mullfort replied.

"Drafty?" Mr. Bray glanced around. "I don't feel a draft. Of course, compared to your Strait of Magellan, I've got the fanciest store in Rosewood! Now what can I do you for this evening? More ledgers, is it?" Mr. Bray dipped below the counter. "I've just received a—"

"I need a journal, actually. I didn't see what I wanted on the shelves."

"What're you looking for, exactly?"

Mr. Mullfort stuck his tongue into his cheek. "How about brown leather with, *say*, reinforced corners? And stitching or some such. Green, perhaps?"

Archer couldn't put his finger on it, but the journal Mr. Mullfort described sounded very familiar.

Mr. Bray laughed. "Well, this is certainly something! No longer going for what's cheapest?"

"Do you have one or not?" Mr. Mullfort asked, tapping his spindly fingers on the counter. "I'm in a hurry."

"All right, all right. Don't get yourself all bent out of shape. I might have something in storage."

Mr. Bray disappeared. Mr. Mullfort stepped away from the counter. Archer could no longer see him, but from the footsteps, he knew Mr. Mullfort was near the front door.

"Bray's right. There's no draft," Mr. Mullfort muttered.

Oliver's smile wilted. "He's searching the shelves. He knows someone came in. We need to hide!"

"But where?" Adélaïde whispered, glancing left and right.

Archer looked to the ceiling.
"Up! Go up!"

The trio took hold of the
slanted shelf and quickly climbed
it like a ladder. Archer hoisted
himself over the top, followed
by Oliver, and then they both
grabbed Adélaïde, whose
wooden leg vanished from view
the moment Mr. Mullfort peeked
down the now-empty aisle.

"Found something!" Mr. Bray
called.

The trio sat wedged together, not three feet from the ceiling,
hidden behind reams of yellowed paper, peering down at Mr.
Mullfort as he rushed back to the counter.

"He's balding," Oliver whispered.

"Forgot I had these," Mr. Bray said, dropping a dusty
box on the counter and brushing himself off. "Will they
work?"

Mr. Mullfort tore the box open and lifted a journal. Archer
recognized it immediately.

"Those are the same journals my grandparents use," he said. "The ones I found inside their trunks."

"This should do the job," Mr. Mullfort replied, almost smiling.

Mr. Bray looked somber, gazing at the journal.

"I've never displayed these. They were a special order—for the Helmsleys. I've sold them those journals for as long as I can remember. Always such *kind* customers. It's terrible to see what's happened, isn't it?"

Mr. Mullfort set the journal on the counter and fetched his wallet. "Don't tell me you believe the story that buffoon at the *Doldrums Press* wrote?"

There was a faint grunt next to Archer. Oliver's teeth were clenched. Mr. Bray wasn't too pleased either.

"Aubrey's not a buffoon! I've supplied his paper for years. But I told him he got this one wrong. I mean, *really*. To claim that Captain Whoever-He-Was left the Helmsleys on an iceberg to freeze to death? There was no *reason* given. And then they went into *hiding*? That sounds like paranoia to me." Mr. Bray leaned across the counter. "You must know more. What's everyone at that Society think?"

"They found the story laughable. We're going to banish them. Rosewood officials should do the same."

Mr. Bray shook his head, staring at the dusty box of journals. "If the whispers are anything to go by, that's a real possibility.

I can't imagine they'll need these journals anymore. Take the entire box, if you want."

"I only need *one*. And a large envelope. And stamps."

Mr. Bray set everything on the counter and took Mr. Mullfort's money. As Mr. Bray put the bills into the register, Mr. Mullfort reached into the box and slipped a second journal into his pocket.

"Did he just *steal* one?" Adélaïde whispered.

"He did," Oliver replied.

"I wish you the best of luck," Mr. Bray said, shutting the register and closing up the box. "And everyone at the Society. I'm glad I don't have to deal with any of this."

Mr. Bray lugged the box into the back of the shop.

Mr. Mullfort tore a page from the journal, scribbled a note on it, and after sealing everything inside the envelope, made for the exit. The trio heard the door open as they climbed down the shelf, and they felt a gust of cold wind when it slammed shut. All three stepped out from the shadow of the aisle—and stopped dead.

"I *knew* I wasn't alone in here." Mr. Mullfort smiled at them, his hand still on the doorknob. He opened it. Another cold breeze blew over them. They'd been tricked. "So you've decided to go swimming, have you?"

Mr. Mullfort lunged, grabbed Archer by the collar, and wrenched him out of the shop.

✦ STEAMING ✦

"Sneaky little wunderkind," Mr. Mullfort hissed, dragging Archer into an alleyway next to Bray and Ink and forcing him up against a brick wall. "Your grandparents have you tailing me, do they?"

"Archer? Archer! Where are you?"

In an instant, Oliver and Adélaïde were at his side.

Mr. Mullfort's darkened silhouette stooped before them. "Now be good children and tell me what you saw. You saw something you shouldn't have, didn't you?" His narrowed eyes caught a bit of light streaming down the alley. They were fiery slits.

"We didn't—we were just—looking for school supplies—" Archer stammered.

"You do *not* want to lie to me," Mr. Mullfort barked. His breath smelled like cabbage. "You were hiding, and we only hide when we *have* something to hide."

"He's—he's not lying," Adélaïde insisted. "We were at DuttonLick's getting chocolate. And then we were going to buy school supplies. We did hide. But only because . . . we were afraid, is all."

Mr. Mullfort tapped his crooked finger against Oliver's forehead. "And what about the loose tongue? Does it have anything to add?"

Archer heard something crinkle. With a shaky hand, Oliver presented a small bag of DuttonLick's chocolate eyeballs.

"Chocolates," he managed.

Mr. Mullfort snatched the bag and bit into an eyeball. A second later, he spat the chocolate into the snow as though it'd been laced with poison.

"You saw nothing," he warned, pouring the remaining eyeballs onto the ground and crushing them under his heel. "Don't forget it. You three are in muddy waters, and you *know* what's lurking beneath your feet."

Mr. Mullfort gnashed his teeth and was gone.

The trio released a tremendous gasp and peeled their backs off the alley wall.

"I thought he was going to smash our heads against the bricks," Adélaïde breathed, staring at the demolished chocolate eyeballs.

"I'm glad those aren't *our* eyeballs," Oliver agreed, turning to Archer, who was pulling something out of the snow. "What's that?"

"It's the journal he stole." Archer brushed the cover clean. "It must have fallen from his pocket."

He crept to the entrance of the alley and spotted Mr. Mullfort slithering down Howling Bloom Street with the envelope tucked under his arm.

"There's a letter in that envelope," Archer said as Oliver and Adélaïde huddled around him. "You don't have to come, but I'm following him."

Oliver and Adélaïde weren't about to let Archer tail Mr. Mullfort by himself. They set off together, sticking to whatever shadows they could find, until Mr. Mullfort stopped, glanced over his shoulder, and shoved the envelope into a postbox. He then set off down Foldink Street.

"Maybe I can grab it," Archer said, sidling up to the box and hooking his arm through the slot. But he couldn't get his fingers all the way down.

"Let me try," Adélaïde said, pushing her hand in. "My arms are skinnier."

"Anything?" Archer asked. She shook her head.

"Stupid box with your tiny slot," Oliver grumbled. He swung his foot at it, but slipped and kicked it much harder than he'd intended to. Adélaïde yelped as Oliver fell backward into the snow. The postbox access door creaked back and forth.

"You did it, Ollie!"

"Don't call me Ollie!"

"You didn't have to kick it," Archer said, inspecting the lock. "It's frozen. The postman couldn't turn the key."

Oliver stumbled to his feet as Archer fished out the envelope.

PRESIDENT BIRTHWHISTLE
23 DEANGOR STREET
ROSEWOOD

"Now we know where he lives," Adélaïde said, peering over Archer's shoulder.

"Can we open the envelope without tearing it?" he asked. "I want to read the letter before we put it back."

"Aren't we keeping it?" Oliver questioned. "You said that's the same journal your grandparents use. I'll bet they're making a forgery or something."

"I think that's exactly what they're doing," Archer agreed. "Mr. Birthwhistle needs fake proof. Even if we kept it, Mr. Bray had an entire box of them. But the letter might tell us something."

"Steam," Adélaïde suggested. "Steam will warm the glue, and the envelope will open. We'll be able to seal it again without them knowing."

"Lots of hot steam out here," Oliver said, staring at the heaps of snow.

Adélaïde spun back to Howling Bloom Street. "The café. We'll open it there."

Amaury was outside the coffeehouse, loading the Belmont Café delivery truck as they approached. It was a tiny vehicle with three wheels, a small cab, and a rear cargo storage area, which Amaury was tossing boxes of coffee into.

"Evening, Adié!" he called, wiping sweat from his large brow despite the freezing temperatures. "What's got you limping, Oliver?"

"I slipped on a patch of ice. It's dangerous out here!"

"Certainly is. I've never seen a winter like this in all my life." Amaury inspected the snow he'd have to shovel out from around the truck in order to make his deliveries. "Hope I never do again. What's in the envelope, Archer?"

"Actually," Adélaïde said, taking the envelope from Archer. "It's about what's *not* in the envelope. We forgot to put something inside. We need to steam it open."

Amaury pointed to the café. "You know the drill."

"Amaury looks exhausted," Oliver said as they entered.

"He's completely overworked," Adélaïde agreed, making for an espresso machine behind the bar. "My father set up a coffee laboratory in our cellar. He's gotten a little obsessed with his new espresso blends. And you know what he's like. He doesn't realize he's left so much to Amaury. I have to talk to him about it."

Adélaïde had been watching her father make espresso for as long as she could remember. Her movements were a blur to Archer and Oliver. Buttons were pushed, levers were pulled; the machine let out a deep groan, and then hot steam shot from a valve. Adélaïde held the envelope in it. The seal loosened and popped open. She gave the envelope to Archer. He stuck his hand in and grabbed the journal. The note came out with it.

Expect me at your house Thursday evening. Six o'clock.
I want the communications.

✦ A GENIUS, YOU SAY? ✦

Archer couldn't tell if Oliver and Adélaïde were thinking what he was thinking, but he was still thinking it after returning the envelope to the postbox and entering DuttonLick's sweetshop.

A bell jingled above their heads, and they closed their eyes to better enjoy the delightful aromas. When Archer opened his, he discovered that the sweetshop had gone sour. Button Factory students stood frozen in place, gawking at him. Gone was all sense of merriment and good tidings toward man.

"What are *you* doing in here?" Alice P. Suggins demanded, lowering her bag of hotter than hot fireballs.

"If you must know, I'm here on business," Oliver said importantly. "Mr. DuttonLick asked me to be his assistant for the party."

"Not you, *Glub*," Molly S. Mellings scoffed. "Why is Archer here? He's not making chocolates, is he? He'll curse them!"

Charlie Brimble snickered with his mouth full of jelly beans and stared up at the ceiling. "Can you make it snow *inside*, Archer?"

Archer's ears were pink. "You *really* think my family is responsible for the snow?"

"Of course they are." Alice snorted. "Don't you read the newspapers? It's a fact."

"Forget them," Oliver said. "Go upstairs. I'll get Mr. DuttonLick."

Adélaïde followed Archer past the many sneering students and down an aisle packed with sweets. Oliver stopped at the counter to speak to Mr. DuttonLick before climbing up the spiraling stairs. He paused halfway up, when he spotted Diptikana Misra, standing at the back of the shop, studying him. She quickly seized a box of blueberry pearl coconut clamshells and pretended to read from it.

On the second floor, Archer and Adélaïde sat together in a large window that bubbled out over Howling Bloom Street, watching Amaury wedge himself into the tiny delivery truck.

"I thought vehicles weren't allowed on Howling Bloom Street," Archer said. "Isn't it too narrow?"

"The city gave us permission," Adélaïde explained as Amaury drove off. "Have you ever seen a tinier truck? I think it's cute. And Amaury looks funny in it."

"Mr. DuttonLick said he'd be here in a minute," Oliver said, joining them. "Did either of you see Kana downstairs? I just caught her staring at me again. She pretended she wasn't by grabbing a box of blueberry pearl coconut clamshells. No one eats those things. That box has been there for at least three years. They're probably toxic."

"You should talk to her," Adélaïde suggested, making googly eyes at him.

"I prefer nonverbal communications with Kana."

"Speaking of communication," Adélaïde said to Archer.

"Have you figured it out? Do you have any idea what these communications Mr. Mullfort wants are?"

Archer turned from the window. "Remember when we saw Mr. Mullfort at the Society? He was searching a desk. Cornelius said that it was Mr. Birthwhistle's office. Maybe he was looking for whatever it is then?"

"But *what* do you think they are?" Oliver asked. "Do you think they have something to do with the iceberg?"

"What else would they be communicating about?"

"And the journal," Adélaïde said. "You're going to tell your grandparents about that, right? If Mr. Birthwhistle is making a forgery, they need to know."

Archer *was* going to tell his grandparents, but there was something he wanted to do first—something that would be dangerous and difficult and worst of all, illegal.

"I want to break into Mr. Birthwhistle's house," he said.

Oliver and Adélaïde stared at him as though he'd suggested they go up to DuttonLick's rooftop and throw themselves into the street.

"Mr. Mullfort said he'd be there at six o'clock. If we can get there before they—"

"Wait," said Oliver, shaking his head. "You want to break into Mr. Birthwhistle's house *while he's inside?*"

"*Before* he's inside. We could find a place to hide and then hear what they have to say. My grandparents need proof.

This could be my chance to get it."

"But *how* are we going to get inside?" Adélaïde asked.

"That's the part I need to figure out. Maybe we could—"

"Here we go, Oliver!" Mr. DuttonLick chirped, his head popping up from the spiraling stair. The chocolatier was as skinny as he was cheerful, and his curly hair bounced up and down as he strode toward them and presented a slip of paper to Oliver.

"I'm so wonderfully excited to teach you all my secrets! Three generations of chocolate mastery await you! I hope you're excited to learn!"

"I am," Oliver said, but instead of taking the paper, he pointed to Archer and Adélaïde. "I was wondering, would you mind if my friends were assistants, too?"

"*Mind?* Why would I mind? There's going to be lots to do! We could use all the help we—" Mr. DuttonLick's chirping collapsed into a croak. "But aren't you . . . aren't you Archer *Helmsley?*"

"Kind of," Archer admitted.

Mr. DuttonLick raised a finger, as though he were about to say something very wise, but for a moment, his mouth hung open like a deep sea bass.

"I don't want to sound . . . It's not that I'm ungrateful, you understand. But it's terribly unpleasant, this whole curse business."

Archer couldn't believe it. Did *everyone* in Rosewood think his family was responsible for the snow? It was completely absurd. And while he wasn't desperate to be Mr. DuttonLick's assistant, it would be a handy alibi with his mother, should he need one.

"Terribly unpleasant," Mr. DuttonLick continued, running a hand through his curly hair. "That poor lemon drop lady, rest her soul. And if something were to happen *inside* my shop . . . possible lawsuits and—"

"*Please,*" Adélaïde pleaded. "What if Archer promises he won't get anyone killed?"

"My dear, it's disturbing that Archer would even have to make such a promise."

Oliver whispered in Archer's ear. "Don't get angry. I'm only saying this to help." He then addressed Mr. DuttonLick. "Archer's grandparents are the curse. Not him. Archer was *thrilled* to hear he could be your assistant. It's all he's been talking about. Right, Archer? What were you saying the other day? Oh, right, you said Mr. DuttonLick was a genius."

While it was true that Mr. DuttonLick was a wonderful chocolatier, Archer had never said he thought Mr. DuttonLick was a genius. Mr. DuttonLick was peculiar. Peculiar doesn't always equal genius. But Oliver knew what he was doing.

"A *genius?*" Mr. DuttonLick repeated, flushing with pride. "I'm not sure I'd call myself a *genius*. But I *do* make wonderful chocolate, don't I? Perhaps you're right! Perhaps I *am* a genius!"

To Archer's amazement, Mr. DuttonLick clicked a pen and added two signature lines to the permission slip.

"What kind of monster would I be if I didn't let you assist your favorite genius? Now, have your parents sign this. And bring it back as soon as you can. We'll begin our work next week!"

Mr. DuttonLick practically floated off, repeating the word *genius* under his breath. Archer and Adélaïde stared at Oliver, who grinned widely.

"Mr. DuttonLick likes to be flattered," he explained. "I come here a lot. I know him well."

"But I think your *genius* comment might go to his head," Adélaïde said.

"I think it already did," Archer agreed, laughing.

⬩ STEALING GLIMPSES ⬩

When Archer returned home, he shut his bedroom door and sat down at his desk, flipping through the blank pages of the journal Mr. Mullfort had dropped. Why did they need two journals? Wouldn't one be enough to make a forgery? And why did Mr. Mullfort *steal* this one?

Archer couldn't make sense of it. He left the journal and his desk and stepped out onto his snowy balcony, his mind focused on breaking into Mr. Birthwhistle's house. Mr.

Birthwhistle's house was also Benjamin's house. But Archer didn't want to think about that. He didn't want to think about Benjamin at all.

Across the way, through the top-floor windows of the Belmonts' home, he saw Adélaïde lying on her bed, reading a book. He glanced next door at Kana's house and nearly slipped backward. When he looked again, the windows were empty. But they hadn't been a moment ago.

Why would Kana be watching me? he wondered.

✦ CONCERNING GLUBS AND MISRAS ✦

At Rosewood Port in Barrow's Bay, an elegant ship, sparkling with morning light, drifted through icy water, approached a private slip, and docked. An old man, as elegant as the ship, disembarked and, with the assistance of a cane, entered the port.

"Passport, please," a port guard groaned, craning his neck to glimpse the immense line before him.

"You're new, I see," the old man replied. He hung his cane on the lip of the desk, searched the pockets of his fine twill vest, and presented his passport.

"You've not been in Rosewood for more than two years, Mr. Dalligold," the port guard said. "How did you know I was new?"

Mr. Dalligold didn't respond. Instead, he adjusted his round glasses and lifted a coffee-stained newspaper from the guard's desk.

Rosewood Chronicle

METEOROLOGIST EXPLAINS
THE SCIENCE OF THE HELMSLEY CURSE

"Mr. Dalligold? *Mr. Dalligold.* May I ask what brings you home?"

"*Ah*, yes." Mr. Dalligold lowered the paper and removed his glasses. "I'm here to defend two *very* old friends from the madness we sometimes call society."

"You mean you're here to appear in court?"

"In a manner of speaking."

The port guard searched the floor. "Where's your luggage?"

Mr. Dalligold raised his cane. "I travel light."

On the other side of the city, through the revolving doors of Rosewood Station, a train squealed to a halt and hissed. Three Society members stepped off and stood side by side in the dissipating steam. Throughout the station, eyes settled on them and took in their tattered appearance, but the three were too steeped in conversation to notice.

"All I'm saying is, the Order of Magellan and the Order of Orion have always hated each other."

"It's true, but I trust Birthwhistle's assessment. Captain Lemurn wouldn't leave anyone behind."

"The Helmsleys lost it years ago. Wigstan Spinler knew it better than anyone."

In the center of Rosewood, through the front door of Helmsley House and up four flights of stairs, Archer opened a drawer, hid a stolen journal beneath a sweater, and took Mr. DuttonLick's permission slip to the kitchen.

✦ BEHAVIORAL CHANGES ✦

Mr. and Mrs. Helmsley were alone at the table, speaking quietly. Archer paused in the doorway to listen.

"Who is this Wally Gold they went to meet?" Mrs. Helmsley was saying.

"I don't know any Wally," Mr. Helmsley replied, staring over his newspaper.

"*Wally Gold?*" Mrs. Helmsley repeated, poking her fork at a fruit salad. "I wouldn't trust him—sounds like someone who runs a carnival scam booth."

Archer tilted his head. Were his grandparents meeting with Mr. *Dalligold?* The man his grandfather had told him about? If they were, Archer was thrilled to hear it.

Mr. and Mrs. Helmsley hushed when he approached the table. After their meeting at the Glubs' house, they acted as though nothing was going on whenever Archer was within earshot. And considering Archer was now plotting to break into Mr. Birthwhistle's house, he was quite content to let his parents think he knew very little.

"You look in good spirits, Archer," Mr. Helmsley said,

sipping his coffee. "Enjoying your break from Raven Wood? Or do you miss that country air?"

While the country air had been nice, there wasn't a single thing about Raven Wood that Archer missed. With the exception of Mr. Churnick. And sometimes, someone else.

"I'm glad to be home," he said, and handed his mother the permission slip. "Mr. DuttonLick is having a holiday party next week. He needs assistants to help him prepare. Oliver and I volunteered. Adélaïde, too."

Archer figured there were many ways his mother could have reacted to this, but he wasn't prepared for the way she did. It looked like she might cry tears of joy.

"Did you hear that, Richard?" She held the paper as though it were a trophy. "Archer has *volunteered* to help at a *party*! *That Mr. Churnick!*"

"That certainly *is* something," Mr. Helmsley said, considering Archer with a pinch of suspicion. "Odd man, Mr. DuttonLick. Awfully smiley."

"If you keep this up, Archer," Mrs. Helmsley continued, beaming as she added her signature to Mrs. Glub's and Mr. Belmont's, "I might let you take over my flower festivals one day."

Taking over the Willow Street Flower Festivals was the last thing Archer wanted, but he forced a smile and said, "That might be nice."

Archer left his house and knocked on the Glubs' front door. Mrs. Glub answered, looking more frazzled than usual.

"Oh, uh, good morning, Archer. Come in. Come in."

Archer watched Mrs. Glub from the corner of his eye as he hung up his coat. Mr. Glub stumbled out of the kitchen, mumbling to himself and staring at a piece of paper covered in numbers.

"Good morning, Mr. Glub," Archer said, waving.

But Mr. Glub passed him without even noticing.

"Is everything all right?" Archer asked.

Mrs. Glub strained a smile. "Never better. Oliver and Adélaïde are across the hall. I've made your favorite. Apple cider turnovers."

Archer poked his head into the great room. Oliver and Adélaïde were seated on the sofa before the fireplace.

"They won't disappear," Adélaïde was saying. "Give it a moment. You're going to burn your tongue."

Between his friends and a cozy fire, resting on an ottoman was the tray of apple cider turnovers. They were still bubbling hot. Archer hurried in and grabbed one. Oliver already had. Both wasted no time chowing down, breathing hard to cool each bite before swallowing. Oliver reached for a second before he'd finished his first. Adélaïde watched with disgust.

"You don't understand," Oliver said, sucking a piece of

caramel from between his teeth. "You've never tried these ones."

"They're the best thing Mrs. Glub makes," Archer agreed.

"I'm sure they're delicious. But that doesn't mean you shouldn't chew."

"Is everything okay with your parents?" Archer asked Oliver, in between bites.

Oliver suddenly looked guilty for eating like a starved pig. "It's nothing," he said, setting his half-eaten turnover back on the tray.

It was clearly not nothing. And Archer was about to push the matter, but Adélaïde made a face that suggested she'd already tried.

"Have you had any ideas?" she asked.

Archer shook his head. Two days had passed since their run-in with Mr. Mullfort, and Archer still didn't know how they might break into Mr. Birthwhistle's house. The meeting was tomorrow evening. And as far as he could see, their only option involved a rock and lots of broken glass. Archer thought it best to save that as a last resort.

"I still think you could ask Benjamin," Adélaïde said, finally reaching for a turnover. "It's his house, too."

Oliver shook his head and turned to look out the window. "What's Archer supposed to say? 'Hi, Benjamin. I'm here to spy on your father and prove he tried to murder my grandparents, so if you wouldn't mind letting us in, this should only take a few minutes and we'll—" Oliver shot to his feet. "I don't believe it!"

"You don't believe what?" Adélaïde asked.

"It's Kana. She's in the garden. She was just staring at these windows. Does she know I'm in here?"

"I thought she was watching me the other night," Archer said, standing up. "But maybe she was watching your house."

Archer and Adélaïde joined Oliver, peering out the window and over the Glubs' garden wall. Kana was in her garden, building a snowman, her silver streak of hair curling down the side of her head.

"Why does her snowman have a base and three midsections, but no head?" Archer asked.

"Because she's a strange one," Oliver replied.

"I'm sure she's perfectly normal," Adélaïde insisted.

"As normal as that snowman," Oliver agreed.

Kana glanced over her shoulder. The trio ducked below the windowsill.

"Did she see us?" Adélaïde asked.

"I don't think so," Oliver said. "But I want to know what's going on. I'm sick of living in fear. Follow me."

At the garden door, Oliver put a finger to his nose. "We'll study her up close before saying anything."

"What do you mean, *study* her?" Adélaïde asked. "She's not a zoo creature, Oliver!"

• WISHING NOT SO WELL •

Earlier that winter, Mrs. Glub had had Oliver shovel the garden patio after every snowfall. Having nowhere to put the great heaps, Oliver had piled the snow against the back garden wall. It had grown into quite a mountain. Now, in perfect silence, Archer, Oliver, and Adélaïde climbed that mound to peek into Kana's garden. Almost immediately, Kana turned.

Archer squirmed under Kana's gaze. Were her bright blue fish eyes looking at him or through him? Adélaïde tried to explain on behalf of the group, but she was just as sheepish.

"We were . . . and then you . . . What I mean to say is, *how did you hear us?*"

"I didn't." Kana giggled. "I felt you."

"That's *perfectly normal*," Oliver mumbled, nudging Adélaïde with a great deal of satisfaction. "We're only here because I want to know why you've been watching me."

Kana twirled her silver streak of hair around her finger. "I was being a bit obvious about it, wasn't I? It's just that I'm worried about you."

Oliver's satisfied grin disintegrated. "*You're* worried about me?" he said almost indignantly. "*You're* the one who falls down wishing wells."

"Is that true, or was it only a rumor?" Adélaïde asked.

"It's true. I forgot to let go of the coin. Or I didn't want to let go. I think that's it. Yes. I threw the coin in but didn't want to let go. And then I tripped over my foot."

"And yet you're worried about *me*?" Oliver asked slowly.

"Very much. I think you're in danger of falling down a well, too. Not a real well, of course. But you worry about lots of things, don't you? Almost everything."

Oliver went bright red, but Kana wasn't finished.

"And I'm worried that one day, you might wish to throw your cares away, but after so much time, you won't be able to let go."

"Are you psychic?" Archer asked with amazement.

"Psycho is more like it," Oliver grumbled.

"I'm not *psycho*," Kana insisted with an intensity that surprised Archer. "I go to the Button Factory. That's how I know you three. Everyone talks about you. You're very popular." She paused. "Maybe *popular* is the wrong word. Nothing they say about you is very good."

"Well, you should hear what they say about—"

Adélaïde elbowed Oliver before he could finish.

"I *know* what they say about me. But I'm not crazy. And I'm sorry if I offended you."

Kana put her back to them and began patting one of her snowman's three stomachs. Adélaïde flashed Oliver a sharp eye and tried to smooth things over.

"Where did you live before moving here, Kana?"

"I used to live on Deangor Street," she replied, keeping her back to them. "That's on the other side of the park. I didn't like that house. I begged my parents to move until we finally did." Kana stared up at her new house as though it had whispered to her. "This one isn't much better. There's something dark about this house, too."

"Probably because it used to belong to Mrs. Murkley," Adélaïde suggested. "What was wrong with your old house?"

"The problem wasn't *my* house. It was the one next door. Benjamin was nice. But his father filled me with terrible feelings."

Archer nearly slipped down the snowbank. "Did you say *Benjamin*? You don't mean . . . You didn't live next to the Birthwhistles, did you?"

Kana turned to face him. "I did. Do you know them?"

Archer picked his jaw up off the wall.

"I'm glad your grandparents are alive, by the way," she continued, once again twirling her silver streak. "I know the papers are saying awful things. But I'm glad my wish came true."

"What wish?" Archer asked.

"I saw the iceberg headline two years ago, like everyone

else. After I did, I began wishing your grandparents were still alive. There's a hidden wishing well inside a Rosewood Park hollow. And for two years, I made that wish almost every day."

Adélaïde tilted her head. "Are you saying *that's* why you fell down the well?"

Kana nodded. "After two years, I thought I should stop. Why are—why are his eyes flickering like that?"

Adélaïde peered at Archer. "He can't hear you. He goes to this place sometimes. We're not sure where it is."

Kana smiled, seeming to know exactly where that place was. "I've gotten lost there."

Oliver paled and shook Archer's shoulder. Archer snapped to and locked eyes with Kana.

"Who lives in your house now?"

"Why do you want to know who lives in her house?" Adélaïde asked.

"He wants to use my old house to get into the gardens and hop over the wall so he can break into the Birthwhistles' house," Kana said. "That's the part I don't understand. Why do you want to break into the Birthwhistles' house?"

"*That's* the part you don't understand?" Adélaïde marveled.

"It's a long story," Archer said. "I'll explain everything, Kana. But we need to investigate something."

Kana bit her lip, thinking it over. "It's a shame you can't ask Digby."

Digby? Archer knew Digby. Digby went to the Button Factory. But why would he ask . . . His eyes widened. *Of course.* Digby's mother was Mrs. Fig, the lady who'd given him an earful at Rosewood Station. Benjamin had stayed with the Figs until his father arrived. Was Benjamin's other neighbor Digby? Archer didn't have to ask.

"I'll fig the phones," Kana said, hurrying away. "I mean, I'll phone the Figs."

◆ A FIG IN THE HAND IS WORTHLESS ◆

"And you're certain Digby is at DuttonLick's?" Adélaïde asked, walking alongside Kana as they set off for Howling Bloom Street.

"I'm sure," Kana replied. "Mrs. Fig said Digby had only just left his house. I think he'll help you. He's nice. Or at least, he doesn't make fun of me."

While making their way north, Archer and Adélaïde had told Kana everything. She listened intently. Archer didn't expect her to believe him. No one else in Rosewood would have. The strange thing was, Kana *did* believe him. She didn't question any of it.

"I've never liked Mr. Birthwhistle," she said. "He frightens me."

Oliver trudged a few feet behind everyone. He hadn't taken kindly to being told he was a worrywart. And he didn't like seeing Archer and Adélaïde being so chummy with Kana.

"Caution is sensible," he mumbled as they approached the sweetshop.

Before entering, Archer asked the others if they wouldn't mind pooling their money together in order to buy Digby some sweets. He wasn't going to force Digby to help him, but a little bribe never hurt anyone. Archer, Adélaïde, and Kana had a few coins between them. Oliver had a single coin and a bent paper clip.

"My parents cut my allowance," he explained.

They scoured DuttonLick's shelves until Archer's arms were overflowing with sweets. At the counter, Oliver handed Mr. DuttonLick the slip with their parents' signatures, and Adélaïde paid for the candy.

"Can't get enough of my *genius* sweets, can you, Archer?" Mr. DuttonLick chirped, winking at him. Archer smiled awkwardly. "Come back next week! We have lots to do!"

They found Digby on the third floor, sitting alone on a couch like a bump on a log. Digby was on the rounder side, like his mother. But fortunately, he hadn't inherited her frightening smile.

"A belated merry Christmas, Digby!" Adélaïde cheered half-heartedly as Archer dropped the sweets into his lap.

Digby's whole face lit up. Archer thought he might explode.

"This was very nice of you!" he said, wasting no time tearing open a box of seahorse bubble gum and popping a handful into his mouth. "I didn't realize I'd spent all my Christmas money until I got here."

"You might not think it's very nice of us in a minute," Archer said as they all sat down before him.

Digby stopped chewing.

Kana had suggested Archer not mention anything about Mr. Birthwhistle being an attempted murderer, so Archer spun a confectioned tale, explaining to Digby that Benjamin had been his roommate at Raven Wood and that he'd gotten Benjamin a Christmas gift, but because Benjamin wouldn't be returning to Raven Wood, he wanted to leave the gift in Benjamin's bedroom as a fun surprise.

Digby popped a few more pieces of gum into his mouth, looking skeptical.

"I have a key, but they'll have to do it for you," he said, wadding the gum in his cheek and pointing at Oliver, Adélaïde, and Kana. "You can't come, Archer. My mother doesn't like you or your family. She says you're strange and dangerous people."

Archer slumped back into the couch.

"But you'll let us in if Archer doesn't come?" Adélaïde confirmed.

"Sure. But you'll have to be quick. My mother can't know."

It was obvious where Adélaïde was going with this. It was equally obvious that Oliver wanted no part in breaking into the Birthwhistles' house without Archer. Perhaps that was what he was about to say when he caught Kana eyeing him. *You worry about everything.*

"Get out of my head, Kana!" Oliver demanded. "It's creeping me out!"

Kana hadn't said a word, and if anyone was acting weird, it was Oliver.

"And you're wrong anyway. I'm not worried." He paused as though not believing what he was about to say. "I'll be in charge of this."

Digby's cheeks bulged with gum. "Why would you be worried about giving Benjamin a gift?"

"We're not," Adélaïde said quickly. "Oliver just worries about everything. Thanks for agreeing to help us. We'll see you tomorrow. Don't forget. We'll be at your house before six."

"I'll be there," Digby replied. "And thanks again for the candy."

Archer led everyone back downstairs, not liking this idea anymore. He had no intention of sending his friends into Mr. Birthwhistle's house without him.

"I'd like to go with you," Kana said. "Especially since you can't, Archer."

"Thanks, Kana. But I'm not staying home. I'm going, too."

"You can't come, Archer," Adélaïde insisted. "You heard Digby. He won't give us the key if you're there. So unless there's some way for you to be there without actually being there, you'll—" She paused, peering out DuttonLick's door and across the street at her father's café. "Actually, I think there is a way for you to be there without actually being there. We could use a radio. Amaury has lots of equipment. It's his hobby."

"I have a radio in the map room," Archer said, perking up as they stepped outside. "I used it once. Someone tried to sell me something. I'm not sure exactly how it works."

"Let's ask Amaury," Adélaïde said. "I'm sure he'll show us. Do you want to come to the café, Kana? *Kana?*"

Kana was standing perfectly still, staring up at the clouds.

"I think I'll go for a walk," she said. "It won't be so easy after the blizzard."

"*Blizzard?*" Archer repeated. He tilted his head and gazed up at the clouds. "How do you know there's going to be a blizzard?"

"I'm not exactly sure. But I can feel it. Can't you?"

The only thing Archer felt was concern. Letting Kana wander the icy streets of Rosewood on her own seemed like a bad idea.

"I'll be fine." Kana giggled. "But thank you for your concern."

"Why are we letting her join us?" Oliver whispered as they left Kana, who was still staring at the sky. "She's completely cracked."

"No, she's not, Oliver," Adélaïde objected. "She's intuitive. You're only being a rotten eggplant because she told you something you didn't want to hear."

"How intuitive can she be?" Oliver asked. "She lived next door to Mr. Birthwhistle and had no idea what he tried to do. *You* only like her because she's as flaky as fresh croissant. And when there's no blizzard, you'll know I'm right."

Adélaïde paused at the café door. "But if there is a blizzard, you're going to apologize to her." She stuck out her hand. "Deal?"

Oliver confidently shook it. *"Deal."*

⬧ AMAURY THE EXHAUSTED ⬧

Belmont Café brimmed with patrons, but aside from clinking spoons and slurps, it was silent. Everyone was hidden behind a newspaper. The *Rosewood Chronicle* was everywhere. Archer glanced at the newspaper rack. A large pile of *Doldrums Press* papers sat untouched.

"That's why my parents cut my allowance," Oliver explained as they followed Adélaïde to the bar. "My father's readers aren't happy he took your grandparents' side. He lost a bunch of subscribers when he ran the true iceberg story. He's losing more every day. Everyone wants to read the *Chronicle*. They think it's more exciting. Don't tell your grandparents. My father said they have enough to worry about."

Archer felt both terrible and grateful. That explained why Mr. and Mrs. Glub were so distracted. "I'm sorry your family got dragged into this," he said, sitting on a barstool.

"Don't be. My father's not sorry. He said the *Chronicle* is like candy—that eventually, too much of it will make people sick." Oliver stared around the café. "I hope that happens sooner than later."

Amaury was leaning against the bar with his eyelids migrating south. They reversed course when he noticed Adélaïde. "Hot chocolates?" he asked over a yawn.

"Only if it's not too much trouble," she replied.

"For you it's never trouble." Amaury went to the hot chocolate machine and pulled levers left and right. Steam shot from valves, the machine groaned, and then, thick, velvety chocolate flowed from three nozzles into three cups. Amaury slid the cups down the bar.

"Your hot chocolate is the best, Amaury," Oliver said, catching his cup and taking a gulp.

"If you want the best, you must use the best," Amaury replied. "We had DuttonLick make us a special chocolate. Very rich. Melts to perfection."

"I know you're busy," Adélaïde said, watching Amaury wipe the nozzles clean with a wet rag. "But were wondering if you had a moment to teach us about radios."

Amaury yawned again. "I'd be happy to," he said. "Why the sudden interest?"

"There's a project we're working on," Archer explained.

"That Button Factory hasn't got you working over the break, have they?"

"No," Oliver said. "It's extracurricular."

Amaury glanced around at the customers still buried in newspapers. "We'd best do it before the next wave arrives."

The back room of Belmont Café was crowded with bags of coffee beans and supplies, worn-out espresso machines, and extra barstools. In the corner, near a window, were a chair and a desk with Amaury's radio equipment on it. Amaury collapsed into the chair, and Archer thought he might fall asleep on the spot.

"I'm going to help you today," Adélaïde said, placing her hand on Amaury's shoulder. "And I promise I'll talk to my father."

"Thank you, Adie." Amaury sat up straight and cracked his knuckles. "Now, the first thing you need to know about radios is—"

"We were actually wondering if you had one that's portable?" Archer asked.

With some difficulty, Amaury bent down below the desk and lifted what looked to be a small metal box with two straps. "This fellow is," he said, sitting it on his lap. "Not sure why I bought it, to tell you the truth. But they're not the easiest to come by. It works the same as a desk radio, except it's hand powered."

Amaury clicked a button, and a handle flipped down on one side. "This is the crank," he said, spinning it rapidly.

"If you need the radio powered for a long time, you'll have to spend a good while charging it." After two minutes, he released the crank. "That'll do for the demonstration."

Amaury unlatched the back panel to reveal the radio. There was a microphone tucked to side and a pair of headphones hanging from a hook. Amaury proceeded to explain everything there was to know about radios. It was more in-depth than any of them had anticipated. Archer's hand kept cramping, trying to write everything down. He was almost certain he heard Oliver snoring at one point.

"Now in order to communicate between two different radios," Amaury said, "you'll have to pair them using a frequency number."

Amaury adjusted a dial on the portable radio, setting the frequency to his desk radio, and then strapped the radio to Adélaïde's back. He handed her the microphone and headphones and instructed her to go to the far wall. Archer sat down at the desk, and Amaury told him to say something into the microphone.

"Hello?"

"Bonjour?"

It worked perfectly. And they went on talking. Amaury laughed, clearly enjoying their interest in his hobby, but his laugh trailed off when a bell jingled at the front of the shop.

"Would you mind if we borrowed this radio tomorrow?" Adélaïde asked, returning to the desk.

"It's yours whenever you'd like, Adie," Amaury said, staring at the radios as though they were a long-lost love. "I haven't had time to use these in ages."

The bell rang again. Amaury lumbered out with the eagerness of a pig headed for slaughter.

"I'll be right there to help," Adélaïde called. "Oliver, Archer, help me get this thing off."

⋆ COUGHING COFFEE ⋆

Adélaïde grabbed her uniform from a peg on the wall and stepped behind a mountain of Belmont Coffee boxes to change. She reemerged in a pale blue dress, and had a yellow apron with the words BELMONT CAFÉ embroidered on it tied round her waist with a deep blue ribbon. Adélaïde's father had it made especially for her, and even though she looked very pretty, Archer and Oliver tried their best not to laugh.

"What?" she asked, flushing as she glanced down at herself.

"I'd like three coffees, dearie," Oliver replied, imitating

a fussy customer. "The first I'd like with extra cream, and the second with three and half tablespoons of sugar. The third I'd like black. Did you get all that or would you like me to write—"

Adélaïde flicked a stray espresso bean from atop a box. It shot straight into Oliver's throat. Oliver coughed, but the bean was lodged. Archer smacked his back until it finally popped out.

"And you say I'm the rotten eggplant!" Oliver said, rubbing his throat. "I was only teasing you. You look nice."

"Thank you, *dearie*."

Adélaïde gave them an abrupt curtsy and made for the front of the café. Archer and Oliver watched her greet a customer with smile far more pleasant than the one she'd left them with.

"One-legged French girls," Oliver grumbled.

"Are you sure *you* want to be in charge of this plan?" Archer asked, grinning.

"Of course," Oliver replied, trying to sound self-assured. "But I might *allow* her to think she's in charge."

The following afternoon, Archer and Oliver went to Adélaïde's house to finalize the plan. Adélaïde and Kana answered the door together. Both were laughing and went on laughing as they walked down the hall.

"Were they talking about us?" Oliver whispered, kicking off his boots.

"I think so. But we were talking about them, too."

"I was just trying to say I think it's a *little* strange that Kana wants to help us. We barely know her. And I'm not sure she will help. She might do something *strange* and get us caught."

"She's already been helpful," Archer said, following Oliver down the hall. "She's the one who knows the Figs. I don't think Digby would give us the key without her."

Archer had never been inside Adélaïde's house before, but as they stepped into the large sitting room, it was quickly apparent Mr. Belmont wasn't much of a decorator. In the center of the room was a simple rug with two elegant couches and two armchairs positioned around an old table. Everything was nice. But that was it. No pictures, no plants, and no knickknacks of any kind.

Archer and Oliver sat down on the couch opposite Kana and Adélaïde. Adélaïde's beagle, Fritz, was resting his head on Kana's lap, and Kana was scratching his ears.

"Here's my radio's frequency number," Archer said, tearing a page from his journal and sliding it across the table to Adélaïde. "But I'm still not comfortable with this."

In a few short hours, Oliver, Adélaïde, and Kana would be breaking into the Birthwhistles' house to help *his* grandparents.

"We'll be fine," Adélaïde assured him. "As long as we get

there before Mr. Birthwhistle and Mr. Mullfort arrive."

"Deangor Street is about a ten-minute walk from here," Kana said, now rubbing Fritz's belly.

"I told Archer we should hide in Mr. Birthwhistle's office," Oliver said. "That's the most likely place they'd go. My father's office is on the second floor of our house."

"So is mine's," Archer added.

"What happens if Mr. Birthwhistle gives Mr. Mullfort these communications you talked about?" Kana asked. "You want those?"

"We're not sure what they are," Archer explained. "But if they have something to do with the iceberg, we need to get them. You'll have to follow Mr. Mullfort when he leaves, and I'll meet you wherever he's going."

"You were his neighbor, Kana," Oliver said, leaning forward hopefully. "Do you know *anything* else about Mr. Birthwhistle that might help us?"

Kana thought it over for a long while, but Oliver's hope became despair when all she said was "He has a beard."

CHAPTER

✦

TEN

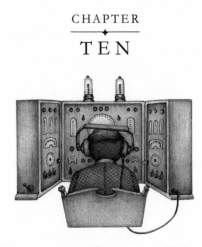

✦ Over the Garden Wall ✦

Archer slipped into the map room and locked the door behind
him. He sat in front of the radio, opened his journal, set the
dial to Adélaïde's frequency, placed the microphone before
him, and secured the headphones. He then anxiously tapped
his pen on the desk, waiting for the static to cut.

ADÉLAÏDE: It's on. I set it to Archer's frequency. Are the straps
           tight? It shouldn't be loose.
OLIVER: Stop jerking them. It's tight enough.
ADÉLAÏDE: All right. Here, put the headphones on. Hold the
           microphone close to your mouth. See if Archer's there.
OLIVER: HELLO? ARCHER? CAN YOU HEAR—

Archer threw the headphones off. His ears were thumping,
and even with the headphones at arm's length, he could hear
Oliver loud and clear.

OLIVER: ARCHER? ARE YOU THERE, ARCHER? THIS IS
OLIVER. OLIVER GLUB. HELLO? ARCHER?

Archer rubbed his ears and waited for Oliver to stop
shouting. Once he did, Archer cautiously put the headphones
back on.

OLIVER: I don't think he can hear me. He's not responding. Are you sure
the frequency is right?

ADÉLAÏDE: Where's the paper with his number?

OLIVER: It's on that box.

ARCHER: I can hear you, Oliver. The frequency isn't wrong.

OLIVER: Wait. I hear something. ARCHER? IS THAT—

ARCHER: It's me! But *please*, stop shouting!

OLIVER: OH! I'M SOOorry. I might have dozed off when
Amaury was explaining how this works. Yes, I can hear him
now. We're about to leave, Archer. Hurry, Kana. We have to
get going.

ADÉLAÏDE: Leave her alone. We still have time.

KANA: That was very good hot chocolate.

OLIVER: Archer, we're leaving the café and should be . . . What are
you—No. I'm in charge of the—

KANA: Hi, Archer. It's Kana. How are—

OLIVER: Give it back. And please don't touch it again without asking.
Sorry about that. We've left the café and—*Oh!*
Hold on.

ADÉLAÏDE: Did he just eat something off the ground?

KANA: He *did*.

OLIVER: It was a lemon drop. Don't look at me like that. It wasn't dirty. It
            was in the snow.

ADÉLAÏDE: But don't you realize where that came from?

OLIVER: DuttonLick's, probably.

ADÉLAÏDE: *Yes*, but it must have belonged to the lady who was hit by
            the bus.

OLIVER: . . .

KANA: He's going to throw up.

OLIVER: I'm fine. Keep going. I'm just rinsing my mouth with snow. . . .
            Pyuck.

ARCHER: What's going on?

OLIVER: Nothing important. We're crossing Foldink Street now
            and heading north around Rosewood Park. We . . . but I
            think . . . the Hollow? . . . it's where? . . . so we're . . .

The signal cut in and out as they crossed Rosewood Park,
and he could barely hear Oliver.

OLIVER: I think I lost him. Archer? Are you still there? Hello?

ARCHER: I can hear you now. Where are you?

OLIVER: We're on Deangor Street.

KANA: That's my old house. Isn't it pretty? That's the Birthwhistles'
            house.

OLIVER: Mr. Birthwhistle's house is completely dark. I don't think
            anyone's home. We're walking up the Figs' front steps. You
            should knock, Kana. You're the one who knows them.

Knock knock knock.

OLIVER: It sounds like someone's—

MRS. FIG: Oh! Kana, dear! What a lovely surprise. We've missed seeing you. But who are . . . Is that a radio strapped to his back?

ADÉLAÏDE: *Uh,* his father runs the *Doldrums Press.* And his father . . . he asked us to do a report on the Rosewood snow for an article. We thought we'd interview Digby to get his thoughts.

MRS. FIG: Yes, this winter has been something, hasn't it? Those horrible Helmsleys have really—

The conversation muffled. Archer guessed Oliver had covered the microphone with his hand, but Mrs. Fig's opinion of the Helmsleys was no secret to Archer.

MRS. FIG: Regardless, it's wonderful to know Digby has *responsible* friends. Keeping busy and working hard over the break. Please, come in! You all look perfectly frozen. Digby! You have friends here!

OLIVER: We're inside, Archer. Mrs. Fig's fetching Digby.

MRS. FIG: They're frozen, Digby. Get them something hot to drink. I'll be upstairs if you need me.

ADÉLAÏDE: We need to hurry, Digby. Do you have the—

DIGBY: Shhh! Wait till she's gone. All right. Here's the key. Bring it back *as soon* as you're done.

OLIVER: We have the key, Archer. We're heading next door and—

ADÉLAÏDE: Go back! Hurry! Get inside!

OLIVER: What's going on?

ADÉLAÏDE: A Society truck just pulled up.

OLIVER: Is it Mr. Birthwhistle?

ADÉLAÏDE: I didn't see. Check the window.

OLIVER: It's Mr. Mullfort. He's waiting on the front steps. Mr. Mullfort's early, Archer.

KANA: Mr. Birthwhistle isn't with him.

ADÉLAÏDE: Digby, does this key open the garden door, too?

DIGBY: Yes, it opens all the doors.

ADÉLAÏDE: Do you have a ladder?

DIGBY: Why do you need a ladder? What's going on? And where's Benjamin's gift?

ADÉLAÏDE: I'll explain in a minute, Digby, but please. We need a ladder. Quickly.

There was a lot of scuffling, and everyone seemed to be talking at once. Archer couldn't make sense of it.

OLIVER: Change of plans, Archer. We're in the garden. We're going over the wall. Where's Digby? Did he get the ladder?

KANA: He's coming now, but look at him. He knows we're lying. He's panicking.

ADÉLAÏDE: He'll be fine.

DIGBY: Will this work?

ADÉLAÏDE: That's perfect, thank you.

DIGBY: What exactly is going on here? Did you . . . I have a bad feeling about this.

KANA: What sort of bad feeling?

ADÉLAÏDE: We don't have time for feelings. Oliver, help me with the ladder. Don't make the angle too steep. Step on the first rung. Wedge it into the snow. Is it steady? Shake it. Good. You go first.

OLIVER: Stand back. I need room to get up.

ADÉLAÏDE: Be careful with Amaury's radio. Clear some of the snow. Don't slip.

OLIVER: There's a small greenhouse in the backyard. It's next to the wall. I think if I . . . Yes, I can just—

ADÉLAÏDE: OLIVER!

OLIVER: I'm fine. The snow was deep. But be careful. The greenhouse roof is slippery. Archer?

ARCHER: I'm here, Oliver. Are you in the backyard?

OLIVER: Yes. The lights are still off. They can't be inside yet. Hold on. Adélaïde's coming now. I've got your foot. Slower!

ADÉLAÏDE: Now hurry, Kana.

OLIVER: Tell her to watch her footing. She's going to knock the ladder. Give me your hand, Kana. We're all here, Archer. We're going to . . . No. I told you not to touch the microphone.

KANA: You need to tell Archer about Digby. He's not going to wait for us. I told you he was panicking.

ADÉLAÏDE: Digby, what's going on?

DIGBY: . . .

OLIVER: Digby, we know you can hear us. We just left you.

DIGBY: I'm sorry. I'm not sure what you're up to, but I can't be a part of this. I promise I won't say anything if you bring back the key. I *need* that key.

OLIVER: Digby, put the ladder back! Digby! No. You can't leave us—

ADÉLAÏDE: He's gone.

OLIVER: Archer?

ARCHER: Yes?

OLIVER: We have a problem. Digby abandoned us. And he took

	the ladder. No, Kana, I don't think he's just getting a drink of water. Look, he turned off the garden lights.
ARCHER:	Oliver?
OLIVER:	Yes?
ARCHER:	How are you going to get back out?
OLIVER:	I have no idea. Change of plans again. We need to focus on getting out of here. We can use the greenhouse to—
ADÉLAÏDE:	Archer, it's Adélaïde. Listen, we're fine. We don't need Digby's ladder. We're over the wall, and I have the key. Getting out was always going to be the tricky part, but we can use the front door. I'm giving the microphone back to Oliver. We have to hurry.
OLIVER:	Adélaïde unlocked the garden door. We're going inside.
ADÉLAÏDE:	Where's the flashlight? Thank you. There. The stairs.
OLIVER:	We're going upstairs. Hopefully Mr. Birthwhistle's office is on the second floor. Their house sort of reminds me of yours. Except it's very neat. I'm afraid to touch anything. Mr. Birthwhistle might notice. Is that an office?
ADÉLAÏDE:	It has to be. Look at it.
KANA:	That's a lot of plants.
ADÉLAÏDE:	Shhh. Do you hear that? Go to the window.
OLIVER:	Mr. Birthwhistle arrived. He looks angry.
KANA:	They're coming inside.
ADÉLAÏDE:	Quick. We need to hide. Oliver—the closet. Can we all fit?
OLIVER:	There's barely room for one.
ADÉLAÏDE:	You get inside. I'll shut the door behind you.
OLIVER:	Leave it open a crack so Archer can hear.
ADÉLAÏDE:	Kana—under the couch.

KANA: What about you?

ADÉLAÏDE: I'm going under the desk.

Archer pressed the headphones tight to his ears and increased the volume. Everything went muffled when Adélaïde shut Oliver in the closet. He thought he heard Adélaïde and Kana scrambling, and then all he could hear was radio static and his heartbeat. His friends were in danger. And he we wasn't with them.

Footsteps entered the office.

⋆ THE RIGHT PLACE AT THE RIGHT TIME ⋆

MR. MULLFORT: Can I talk now? You're being awfully dramatic. And why do you keep scratching your arm?

MR. BIRTHWHISTLE: I brushed against two things I shouldn't have, and one of those things was you. Now tell me, how long were you standing outside my front door for anyone to see?

MR. MULLFORT: I arrived a few minutes before you did.

MR. BIRTHWHISTLE: I told you we were not to have direct contact. Why do you insist on failing me?

MR. MULLFORT: I've done everything you've asked. I'm the one who has been failed.

MR. BIRTHWHISTLE: Were you not given Strait of Magellan? Did you not cash out on your bets?

MR. MULLFORT: Everyone wants their money back.

MR. BIRTHWHISTLE: I told you not to get carried away.

MR. MULLFORT: Don't lecture me. I don't care about the money anymore. I just want this over with. Where's the journal?

MR. BIRTHWHISTLE: That's no longer your concern. Your concern is keeping the stolen journal safe. That is your alibi in case Mr. Bray becomes suspicious after the forgery leaks. Be ready. . . . Why are you tapping your pocket like that, Eustace?

MR. MULLFORT: No reason. And don't worry about Bray. I'll deal with him if he becomes a liability. But he wasn't the only one in the shop the night I bought it. The Helmsleys' grandson was there, too. And his friends.

MR. BIRTHWHISTLE: They saw you buy the journal?

MR. MULLFORT: I'm not sure what they saw. But it wasn't my first run-in with them. They were in your office at the Society before the Helmsleys were ostracized.

MR. BIRTHWHISTLE: How would you know they were in my office unless you were also in my office?

MR. MULLFORT: Where are the communications?

MR. BIRTHWHISTLE: You thought I would be careless with such a thing? I'm a little insulted, Eustace.

MR. MULLFORT: We agreed to destroy them. Why keep something that connects us to the iceberg?

MR. BIRTHWHISTLE: I always have a reason. They're tucked away at the Society. But this is becoming messy, and you know how I feel about messes. One thing at a time. First, is Captain Lemurn ready for Suplard's test?

MR. MULLFORT: He'll be fine. Lemurn has the heart rate of a whale. Dalligold was trying to pick off the crew, trying to get them to testify against us, but none would.

MR. BIRTHWHISTLE: *Dalligold.* He's the one I should have put on the iceberg.

MR. MULLFORT: Why?

MR. BIRTHWHISTLE: Ralph's an ox. I think he was pulling a plow that
                      Dalligold was steering. Regardless, about the
                      grandson—

MR. MULLFORT: I wouldn't worry about him. If I had to guess, I'd say
                      they were in the right place at the right time.

MR. BIRTHWHISTLE: We don't make guesses, Eustace. We make certain.
                      Being in the right place at the right time can happen
                      once, but *twice*? The eyebrow rises. They might be
                      tailing you. And if it continues, you'll have to deal with
                      them as well. But this will be more delicate. Do you
                      remember what I told you about fingerprints?

MR. MULLFORT: If we use other people to do what we want done, we
                      won't leave any.

MR. BIRTHWHISTLE: Precisely. And there's someone inside Helmsley House
                      who can take care of the boy *for* you.

MR. MULLFORT: Who?

MR. BIRTHWHISTLE: Mrs. Helmsley. That family's story is no secret. She
                      kicked Ralph and Rachel out of their own house.
                      When news of their survival reached Rosewood, she
                      sent the boy up to Raven Wood. Benjamin wrote
                      me the moment he arrived. *Yes*, I know. Quite the
                      coincidence.

MR. MULLFORT: But how is that going to help me? And what about the
                      other two?

MR. BIRTHWHISTLE: If Mrs. Helmsley thinks the boy's in danger, *she'll*
                      take him away. Clean and simple. As for the other two,
                      when you cut out the root, the plant will die.

MR. MULLFORT: How are we going to make her think the boy is in
                   danger?

MR. BIRTHWHISTLE: *We're* not. It's *you* they might be tailing. It's *you* who
                   should be concerned. And should it be necessary, it's
                   you who will take care of this. And while I know it's not
                   your strong suit, this will call for *subtlety*. We don't use
                   a spear to make a pinprick. And a pinprick is all you'll
                   need.

The room grew very quiet. Archer's mind was racing. Was Mr. Mullfort really going to come after him? He pushed that thought away and pressed the headphones even tighter. His friends were the ones in danger. He could hear Oliver breathing, but why was no one talking? What was—

MR. MULLFORT: Why are you smiling at me?

MR. BIRTHWHISTLE: We mustn't turn on each other, Eustace. We are allies.

MR. MULLFORT: Who said I was turning on you?

MR. BIRTHWHISTLE: Listen, Eustace. Do you not you hear that?

MR. MULLFORT: . . .

MR. BIRTHWHISTLE: What are you up to? What's in my closet?
                   It wasn't humming when I left this morning. Why is it
                   humming now?

MR. MULLFORT: You're completely paranoid.

MR. BIRTHWHISTLE: Or are you trying to be clever? Let's see what you have
                   in—WHAT IN THE—

CLICK

Archer didn't move. He didn't breathe. He stared at the glowing radio dials. How could they not have noticed the radio had a hum?

"Oliver?" he whispered into the microphone.

There was no reply. Only static. What had he done to his friends? He tore off the headphones. He had to tell his grandparents.

Archer hurried across the hall, but stopped, hearing his grandparents downstairs. He raced to the second floor and stopped again. Why was Mr. Suplard down in the foyer, speaking to his grandparents?

"It's an *evaluation* of what?" his grandmother was saying.

Mr. Suplard motioned to one of the Deputies with him. The Deputy clicked open a black case and revealed a complicated machine.

"A *lie detector?*" Grandpa Helmsley asked.

"It's policy, Ralph," Mr. Suplard said in his nasal voice. "Part of our Inquiry. You know that. In cases of contradicting testimonies. And while personally, I don't believe you two are . . . *well* . . . I'm not convinced you are telling the whole—"

Grandpa Helmsley raised himself to his full height. Mr. Suplard and the Deputies took a step back. Archer thought his grandfather might launch them out into the snow.

"*Please*, Ralph. Let's not do anything rash. The Inquiry Department is impartial. We're not for *or* against you."

"You expect us to believe that? The banquet was a setup! You knew Birthwhistle's plan was to force an Ostracization."

Mr. Suplard seemed genuinely insulted at this accusation.

"Strap Lemurn to the lie detector," Grandma Helmsley insisted. "Ask him if he left us on the iceberg."

"Captain Lemurn will be evaluated tomorrow. This evening it's you. If you have nothing to hide, this test should *help* you."

"We have nothing to hide," Grandpa Helmsley replied, directing everyone up the stairs. "We'll do it in the map room. But I need to call Dalligold. I want him here for this."

Archer's heart was beating wildly as Mr. Suplard passed him on the second floor.

"Please allow my Deputies room to pass, Master Helmsley. Thank you."

Archer grabbed his grandfather's arm, wanting desperately to shout what was happening across town, but how could he tell his grandfather that his friends had broken into Mr. Birthwhistle's house while the head inquirer of Society Codes and Conduct was there? Mr. Suplard might think his grandparents had put them up to it.

"You look like you've seen a ghost, Archer," Grandpa Helmsley said. "Don't get yourself worked up. We'll be fine."

"I have to talk to you," Archer pleaded. *"Privately."*

"It'll have to wait, Archer," Grandma Helmsley said, ushering his grandfather up the stairs. "We won't be long."

Archer watched helplessly as they disappeared. Should he go to the Birthwhistles' alone? He rushed to the front door, pulled on his coat, shoved his feet into his boots, reached for the knob, and—

"What's going on?" Mrs. Helmsley asked, pressing her hand firmly against the door.

"You have to let me go! It's important! I can't explain. But please! You have to let me go!"

Mrs. Helmsley glanced at the clock. "I'm sorry, Archer, but you're not going anywhere—especially if you can't give me a reason. Does this have to do with Mr. DuttonLick's party?"

"No. It's Oliver and Adélaïde. They're in trouble!"

"And how would you know they're in trouble?"

"I heard . . . I have . . . It's a feeling."

A *feeling* wasn't going to get him through that door. The truth wouldn't get him through it, either.

"If something's going on, Archer, you need to tell me right now."

Archer wanted to tell his mother. He wished he could. But he never *could* tell his mother the truth—about anything. And she hadn't lifted a finger to help his grandparents. Did she even care what happened to them? If he told her what he'd done to try to help, he'd never see his grandparents or Helmsley House again. And that was exactly what Mr. Birthwhistle wanted.

"It's nothing," Archer said bitterly, pulling off his coat. "I imagine things, that's all."

✦ HALLUCINATING BEACONS ✦

Upstairs in the map room, Mr. Suplard and the attendants were setting up their equipment. Archer's grandmother was standing before the glowing radio. Archer tried to get his grandfather's attention, but he was on the phone. And one of the Deputies, seeing Archer first, abruptly shut the door. Archer ran to his room. The polar bear shouted after him.

"You got your friends killed!"

Archer threw his new binoculars around his neck and climbed the ladder to the roof. Maybe they had escaped somehow and were making their way home? He pointed his binoculars across Rosewood Park, at the Birthwhistles' house, but he wasn't high enough to see anything. He took hold of the chimney, pulled himself to the top, and stood like a beacon, as tall as he could, binoculars raised. He still couldn't see north of Rosewood Park, but he didn't move from that spot.

Time moved both very quickly and very slowly. Archer didn't know how long he'd been standing atop that chimney, but he was shaking and his fingers were frozen. He couldn't hold his binoculars steady. Twice now he'd poked himself in the eye. Below, Adélaïde's bedroom was dark. Kana's, too. Oliver's balcony, jutting out beneath him, was also in shadow. He turned and spotted the dented metal bowl. If his friends were okay, if they *had* made it out, he was certain they'd come to the roof. And he had to be here, preferably not in iceberg form.

Dismounting the chimney was difficult. Archer was frozen stiff. When his feet found the roof, he continued to the ladder and disappeared into his house. The door to the map room was still closed. Archer was back on the roof a few minutes later with his coat, a newspaper, an armful of logs, and a matchbook in his pocket. He scooped the fresh snow out of the metal bowl, crumbled the newspaper into balls, set the logs on top, and struck a match.

Soon firelight flickered on Archer's face as he stood there thawing. Adélaïde's and Kana's rooms were still dark. Archer's thoughts were darker. His friends hadn't escaped. He couldn't wait for them any longer. He was wrong not to tell his mother. He had to tell someone.

Archer turned away from the fire and took hold of the ladder. The cold metal stung his hands. As he reached the final rung, Oliver's room lit up. Then Oliver's balcony door opened.

"Look at my hand," Oliver said, stepping outside. "I'm still shaking!"

"So am I," Adélaïde replied.

Archer stayed motionless, certain he was hallucinating.

"We were just coming to see you, Archer," Adélaïde said when she spotted him. "We tried to get you on the radio.

Kana went straight home."

"But how—*how are you here?*"

"Benjamin," Oliver said, and sniffed the air. "Is my house on fire?"

◆ RADIO SILENCE ◆

Archer, Oliver, and Adélaïde huddled around the fire for a long while before anyone said anything. Archer was amazed his friends were safe. Adélaïde and Oliver were equally surprised.

"I don't understand," Archer finally said. "I thought you . . . Didn't Mr. Birthwhistle open the closet?"

"Almost." Adélaïde's voice was still a little shaky as she rubbed her hands over the fire and explained everything.

Mr. Birthwhistle and Mr. Mullfort had entered the office not one minute after she wedged herself beneath the desk. All she could see were their shoes, but it was easy to tell who was who. Mr. Mullfort's boots were pitiful. He plopped himself on the couch, which sagged to the top of Kana's frightened head. Mr. Birthwhistle remained on his feet, leaning against the front of the desk. Adélaïde could count the stitching on his perfectly polished, fine leather shoes.

Her eyes were glued to Kana's throughout the men's conversation. But when they fell silent, her attention went straight to the closet. She heard the hum before Mr. Birthwhistle did.

But Mr. Birthwhistle and Mr. Mullfort weren't the only ones in the house. Benjamin had also arrived home with his father, and Adélaïde saw his head poke over the landing as he came upstairs. She waved furiously to get his attention. Benjamin almost tripped backward. Adélaïde mouthed, *"Please help us!"* But Benjamin simply stared. Then he spotted Kana under the sofa. After that, he went back downstairs, and Adélaïde closed her eyes, certain they were doomed.

Mr. Birthwhistle approached the closet door. Adélaïde glanced at Kana and couldn't believe what she was seeing. Kana was reaching for Mr. Mullfort's ankles. But just as she was about to grab them, there came a thunderous crash from downstairs. It startled Kana and Adélaïde as much as it did Mr. Birthwhistle and Mr. Mullfort. The men bolted from the room, and Adélaïde wasted no time. She crawled out from beneath the desk, yanked a ghostly pale Oliver from the closet, and when Kana was freed, all three crept to the top of the stairs. Benjamin was staring up at them.

"Hurry!" he whispered sharply.

Kana tried to thank Benjamin for his help, but he practically shoved them out the front door and into the snow. Digby was wallowing in despair on the Figs' front steps. They tossed him the key, but from his expression, you'd think they had tossed him a gold bar.

"I know you and Benjamin disagree," Adélaïde told Archer,

still rubbing her hands over the fire. "But we would have been in terrible trouble without him."

"I'm not sure why he helped us," said Oliver.

Archer was beyond grateful and wished he could thank Benjamin himself.

"You heard what Mr. Birthwhistle said about coming after you?" Adélaïde asked. "We need to tell your grandparents."

"We'll tell them about the journal," Archer said, trying to digest everything. "We can't tell them about the communications yet. They're going to ask me how we know and they can't find out you were inside Mr. Birthwhistle's house. Mr. Suplard was here. Maybe he still is. He hooked my grandparents up to a lie detector. The less they know about what we did, the better."

Adélaïde and Oliver followed Archer down the ladder, into his bedroom, and to the top of the stairs. One floor down, Mr. Suplard and his Deputies stepped out of the map room.

"This is all confidential, of course," Mr. Suplard said, shutting a notepad. "But you both should know you did well. Barring any new evidence . . . *well*, let's not get ahead of ourselves."

✦ Mr. Dalligold ✦

The trio entered the map room, and for a moment, Archer's grandparents didn't notice them. Grandma and Grandpa Helmsley were seated at a long table that was covered in maps and globes, deep in conversation with a man even older than them. Archer cleared his throat.

"Come in, Archer!" Grandpa Helmsley said, pushing up from the table. "I'd like to introduce you to the wonderful Mr. Dalligold."

Mr. Dalligold rose to his feet with much elegance and a cane in one hand. His face was filled with wrinkles, but dust had settled into the cracks and softened them a bit.

"It's a pleasure to meet you, Archer Helmsley," Mr. Dalligold said in a regal tone.

Archer couldn't explain it, but he knew in an instant that Mr. Dalligold was someone to be greatly respected. Archer was also a little nervous. Mr. Dalligold's kind eyes were penetrating. He didn't seem like someone easy to keep secrets from—like his grandmother.

"Now what had you in such a tizzy before?" Grandma Helmsley asked as everyone sat down.

"There's something we need to tell you," Archer began. "We were at Bray and Ink four days ago. We saw someone buy a journal identical to the ones you used—the ones I'd found inside your trunks. We thought it was odd, and we followed him and he immediately mailed the journal somewhere."

"He actually took two journals," Adélaïde added. "One he stole without Mr. Bray noticing."

"Can you describe this man?" Mr. Dalligold asked.

"He's *crooked*," Oliver said. "But we don't have to describe him. His name is Eustace Mullfort. We'd seen him before. He owns a shop called Strait of Magellan. He once threatened to cut my tongue out."

Archer didn't look at his grandfather directly, but he could feel heat pouring off him.

"*Mullfort?* That third-rate, crusty, no-good—"

"Calm down, Ralph," Grandma Helmsley insisted, turning to Mr. Dalligold. "You were right."

Mr. Dalligold nodded thoughtfully "You would have been suspicious too, Rachel. After you and Ralph vanished, Mr. Birthwhistle gave Strait of Magellan to Mr. Mullfort and then kicked him out of the order. I overheard Mr. Birthwhistle telling Mr. Suplard he had misgivings about Mr. Mullfort. Strait of Magellan was virtually blacklisted and has since fallen into disrepair."

"That doesn't sound like people who are working together," Grandpa Helmsley said.

"No," Mr. Dalligold agreed. "But it *does* sounds like Mr. Birthwhistle."

"But the journal," said Grandma Helmsley.

"They're making a forgery, of course," Mr. Dalligold said. "A banishment vote won't pass without hard proof. Mr. Birthwhistle knows that. But should someone discover one of Ralph's own journals corroborating that the iceberg incident was a hoax . . . well, that would convince many to side with Mr. Birthwhistle."

"You could have Mr. Bray testify," Archer suggested.

Mr. Dalligold tapped his cane's handle against the bottom of his chin. "Adélaïde said Mr. Bray sold Mr. Mullfort one journal. If Mr. Bray testifies, Mr. Mullfort can present the stolen journal and no one would be the wiser."

"No, he can't!" Archer dashed from the room and was back a moment later with the stolen journal. "Mr. Mullfort dropped it."

"Well, that's certainly a bit of luck," Grandpa Helmsley said, looking as though he might kiss Archer.

"For us," Mr. Dalligold clarified, taking the journal. "*Not* for Mr. Bray. What will Mr. Mullfort do when he discovers he doesn't have this? He can't *buy* another. Mr. Bray could be in danger. I'll put eyes on the shop, but we mustn't raise suspicion. Mr. Birthwhistle *must* complete his scheme with the journal before we do anything with Mr. Bray. If he suspects the forgery is compromised, he'll do something else. And we'll no longer be one step ahead of him."

"We need to check on Mr. Bray," Grandpa Helmsley said, standing up and gripping Archer tightly on the shoulder before leaving. Mr. Dalligold nodded at the trio and followed him out.

"Not so fast, you three."

Archer, Oliver, and Adélaïde turned back from the door. Archer's grandmother went to the radio, clicked it on, and read the frequency aloud.

"The radio was on when we came in, Archer. Were you using it? *Who* might I find on the other end of this frequency?"

Archer was perfectly silent. Oliver and Adélaïde didn't say a word either.

"And I'm curious," Grandma Helmsley continued, turning off the radio and facing them. "You said you'd been upset earlier because you wanted to tell us about the journal. That happened *four* days ago. What made you so eager to tell us about it tonight? Is there something *else* you'd like to tell me?"

Archer was a statue. There were many things he wanted to tell his grandmother. Mr. Bray wasn't the only one Mr. Mullfort might go after. There was proof of their innocence, hidden somewhere at the Society. And he knew all this because he'd heard it from Mr. Birthwhistle's own mouth. *That* was the problem.

"There's nothing else," he finally said.

His grandmother clasped her hands tightly, looking concerned.

"Very well. But if you three are up to something, it must end now. It's not that I'm ungrateful, Archer. I'm quite the opposite. All of you have helped us a great deal. But Mr. Birthwhistle is not someone I want you tangled up with. You might think you know where you stand with him, but I'll warn you, with that man, things are rarely what they seem."

✦ FEARING DISAPPEARING ✦

Archer searched Helmsley House many times over the next two days. He peeked around corners and behind doors, frightened he might find Mr. Mullfort lurking inside. He tried to reason with himself, but it wasn't working. Mr. Birthwhistle had told Mr. Mullfort to do something if Archer was found in the right place at the right time again. Breaking into Mr. Birthwhistle's house *was* the third time. Thanks to Benjamin, they hadn't been caught. But that wasn't a great consolation. What if Mr. Mullfort decided to do something regardless?

The only good thing, as far as Archer could see, was that things couldn't get any worse. But when he met with Oliver and Kana at Adélaïde's house, he realized he was wrong.

"What do you mean you haven't told your grandparents?" Adélaïde asked, sitting next to Kana on the couch. "You *have* to, Archer. You're wasting time. They need to search. Those communications *prove* Mr. Birthwhistle was behind the iceberg."

"But if my mother finds out what we did, she'll take me away and I'll never see my grandparents or any of you again."

"Your mother's the last person who should know," Oliver agreed. "Maybe you could tell the Eye Patch—Cornelius, I mean. Have *him* tell your grandparents. No one will know it was us."

Archer would've told Cornelius in a heartbeat. "But how are we supposed to find him?"

Kana hadn't said word since they'd sat down. She kept reaching into a pocket of her dress but never pulled anything out. Adélaïde prodded her.

"What do you think Archer should do?"

"Nothing," Kana warned. "And it's good he didn't tell anyone. Digby knocked on my door this morning. Mr. Birthwhistle knows everything."

Kana leaned forward and lowered her voice.

"We left footprints all over Mr. Birthwhistle's backyard. It was obvious we'd come over the Figs' wall. After we left, Mr. Birthwhistle interrogated Digby, promising Mrs. Fig wouldn't find out if he explained. Digby told him it was Oliver, Adélaïde, and me. And that you were listening over a radio."

Adélaïde and Oliver sank a little deeper into the couch.

"That doesn't mean Mr. Birthwhistle knows we heard

anything," Archer said. "Maybe he thought you were the ones who caused the crash downstairs?"

"We left the closet door wide open," Kana said, shaking her head and reaching into her pocket again. "I found something in my mailbox."

Kana removed a letter and set it on the table. There was perfect silence as Archer read it aloud.

> "When I hide something, it's never found. But should I discover the Society is being searched, that search will be redirected. The four of you will vanish. And while I don't like to repeat myself: when I hide something, it's never found."

The silence grew as thick as Raven Wood oatmeal. Adélaïde and Kana were staring at each other. Archer glanced at Oliver. He'd never seen his friend look gloomier. Archer turned back to the letter. The writing matched Mr. Mullfort's, but these were obviously Mr. Birthwhistle's words.

"We didn't tell anyone about the communications," he said, trying to keep everyone calm. "We're not in danger unless someone is caught searching."

"But think about it, Archer," Adélaïde said, lowering her voice as though someone were listening. "Mr. Dalligold has eyes watching Mr. Bray. If Mr. Birthwhistle or Mr. Mullfort realize that, they'll *know* you told your grandparents about the journal. And they'll have no reason to think you didn't tell them about the communications, too. They'll come after us."

"I wish I could vanish right now," Oliver mumbled.

Kana twirled her silver streak of hair around her finger, her eyes fixed on Archer. "What are you going to do?"

Archer didn't know. But Mr. Birthwhistle was not someone who made empty threats.

Adélaïde reached out for the letter.

"Why did he give this to you, Kana?" Archer asked, passing it over.

Kana shrugged, gazing at the floor.

"Whatever we decide," Adélaïde said, reading the letter to herself. "From now on, we shouldn't go anywhere on our own. It's too easy to pick us off one by one."

"And we can't hide." Oliver groaned. "Mr. DuttonLick is expecting us tomorrow."

Archer spent most of the day feeling stuck. It wasn't until later that evening that he thought he might have a solution. He wasn't thrilled at the idea, but what if *he* searched for the communications? It made sense. He wouldn't have to tell anyone. If he went to the Society by himself and if something went wrong, he'd be the only one who vanished. Of course, Archer would prefer not to vanish either.

He sat on his bed, his journal in his lap, reviewing his notes from the radio expedition. Mr. Birthwhistle had said the communications were tucked away at the Society. That wasn't much to go on. It'd be like trying to find a corn kernel on a sandy beach. Archer shut the journal and tapped his fingers on it.

✦ MEEGFLOG, WOLPSHURE, FISHPERG, GLOOP ✦

The sun made a rare appearance the following morning, glistening through icicles hanging above DuttonLick's sweetshop windows. Archer and Oliver were inside, waiting to begin their work with Mr. DuttonLick. They were also waiting for Adélaïde.

"Where is she?" Oliver said, pacing back and forth.

Both grew paler by the minute. It was the final free chocolate day (DuttonLick's signature seahorse lollipop), and the bell jingled frequently as cheerful customers entered. Every time it did, Archer craned his neck, but it was never Adélaïde.

"You don't think Mr. Mull—"

"Don't say it!"

Before setting off that morning, they'd stopped at Adélaïde's house to pick her up. Mr. Belmont had answered the door with espresso beans in his hands. "I haven't seen her since first thing today." Archer and Oliver had knocked on Kana's door, but there had been no answer. They continued to DuttonLick's then, hoping Adélaïde was already there, only to discover she wasn't.

"I'm going to check the café," Archer said, not wanting to

stand around anymore. "Maybe she's with Amaury. You stay here in case she shows up."

Just as he took a step toward the door, Adélaïde burst through it. The bell spun like a top.

"Where were you?" Oliver said, nearly shouting as she dashed down the aisles with a newspaper in her hand. "You're the one who said we—LOOK OUT!"

Molly S. Mellings stuck her foot out, hooked Adélaïde's wooden leg, and sent her somersaulting into a mountain of perfectly stacked chocolate bars. Candy flew everywhere and the students erupted in laughter as Adélaïde, still  clutching the newspaper, scrambled to her feet.

"Are you okay?" Archer asked, taking her arm. Oliver grabbed the other one.

"I'm fine," she said, but she clearly wasn't. She had a nasty scrape across her forehead, and it was bleeding. The others stopped laughing when they saw that—except Alice, Molly, and Charlie. Adélaïde pressed her hand to the cut as the terrible three stood before them.

"I'll bet you haven't leaped that high since you were a ballerina!" Charlie said.

"But you *do* need to work on your form," Alice added. "It wasn't very elegant."

Archer grabbed Oliver, who was about to swing a punch.

"I'm going to have Archer curse you!" Oliver warned.

Alice feigned dismay. Mr. DuttonLick swooped in, and Molly became a beacon of virtue.

"I think you made a mistake allowing them to be your assistants for the party," she said, pointing a dainty wouldn't-harm-a-fly finger at the trio. "They make a mess of *everything*."

Mr. DuttonLick hastily ushered the trio into the back of the shop. For the first time, the cheerful chocolatier looked anything but.

"I'm not sure what happened out there, but *please*, do not make me regret taking you on. We have much to go over. So cool your little heads. I'll return shortly."

Oliver grumbled, searching for a first-aid kit. Archer found one above the sink and bandaged Adélaïde's forehead as she waved the newspaper at them.

"Did you see it?" she asked. "Kana got into my bedroom from the rooftops and woke me up with it. I knew I shouldn't, but I wanted to check the café. The news is all over Rosewood."

ROSEWOOD CHRONICLE

THE ICEBERG IN HIS OWN WORDS

While we at the *Chronicle* are not ones to gloat, we hope those at the *Doldrums Press* are reading. A parcel was delivered to our office late yesterday afternoon. The parcel contained photos of a journal that prove Ralph and Rachel Helmsley's iceberg was, as we've reported, a fabrication from the beginning.

On the first four pages of the journal, Ralph Helmsley wrote his own name six hundred times. His signature, which began very neat, becomes completely illegible at the end. On the following page, he scribbled the words: *Meegflog Wolpshure Fishperg Gloop*. We've confirmed these aren't actual words. Then comes a page revealing what appears to be a hit list, with one name crossed out. Wigstan Spinler. The final page of the journal is the most disturbing. Ralph laments being unseated as president. "This has only happened to one president before me. Antarctica. Better to die than be unseated," he wrote.

We phoned the Society for confirmation and were connected to a man named Mr. Suplard. He immediately hung up on us. An hour later, we received an anonymous call back. The caller confirmed that after analysis, the journal was deemed authentic. We asked where it was found.

"In the deceased members' section of our Archives, among Ralph's other possessions left behind in the President's Office."

"Mr. Birthwhistle had *fun* with this," Archer said, lowering the paper.

"And the *Chronicle* is going to ruin my father," Oliver added. He turned to Adélaïde. "What about Mr. Bray? Is he still at Bray and Ink?"

Adélaïde nodded, rubbing her bandaged head. "I checked on my way here."

Archer read the article again and again and didn't notice Mr. DuttonLick return.

"Have we cooled down? Yes? Very good! We have lots to do! But first, the bad news. I will not be teaching you how to make chocolates. *Yes*, I'm upset too, Oliver! The snow has caused a *slight* hiccup. No cocoa beans. So today, you'll do an inventory to see what we can melt down into smaller treats. Can't give away the whole shop! I'll go bankrupt! Tomorrow, I'll rope off the top two floors and you will clean those. And the morning of the party, we'll melt chocolate and decorate! Very good? Do we all . . . Archer? Are you listening, Archer?"

"*Uh*, yes," Archer said, peeling his eyes from the paper. "Sounds perfect."

"That's the spirit! Now take this clipboard! Time to count!"

"*Sounds perfect?*" Oliver groaned, following Archer and Adélaïde out of the back room. "Inventories and cleaning and melting chocolate into smaller chocolate? That's not what I signed up for. I thought we were going to learn how to *make* chocolate. Mr. DuttonLick sold me a vacuum cleaner!"

"A chocolate-coated vacuum cleaner," Adélaïde sighed, sizing up the three stories of chocolate bars and mountains of sweets that needed counting.

Archer was now reading the article a sixth time, but he put it aside when they set to work.

The trio spent the entire day counting chocolates. It was

a tedious task made worse by Alice, Molly, and Charlie, who hovered around them like gnats. Charlie kept popping out from behind shelves, grabbing his own throat, and shouting, "Archer cursed me! I've been cursed!"

Molly had memorized the gibberish line from the *Chronicle* and began chanting it to a tune. "Meegflog! Wolpshure! Fishperg! Gloop!"

"I finally figured out what it means!" Alice said, laughing. "That's Helmsley for 'our minds are rotting! Put us on ice!'"

Archer did his best to ignore them, but he thought Adélaïde might deck Molly if her singing caused them to lose count one more time.

"Fifty-three," he said, hoisting an armful of chocolate bars back onto the shelf.

Adélaïde grabbed the clipboard. "DuttonLick's triple dark darker-than-dark chocolate bars—fifty-three," she wrote.

"You know who'd be great at this?" Oliver said as they moved down the aisle. "That pale man we saw at the Society—the one who couldn't finish his sentences. What was his name?"

"I think it was Mr. Harptree," Adélaïde said.

"Why would he be great at this?" Archer asked.

"Your grandfather said the Society's Archives are so huge that few enter without getting lost. But Mr. Harptree could see it all at once. I bet he'd know exactly how many chocolate bars Mr. DuttonLick has, simply by looking at these shelves, and we'd . . . why are you staring at me like that? I'm not suggesting we actually ask Mr. Harptree to help us."

"We couldn't even if we wanted to," Adélaïde said, setting the clipboard down and reaching for more chocolate bars. "Didn't he go to Scotland? He said there was an archival emergency, whatever that means."

Archer was still staring at Oliver, his mind humming as he searched his pockets. He'd left his journal in his coat. "I'll be right back," he said, and hurried off.

"I think he snapped." Oliver sighed. "But I don't blame him for abandoning us. What's next?"

"DuttonLick's triple-cherry whipped-cream swirl bars."

Oliver stared at the bars in their red wrappings. He wrinkled his forehead in concentration, but his eyes fell to the floor. "It's getting worse. I used to love those. Now I can't remember why."

Archer knew he was useless when he'd finally returned to his friends, but they didn't make a big deal of it. As they pressed on with the inventory, Archer continually excused himself, dipping behind random shelves and keeping out of their sight as he thumbed carefully though the pages of his journal. "The communications . . . maybe they're hidden in the . . . Could it be?" Archer bit his lip. Had he actually found the corn kernel?

"Thirty-one caramel glob bars," Oliver said to Adélaïde as

Archer approached them. "I'm afraid to ask, but what's next?"

Adélaïde lowered the clipboard and smiled. "We're done!"

Oliver practically cheered as they brought their inventory list to Mr. DuttonLick. He thanked them with a large bag of chocolate snurples. The last thing any of them wanted was to eat chocolate, but they indulged Mr. DuttonLick. Immediately, Oliver's love resuscitated.

"I don't get it," he mumbled, and closed his eyes.

"What don't you get?" Mr. DuttonLick asked.

"The teachers at the Button Factory," Oliver explained. "They spend loads of time teaching us about the invention of electricity, but they've never mentioned anything about the invention of chocolate. I know electricity is important, but it's also dangerous. Electricity has killed people. Chocolate never killed anyone."

"I'm sorry to say that's not entirely true," Mr. DuttonLick replied. "Chocolate *has* been used for sordid purposes. Sometimes, even as a vehicle to deliver poison! Yes. Its richness can hide *many* things!"

Oliver gulped the snurple and seemed to be wondering if Mr. DuttonLick had not only sold him a vacuum cleaner, but now, had also poisoned him.

They climbed to the third floor, hoping to rest their aching legs on a couch, but Alice, Molly, and Charlie quickly spread out, leaving not an inch of room.

"They've been here *all day long*," Adélaïde whispered. "Don't they have anything better to do than annoy us?"

"I wish you could actually curse people, Archer," Oliver sighed as they all squeezed together in a window seat overlooking Howling Bloom Street.

✦ BAND OF OUTSIDERS ✦

Archer sat quietly with his journal on his lap, trying to ignore Adélaïde. He wouldn't look at her, but he could feel her eyes bouncing between him and his journal.

"Is there something you'd like to tell us, Archer?" she finally asked.

Archer tried to play the fool, but fooling a one-legged French girl is no simple task.

Adélaïde's eyes rolled and then narrowed. "Honestly, Archer, you can't lie to me. I'm your friend. I know you've been planning something all day." She turned to Oliver. "I think he's going to the Society."

Oliver looked skeptical. "She's been spending too much time with Kana, hasn't—"

"When were you going to tell us, Archer?"

"I wasn't," Archer admitted. "Neither of you are coming. But I think I know where to find the communications." He opened his journal and pointed to the iceberg hoax story. "Both of you were talking about Mr. Harptree. He left for

Scotland the night we arrived." Archer held the journal toward them. "Read that line."

President Birthwhistle said via telephone from the Scotland Society.

"I think Mr. Birthwhistle got Mr. Harptree out of the way so he could plant the journal in the Archives. But I also think that's where he hid the communications. 'Few go in without getting lost.' Doesn't that sound like a good place to hide something?"

"Because it might be impossible to find them," Adélaïde said, nodding.

"I'll be honest," Oliver sighed, looking up from Archer's journal. "I wasn't expecting to nearly die in a closet over the winter holiday. It's supposed to be a relaxing time. I thought we'd learn how to make chocolates and maybe have a snowball fight. But the closet happened. And I'm not stopping now. If you're going to the Society, I'm coming with you."

"We both are," Adélaïde agreed.

Archer shook his head. "I have to go alone. This is my problem. I don't want anything to happen to—"

"But it's not *just* about your family anymore," Oliver insisted, holding up the *Rosewood Chronicle*. "They're out to destroy my father's paper, Archer. And they will if I don't prove them wrong."

"We're coming with you," Adélaïde insisted before Archer

could respond. "So let's talk. How are we going to get there? The buses aren't running. Remember the lemon drop lady?"

"I was going to walk," Archer said.

Oliver almost laughed. "That's a terrible idea, Archer. We can't stroll into the Society, find the communications, and stroll back out again. Someone might spot us. We don't know who we can trust in there."

"It would help if we could get our hands on Greenhorn uniforms," Adélaïde suggested. "We'd blend in."

"That's *good*," Oliver agreed. "But if we do find the communications, we'll have to get them to your grandparents as fast we can. And knowing our history, probably while being chased. We can't go on foot."

Oliver was right, and Archer didn't argue. Adélaïde turned to the window, thinking it over. A single headlight was flickering down Howling Bloom Street. It was the Belmont Café delivery truck. It swerved around pedestrians and slid to a halt just outside the café. Amaury wrenched himself from the cab, scaled a snowdrift, and shivered into the coffeehouse.

"That's how we'll get there," Adélaïde said, pointing to the vehicle.

"We can't drive a truck," Oliver said.

"It's *barely* a truck. Look at it. It's like someone put a normal-sized vehicle into a washing machine and accidentally shrank it."

"It doesn't matter how small it is. It's illegal. That means we can't do it."

"No," Adélaïde said, her eyes glinting. "That means we can't get *caught* doing it."

Oliver ran his fingers through his hair. "I don't mean to be rude. But you don't *exactly* have the greatest history with delivery trucks."

"Would Amaury notice it was missing?" Archer asked.

Adélaïde slumped. "He would. I'd say we could ask him, but he'd never think of letting me drive it."

"Because we'd probably crash it," Oliver said. "And possibly kill ourselves."

"Amaury would be worried we'd hurt ourselves," Archer agreed, nodding slowly. "What if he didn't care? Or better yet, what if he *wanted* us to hurt ourselves?"

Adélaïde blinked at him. "That's the exact opposite of what Amaury would want."

"And we can make him become his opposite. Oliver, do you remember the crate you found in my grandfather's trunk? Those jars filled with colorful powders and liquids?" Oliver vaguely remembered. "It's the work of that botanist Benjamin loves. Mr. Wigstan Spinler," Archer said, and went on to explain what Doxical Powder did.

"I just want to make sure I'm clear about what you're suggesting here," Oliver said. "If this Doxical Powder *does* do what your grandfather said it could, are you saying we should . . . I mean, in order to get the truck, it *sounds* like you're saying you'd like to *drug* Amaury."

"We have to know it's safe," Adélaïde agreed. "We're not giving Amaury Doxical Powder without testing it first."

"I'm not going to be the guinea pig," Oliver said, reaching for the bag of snurples. "*Doxical Powder.* That doesn't sound like something that tastes good." He peered sideways at Adélaïde. "Fritz might eat it."

"You're not doing anything to my dog! And what would that tell us anyway?"

"If he meowed like a cat, we'd—"

"A snurple," Archer said, watching Oliver pull one from the bag. "Mr. DuttonLick said chocolate's richness could hide many things. What if, when we're melting chocolate, we add Doxical Powder to a few? No one would know. We can test it during the party. We'll test it on—"

"Meegflog! Wolpshure! Fishperg! Gloop!" Alice, Molly, and Charlie, still lounging comfortably, erupted into laughter.

Archer, Oliver, and Adélaïde smiled.

"But we shouldn't," Adélaïde whispered.

"We need to test it." Archer said.

Oliver tossed his snurple into the air and caught it in his mouth. "It's just dessert."

✦

◆ GOOD ADVICE? ◆

Archer overheard his mother on the phone when he shut the front door of Helmsley House. She was speaking to his father.

"Did you read it, Richard? I knew it was falling apart, but I wasn't expecting this! What are we supposed to do with him now?"

Archer frowned and climbed the stairs. She must have seen the *Rosewood Chronicle*, but what did she mean, *do with him*? Did she actually believe the story? He poked his head into his grandparents' bedroom. They weren't there. Ever since Mr. Dalligold had arrived, he hadn't seen much of them. But they must have seen the *Chronicle*, too. They were probably with Mr. Dalligold now, discussing what to do about Mr. Bray. Archer stepped into their room and shut the door behind him.

As Archer searched the crate atop the wardrobe, he caught the hedgehog staring at him with

disapproval. "Is there something you'd like to say?" he asked impatiently, clinking through the jars.

"It's nothing," the hedgehog replied.

"It doesn't look like nothing," Archer said, grabbing the bottle of Doxical Powder. "Don't be coy."

"Let's get one thing straight,"

the hedgehog hissed. "I'm no koi. As to the matter at hand, it's none of my business, but you should be very careful. Tampering with things you don't understand is dangerous."

"But I understand this," Archer said, slipping the jar into his pocket

"You understand it in theory. You don't understand it in practice. Those are two very different types of understandings."

"That's why we're going to test it."

"Yes, you're going to test it on three people who will know *nothing* about it. Do you think your grandparents would approve? I don't. And I know them well. I've lived in this room a long time. Your grandfather's the one who told you, 'The best you can do is what you think's right and hope others will do the same.'"

Archer tried to put the hedgehog's words out of his mind, but they followed him all the way to his bedroom. And they were still with him when he sat down on his bed, fiddling with the jar of Doxical Powder. Archer wasn't sure if he should take the advice of a stuffed hedgehog, but the critter had a point. Maybe he shouldn't test it on Alice, Molly, and Charlie, as much as he'd like to. There was really only one person it seemed *right* to do the experiment on.

Archer set the jar on his nightstand and slid off his bed. He stood before his mirror and studied his face. He scrunched it up. What would his opposite be like?

TWELVE

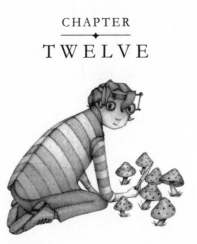

⋆ THE BUDDING BOTANIST ⋆

"Why are we going to the library?" Oliver asked Archer over a yawn the following morning as they slogged their way up Foldink Street. "We're supposed to avoid school during the winter holiday."

Archer hadn't told Oliver or Adélaïde that he was going to test Doxical Powder on himself, but he had told them about a book he was hoping to find.

"Benjamin had it on the train. He was always reading it. I don't remember the title, but it's hard to miss. It has an emerald-green cover. Maybe Wigstan Spinler wrote it. I'm not sure. But I'm guessing it will tell us more about Doxical Powder. And I'd like to know more."

They stepped beneath the giant wrought-iron Willow Academy gate (which still said BUTTON FACTORY). Archer took a crumpled cap from his pocket and pulled the brim low to hide his face. Miss Whitewood had warned him not to be spotted if he came for a visit. They climbed the barely shoveled front steps and pushed through the heavy front doors.

"This is eerie," Oliver said, peering around the empty entryway. "It's never been so quiet."

"Keep your head low," Adélaïde advised, placing her hand on Archer's shoulder. "We'll guide you to—"

A door creaked open. Footsteps hurried toward them.

"School is not in session! May I ask what you children are doing here?"

Archer knew that voice, but with the brim of his hat pulled low, he could only see Mrs. Thimbleton's shoes. They were lime green with tiny bows. Adélaïde and Oliver presented Miss Whitewood's library passes to the head of school.

"How many of these did Marion hand out?" Mrs. Thimbleton mumbled.

Archer also revealed his pass. But instead of taking it, Mrs. Thimbleton placed her finger beneath his hat's brim and lifted it. Immediately, her tiny head reeled back as though avoiding a misdirected snowball.

"*Archer Helmsley?* What are you doing here? You were expelled after that tiger stunt."

"We didn't plan—" Archer said.

"Like your grandparents didn't *plan* the iceberg?" Archer reddened and bit his tongue. "Your actions had many consequences, Archer. The Murkleys had to sell their house just to pay the medical bills. They now live in a miserable two-room hut in the Thickets. *The Thickets!* That's the worst neighborhood in Rosewood."

"How is Mrs. Murkley?" Adélaïde asked, feigning concern.

Mrs. Thimbleton shook her head in dismay. "They say she's making progress, but I don't see it. She can only communicate by blinking. The dear must feel like a strobe light! Now please, Archer, see yourself out immediately. And you two, straight to the library. Tell Miss Whitewood I need to see her before she leaves. Honestly, giving library passes to expelled students?"

Adélaïde and Oliver stepped behind Mrs. Thimbleton. Adélaïde mouthed, "Go straight to DuttonLick's. Don't stop." And they disappeared down the hall.

Mrs. Thimbleton tapped her foot harder and harder until it almost became a stomp. She was also pointing at the door, which suddenly shot open as though she'd willed it.

"ARCHER! What a surprise!"

Archer nearly tripped over his feet as he reeled around. Mr. Churnick stumbled in with a worn suitcase in one hand and a soggy pastry box in the other. His overgrown teeth were on full display in his wide smile.

"What are you doing in Rosewood, Mr. Churnick?"

"I've got a meeting with the lovely Mrs. Thimbleton." Mr. Churnick dropped the soggy pastry box into Mrs. Thimbleton's hesitant hands. "Brought you a cheesecake, Thimble, my dear. Stonewick's finest!"

Mrs. Thimbleton fumbled with the box, keeping whatever was dripping from its corners well away from her lime-green shoes.

"Never had a chance to thank you for *my* cheesecake, Archer!" Mr. Churnick continued, turning back to him. "Terribly kind of you. A wonderful surprise. Wish I had time to chat, but I'm in a bit of a hurry. Have to catch a train back to Stonewick before they suspend service. Apparently there may be a blizzard on the way. Just as well. I didn't want to spend another night in that hotel. It was packed to the gills with peculiar characters. But all the others were booked! Oh, and I hope your parents weren't too—"

Mrs. Thimbleton cleared her throat as though it were clogged with a wet toad.

"Something wrong, Thimble, my dear?"

"Please stop calling me *Thimble, my dear*, Mr. Churnick. Archer must leave the premises. He was expelled following the *incident*."

Mr. Churnick shook with laughter. "The polar bear! Who could forget?"

"*We* haven't."

"*Oh*, come now, Mrs. Thimbleton. Give the boy a break. He gave that bottom dweller exactly what she deserved. Miss

Whitewood suspects you don't know the half of it. That pit of misery *destroyed* my school. And while I can't say I'd blame him if he did, I don't believe Archer *wanted* to crush her with that polar bear."

"I'm not so sure of that," Mrs. Thimbleton said, eyeing Archer. "Now please, we have details to iron out. And Archer, *the door!*"

Mrs. Thimbleton marched to her office. Mr. Churnick slapped Archer on the back and left him with a grin. "I think it's time I make another detention slip disappear. Or in this case . . . I suppose it would be an expulsion slip."

✦ Muddied Thoughts ✦

Archer paused halfway down the school steps, spotting a silver button glistening in the snow. He pocketed it and froze. Across the street loomed the dark forest called Rosewood Park. He searched the crooked trees and their crooked shadows. Was Mr. Mullfort in there? The moment Archer had decided he'd go to the Society himself, he feared Mr. Birthwhistle might somehow already know his plans. He took a cautious step, glanced both ways down Foldink Street, and didn't stop running till he was inside DuttonLick's.

"Something got you all flustered?"

Archer spun from the window. It was only Mr. DuttonLick. He'd never been so glad to see the chocolatier.

"It's nothing," he said, breathing heavily. "Oliver and Adélaïde will be here soon. I just wanted to—"

"Have some alone time with your favorite genius?" Mr. DuttonLick guessed, winking and wrapping his arm around Archer's shoulder. "That's what has you all flustered, isn't it? Afraid you might disappoint me? Don't fret! You're doing great!"

Next thing Archer knew he had a mop in one hand and a bucket in the other and was on the third floor, which Mr. DuttonLick roped off behind him. Archer glanced at the empty couches and chairs and then at the floor. It was a disaster. 'Twas the season of wet boots, after all. Archer groaned, plopped the mop into the bucket, and slapped it on the floor.

Why was Mr. Churnick meeting with Mrs. Thimbleton? And what did he mean when he talked about making an expulsion slip disappear? Even if Mr. Churnick somehow convinced Mrs. Thimbleton to lift Archer's expulsion, his mother would still want him up at Raven Wood. Mr. Churnick said he hoped his parents weren't too . . . *too what?* He'd never finished his sentence.

Archer sploshed the mop into the bucket. The water instantly turned a disgusting brown. He wrung it out and plopped it back on the floor.

What if something went wrong with the Doxical Powder? What if *he* did something wrong? What if he turned into his opposite permanently?

Archer dipped the mop back into the bucket, watching a spider scurry across the floor to escape the burgeoning puddle. Archer wished he could ask Benjamin about Doxical Powder. Benjamin knew more about plants than anyone he'd ever met. Not only that—wouldn't Benjamin be able to help them get their hands on Greenhorn uniforms? And while Archer was convinced the communications were hidden in the Archives, he wasn't sure where the Archives were. He couldn't ask his grandparents if they had a Society map. "Oh, I'm just curious, is all." They'd never buy it. But maybe Benjamin had one.

Of course, the only reason he wanted Benjamin's help was so he could take down Benjamin's father. And even if Benjamin would help him, Archer wasn't sure he wanted to ask.

Archer had been miserable during the train ride to Raven Wood. He'd grown more miserable still when gravel popped beneath bus tires and he'd glimpsed his new school—that dilapidated ruin. It was true that his first week with Benjamin had been strange and awkward, but after that, Archer had almost forgotten about the terribleness of Raven Wood.

"Rub your palm against your forehead," Benjamin had said as they made for the Raven Wood nurse's office one morning that fall. "Make it as hot as you can."

"It's a fever, boys," the nurse concluded, ushering

them into beds. "We'll keep you here till it breaks—can't have you spreading it throughout the school."

When the nurse sealed them off with a curtain, Benjamin hopped out of bed, slid open a window, and Archer followed him out. They crossed the school grounds, making their way toward the thick pines that surrounded Raven Wood.

"I've never had much luck finding interesting specimens in these forests," Benjamin said as he fixed a brass magnifying contraption to his head. "But if you see anything that looks special, bring it to me."

They split up upon entering the shade of the towering evergreens. Archer wandered the forest ground, covered in yellow pine needles, and kicked a pinecone, watching as it tumbled into a curious plant. The plant's leaves were grouped in three—two small ones surrounding one large one. They had a slight sheen, and their tips were orangish. He wasn't sure if it was anything special, but he plucked a few anyway and found Benjamin hunched over a troop of purple-spotted mushrooms.

"I think I found something," Archer said, crouching next to him.

Benjamin inspected the leaves through his magnifying lenses. Then he stared at Archer. The lenses made Benjamin's eyes twice their normal size and their concern twice as alarming.

"That's poison ivy, Archer."

Benjamin pushed the lenses from his eyes as Archer dropped the leaves.

"You're going to have a nasty rash. You need to wash the oils off. Hurry! To the ocean!"

Archer and Benjamin sprinted from the pine forest, passed the crushed topiary where a boy had nearly died, and continued down the stone walkway to the shimmering sea. Archer bent down at the water's edge, dipped his hands in, and didn't notice the wave until it swallowed him. His nostrils flared with salt and he sat up, perfectly drenched, spitting seawater from his mouth. Benjamin laughed so hard the magnifying lenses dropped over his eyes again.

"You're the only fountain at Raven Wood that still works!"

Either Benjamin didn't notice the second wave, or thanks to the magnifying lenses, he thought it was farther away than it appeared. Whatever the reason, a moment later, he too was soaking wet, sitting in the sea next to Archer, spitting.

"Make that *two* fountains," Archer said, both of them grinning wide.

———————◆———————

Archer stood quietly on DuttonLick's third floor, staring into his muddy bucket. Why did Benjamin's father have to be Mr. Birthwhistle?

✦ NATURALLY UNNATURAL ✦

Archer set the mop into the bucket and hurried over to the stairs, hearing Oliver's and Adélaïde's voices.

"I'm not going to make it!" Oliver was saying. "Help me!"

"You'll be fine," Adélaïde replied.

Archer lifted the rope for them. Adélaïde stepped under it with a bulging bag. Oliver stepped under it with two more buckets, another mop, a broom, a brush, rags, and a few spray bottles. He barely managed it.

"Did you find the book?" Archer asked, giving Oliver a hand.

"Not the one you wanted," Adélaïde replied, spilling books onto a couch. "Miss Whitewood had these, but I don't think they're going to help us."

"It was good you weren't there," Oliver

added as Archer sifted through the pile. "Miss Whitewood practically interrogated us. She thought it was odd—us being interested in books on plants and gardening in the middle of winter."

Archer lifted a book called *How Does Your Garden Grow?* It was pink and there was a lady on the cover, smiling in a way that made him think she was in need of a psychological evaluation. Another was titled *Tulips Unsealed: Gardening Secrets.* It was yellow and there was a picture of a bloated, red-faced man, clutching a pair of binoculars, partially hidden deep in a garden overflowing with tulips. These two would love his mother's flower festivals.

"I know," Adélaïde said, seeing his expression. "But these were all she had. She'd never heard of the book you described."

"This one might help," Archer said hopefully, opening a book called *The Plant Dictionary.* He carefully removed the jar of Doxical Powder from his pocket and searched for the plants listed on the back. They weren't in there. Not one of them. Archer frowned at the jar. "It's like they haven't been discovered yet."

"Can I see that?" Oliver asked.

Archer handed him the jar.

Oliver held it up to the light, cautiously shaking the fine blue powder and pink specks. "This can't be natural."

"Technically it's completely natural," Adélaïde said, leaning over to see better.

"How can making someone go against their nature be natural?"

"If you go against your nature with the use of nature, then it's natural."

"I don't think that's right. And I still don't understand why you suddenly want to know more about Doxical Powder, Archer."

"There is a chance we might permanently damage Alice, Molly, and Charlie," Adélaïde said.

"We'd be doing Rosewood a favor if we permanently turned them into their opposites."

"We're not testing it on them," Archer said, shutting the dictionary. "We're testing it on me."

"I hear lots of chatting, but no scrubbing!" Mr. DuttonLick chirped from the second floor. "Scrub! Scrub! Scrub!"

"I love his shop," Oliver said, grabbing a brush and dropping to his knees. "But Mr. DuttonLick is getting very old very fast."

"Why are we testing the Doxical Powder on you?" Adélaïde asked, taking hold of the mop.

"It just seems right," Archer explained. "We'll know more about it with a firsthand account. I'll do it tomorrow during the party. We can't do it around my grandparents or my mother or Amaury."

"I was looking forward to watching the transformation

of the terrible three," Oliver sighed, struggling to pry a piece of gum stuck between the floorboards. "I wonder what *you'll* be like."

Archer was still trying to figure that out, too. He was a Helmsley. But who was *Archer* Helmsley?

"Well," Adélaïde said, thinking it over. "You're loyal and brave, so maybe you'll become a treacherous coward?"

"Or sometimes," Oliver suggested, "when we're together, it's like you're not really with us—like you're off somewhere far away. So maybe you'll be *very* present." He stared at Archer. "That could be intense."

Archer grinned and took the rags and spray bottles to the windows. While polishing the glass, he saw a Society truck squeal to a halt just off Howling Bloom Street. It was much larger than the one Cornelius drove. Archer froze, half expecting to see Mr. Birthwhistle and the Society attendants get out. But when the doors opened, Greenhorns rushed out instead. They separated into groups and scattered down Howling Bloom Street, entering different shops. He spotted Darby, running to keep up with two older Greenhorns who entered Trumm and Drumm, while the cinder block named Fledger made for DuttonLick's alongside a boy who resembled a piece of driftwood.

Then Benjamin hopped down from the truck by himself, looking unsure about which way to go. Archer hesitated, then tapped on the window. He tapped louder. He almost banged.

Benjamin looked up. Archer motioned for him to come inside. Benjamin hesitated, but followed the cinder block and driftwood into the sweetshop.

"What's going on?" Oliver asked, now trying to pry the gum from his brush as Archer hurried to the stairs.

"Benjamin's here. I need to ask for his help."

Adélaïde nearly dropped the mop. "What do you mean, ask for his help? You can't tell him what we're doing, Archer. If you tell Benjamin we're going to the Society and he tells his father . . ."

"You can't tell him the truth," Oliver agreed.

It was a risk, but Archer went to get Benjamin anyway.

⋆ A Pungent Odor ⋆

Tense was about the only word to describe the second post-Raven Wood reunion. Benjamin sat on the couch across from the trio, his leather satchel in his lap, looking everywhere except at Archer.

"I saw Mr. Churnick this morning," Archer tried. "He was at the Button Factory. I'm not sure what's going on."

Benjamin couldn't have cared less.

"Why are Greenhorns here?" Adélaïde asked.

"The Society is overflowing," Benjamin finally said. "They want us out of the way. They've been carting us all over Rosewood."

Oliver cleared his throat, certain he knew the reason for the tension. "You might be angry that we broke into your house, and you're probably wondering why we—"

"My father had nothing to do with the iceberg," Benjamin insisted, locking eyes with Archer. He opened his satchel and dangled a newspaper before him. "I'm only here to show you this. They found a journal, Archer. They proved your grandfather lost his mind."

Archer would rather eat a rotting fish than read that article again. "That journal was forged."

"Why would anyone forge a journal, Archer?"

"Because the iceberg wasn't a hoax. There's proof. It's hidden inside the Society. And I'm going to find—"

Benjamin was on his feet, stuffing the newspaper back into his bag.

"Good luck," he said. "But if you ask me, you're wasting your time. I know you don't want to, Archer, but you need to accept it. The truth isn't hidden anywhere. It's sleeping in your house."

Archer stood up before Benjamin reached the stairs.

"Don't leave, Benjamin. Please. I know you don't like my grandparents. I know you're angry they tried to banish Wigstan Spinler. You won't believe me, but my grandfather didn't want to do that. He was trying to do something else. But my grandparents shouldn't be banished either. Please,

Benjamin. I need your help."

Benjamin turned from the stairs and pushed his leafy hair from his eyes. "You're going to be disappointed," he said, returning slowly to the couch. "But if it means you'll finally accept that my father is the one telling the truth, then sure, I'll help you. What do you need?"

The offer was as quick as it was unexpected. Archer was perfectly silent.

"What do you need help with?" Benjamin repeated.

"Can you get us Greenhorn uniforms?" Adélaïde asked, glancing sideways at Archer.

Benjamin nodded. "How many do you need?"

"Four. Two girls and two boys."

"And do you know if there's a map of the Society?" Oliver asked.

"There is," Benjamin said. "It's a very elaborate, but I can—"

"Wait." Archer raised his hands to hush everyone. "You *do* understand what you're helping me with, don't you, Benjamin? I'm saying there's proof that my grandparents didn't want to vanish. I'm saying there's proof that someone tried to kill them. I'm saying that someone is your father."

Benjamin sighed and slouched back into the couch. "I know you blame my father, Archer. And I wish you'd believe me. But you won't. Not until you see for yourself. I don't know what you're expecting to find, but you're—"

All of a sudden, Benjamin fell silent. They'd left the jar of Doxical Powder on the table.

"Where did you get *that?*" he asked, trying to grab it. Archer got it first. "You didn't steal it from Mr. Spinler's collection, did you?" Archer shook his head. "But no one else knows how to make it. How did you get it?"

"My grandfather had it," Archer explained, and pointed to the pile of useless gardening books. "We're trying to learn more about it. My grandfather told me it could—"

"I know what Doxical Powder does."

Benjamin reached into his satchel once again. Archer saw a brilliant flash of emerald green, and then, on the table before him, was the very book he'd been hoping to find. Its title, gold lettering stamped into the velvet, glittered as it caught the light.

WIGSTAN SPINLER'S
COMPENDIUM ON PLANTS
THIRD EDITION
WIGSTAN SPINLER • ORDER OF MAGELLAN

"What's a plant listed on the bottle?" Benjamin asked as he opened the book.

"The first one is slate leaf," Archer said, leaning forward.

.*SLATE LEAF*.

Slate leaf is typically found in warm, swampy regions. My first encounter with these fascinating viridiplantae was in the Amazon, where they grew in a bit of still, stagnant water. The roots were buried deep in mud and the leaves sprouted no more than an inch above the water line. It was the leaves that first drew my attention. Their thickness was notable—some of the densest I've encountered to date. I plucked one and split it, and there arose a pungent odor. I've since collected a great deal of slate leaf during my travels, and while I've found its effect to be quite versatile, I believe it is at its most potent when mixed with yellow hotus and pugwort. *See*: Doxical Powder, page 253.

———◆◆◆◆———

"Mr. Spinler has a tendency to understate things," Benjamin explained, gazing at the jar in Archer's hand. "Slate leaf is more than pungent. It's *awful*. Have you smelled that powder?"

Archer hadn't. He popped the cork and nearly collapsed off the couch. "It smells like an old sponge soaked in rancid milk!" he gasped, handing it to Oliver, who, for some reason, felt enticed to sniff it, too.

Oliver's eyes watered immediately. "That's the worst thing I— I think it melted my nose hairs!"

Adélaïde grabbed the jar and took a casual whiff. Her eyes bulged. "That *is* disgusting. I hope the chocolate will mask it. You might not be able to swallow it, Archer."

Adélaïde realized her mistake the minute Benjamin's smile faded.

"What do you mean, *swallow* it?" he asked. "What's going on?"

Archer wasn't about to tell Benjamin their whole plan.

"I need to test it for something," he said. "We want to make sure it's safe."

Benjamin became very serious. "Greenhorns aren't allowed to conduct practical tests without supervision," he warned. "I'd *love* to see Doxical Powder at work, but to do it outside the Society . . . Mr. Spinler's work is Society Restricted. That means it can't be known to non-Society members."

"Why not?" Adélaïde asked.

"Can you imagine if everyone had bottles of Doxical Powder?" Benjamin said incredulously. "It'd be chaos."

"But *I'm* testing it," Archer said. "And I'm not a Greenhorn.

We're going to put it into chocolate, and I'm going to eat those chocolates tomorrow during DuttonLick's party." He fidgeted with the jar. "I never understood why you liked plants so much. I thought plants were boring. But I was wrong. Plants *are* incredible."

Benjamin glanced at him.

"We'll be careful," Archer continued. "If the Society finds out, I'll take all the blame."

Benjamin wasn't smiling, but as he turned his attention back to the book, it looked like he wanted to. He flipped to page 253. *Doxical Powder.*

"Mr. Spinler is never specific when it comes to dosage," he explained almost breathlessly. "I'd recommend you make three small chocolates and put one pinch into each. It'll be better to have a little extra than not enough."

Benjamin shut the book, tucked it back inside his satchel, and stood up smiling. "I'm not missing this. I'm coming to the party. But we *do* have to be careful, Archer. *No one* can know."

"Don't forget the uniforms and the map," Adélaïde reminded him.

Benjamin nodded and followed Archer to the stairs.

"I told you you'd find plants interesting if you knew more about them," he said, still smiling. "And Doxical Powder is only *one* example. You should see what *else* they can do."

Archer's smile was less enthusiastic. He was still nervous about eating Doxical Powder, but knowing Benjamin would be there made the idea digestible. Hopefully, chocolate would make the Doxical Powder digestible.

"I'm not sure if I'm comfortable with this," Adélaïde whispered to Oliver as Archer led Benjamin downstairs. "I know Benjamin denies his father had anything to do with the iceberg. But what if he knows more than he's saying?"

"Then he'd have to be a terrific liar," Oliver replied.

"As terrific a liar as, say, *his father?*"

Oliver's face drooped. "I never thought of that."

"Think about it," Adélaïde continued. "After we told Archer's grandparents about the journal, his grandmother warned us about Mr. Birthwhistle. She said things are rarely what they seem with him. What if it's the same for Benjamin?" She bit her lip. "Maybe it's only my imagination, but during the party, let's keep our eyes on him. Don't say anything to Archer. He's got enough to worry about with the Doxical Powder test."

When Archer returned, they pressed on with their work. They scrubbed the third floor and polished the second floor. Their buckets were almost entirely mud when they'd finally finished, and it was dark outside. Inside, everything was sparkling. Especially Mr. DuttonLick.

"What a wonderful job!" he chirped, running his finger

along a shelf. "Not a speck of dust! Can't remember the last time my shop looked so good! I'd love to have you three full-time! Perhaps we can arrange it? We'll talk about that later! Now, be here *first* thing in the morning! We have lots of chocolate to melt before the party!"

The trio grabbed their coats and stepped outside. They found the cold night air invigorating on their hot and sweaty faces. They did not find the crowd gathered outside Bray and Ink equally pleasant.

"Why isn't anyone going inside?" Archer asked, afraid to know the answer.

They heard whispers as they got closer.

"I was supposed to meet Mr. Bray for coffee tonight."

"It looks like someone broke in."

They didn't need to go any farther to see what everyone was staring at. The pane of glass in the green door was smashed, and a sign hanging there said BRAY AND INK WILL BE CLOSED UNTIL FURTHER NOTICE.

THIRTEEN

✦ GOOD KING OLIVER ✦

Everyone says there's a calm before a storm, but this is almost never the case. Before a storm, especially a terrible one, most everyone is frantic, rushing this way and that, collecting and hoarding supplies before Mother Nature throws her tantrum. Shovel factories kick into high gear, newspapers declare doom is upon us, and grocery stores are ransacked. If anything, the storm itself is the quiet part. Streets lie deserted, warm bowls of soup are slurped, and shovels sit quietly by the door, awaiting the aftermath.

The citizens of Rosewood were not calm before the storm. A bleak sky shrouded the city, turning everything an ominous gray.

ROSEWOOD CHRONICLE

THE WORST BLIZZARD YET?

It would appear the Helmsley Curse is far from over. Barometric pressure is dropping. Snow and high winds will soon collide. That can mean only one thing: a blizzard.

"This is ridiculous," Adélaïde said, peering out the windows of DuttonLick's sweetshop. Howling Bloom Street was a hectic scene, everyone dashing this way and that, gripping shovels and bags of groceries. One man even hurried by pushing a wheelbarrow filled with electric heaters. "There might be a lot of snow coming, but it's *just snow.*"

"You'd think the sky was about to spit fire," Oliver agreed.

Archer was studying the Belmont Café delivery truck, parked across the street. The blizzard was supposed to strike the night of the Inquiry. If all went well with the Doxical Powder, they'd have a day to search the Archives before that. He hoped a day would be enough. He couldn't imagine that tiny delivery truck would see them through a blizzard.

"I hope Mr. Bray is all right," he said, turning from the window.

ROSEWOOD CHRONICLE

EDMUND BRAY LED ASTRAY?

An apparent break-in took place on Howling Bloom Street. Edmund Bray of Bray and Ink has not been seen since early last evening. Rumors suggest Mr. Bray's shop was a front for a Rosewood crime syndicate.

The previous evening, after seeing the shattered window, Archer had raced home alongside Oliver and Adélaïde, desperately hoping it was his grandparents and Mr. Dalligold who'd decided to hide Mr. Bray before the Inquiry. But his grandparents weren't there. Archer hadn't seen them till this morning at breakfast. His parents were at the table too, reading the headline for themselves.

"I would never have thought that Mr. Bray was involved in a criminal operation," Mr. Helmsley said, staring over the paper at Archer's grandparents.

"It just goes to show how you never know a person," Mrs. Helmsley agreed, leaning over Mr. Helmsley's shoulder to read the article. "I wonder what he was peddling. Hand grenades? Exotic fish? Black market chewing gum?"

Neither of Archer's grandparents said a word, and neither touched their breakfast. Archer couldn't ask them what had happened, but he didn't have to. His grandparents' miserable expressions said it all. It was clear that Mr. Mullfort had broken into Mr. Bray's shop. Archer had told Oliver and Adélaïde as much as they'd made their way to DuttonLick's.

Oliver was especially upset. Mr. Bray had long supplied his father's newspaper with paper and ink, and when Oliver was younger, Mr. Bray always had a piece of candy for him when delivering spools of newsprint. His sister, Claire, was now the recipient of those sweets.

"I still don't get it," Adélaïde said, lugging a box of decorations from DuttonLick's closet. "Mr. Dalligold promised he'd have eyes on Mr. Bray. How did Mr. Mullfort get to him?"

"Maybe whoever those eyes belonged to went missing as well?" Archer suggested, grabbing a second box.

"Mr. Mullfort was probably thrilled to take him," Oliver muttered. "He probably has him tied up somewhere. Who knows what he'll do?"

The last thing on any of their minds was chocolate, but chocolate was now their only hope.

"I'd better get into the kitchen," Oliver said as Archer and Adélaïde readied buckets and mops. Oliver would spend the day melting chocolate with Mr. DuttonLick while Archer and Adélaïde cleaned the first floor, decorated, and set up tables.

"Don't let Mr. DuttonLick see it," Archer said, handing Oliver the Doxical Powder.

"And remember, one pinch into three small chocolates," Adélaïde added.

Oliver pocketed the jar and stepped into the kitchen.

⟡ INVENTING CHOCOLATE ⟡

Mr. DuttonLick was flitting around in a particularly cheery mood.

"I'd like to teach you something before we begin," he said, ushering Oliver to the far side of the kitchen, where two etchings, ornately framed in gold, hung crookedly. "The other day you mentioned none of your teachers has taught you about the *invention* of chocolate." He pointed to the first etching. "Chocolate was not *invented*. It was discovered!"

"*Discovered?*" Oliver repeated. Perhaps there was more to this whole exploration thing than he'd anticipated.

"Yes, *discovered*. Those are Aztecs, and they believed the cocoa bean was a gift of the gods. The Aztecs mostly drank it mixed with spices. And if you were to drink Aztec chocolate, you'd likely find it incredibly bitter."

Mr. DuttonLick pointed to the second etching, which was of Mr. DuttonLick's own shop.

"It wasn't until sugar was added to the cocoa bean that one could say a little *inventing* happened. And the rest, as they say, is sweet, *sweet* history!"

Oliver didn't say it, but as they set to work, all he could think was that he was about to do a little *inventing* of his own. After breaking a mountain of DuttonLick's triple dark darker-than-dark chocolate bars into small pieces, Oliver dumped them into a glass bowl and set it over a pot of boiling water.

"Keep the heat low. . . . Stir slowly . . . overstirring can cause it to crystallize."

Mr. DuttonLick dug through a cabinet.

"Turtles! We'll start with turtles! Slow and steady wins the race!"

Mr. DuttonLick lined up turtle molds and instructed Oliver as Oliver ladled the chocolate into one mold, then took a long metal spatula and scraped the excess chocolate back into the bowl. Oliver banged the mold on the counter—"to eliminate air bubbles"—and the chocolate was left to harden.

"Won't take but ten minutes! Now you finish the turtles. I'll prepare the rest."

While Mr. DuttonLick was on the other side of the kitchen, Oliver ladled chocolate into another mold, filling only three turtles, and uncorked the Doxical Powder. Even with the jar far from his nose, he could smell the despicable slate leaf. He dropped a pinch into each turtle and watched the blue powder and pink specks vanish into hardening chocolate puddles. He then hid that mold beneath the counter and set to work filling the others.

After that first batch, many more followed. By the time Oliver and Mr. DuttonLick had finished, the entire kitchen was piled with delectable sweets. And everything was covered in a great deal of chocolate. Oliver reached below the counter and pressed his finger to the Doxical Powder turtles. They were hard. He discreetly popped them from the mold and hid them in his pocket.

"That was almost too easy," he mumbled. Then he and Mr. DuttonLick cleaned up the mess and grouped the sweets to be set out on tables throughout the shop.

"Go get Archer and Adélaïde to help you! I'll take care of the . . ."

Mr. DuttonLick paused, staring at Oliver in a more peculiar

way than normal. Did he suspect something? Oliver hurried out.

Archer and Adélaïde erupted with laughter and nearly fell off their ladders when Oliver arrived.

"What's so funny?" he asked.

"Were you trying to turn yourself into a chocolate bar?" Adélaïde jested, peering down at him with a spool of steamers in her hand. "Are we supposed to serve *you* at the party?"

Confused, Oliver wiped his forehead and was shocked at the amount of chocolate that came off. "*That's* why Mr. DuttonLick was staring at me. But no, you're not serving me to anyone, thank you very much."

"It's just as well. You're going to taste like a rotten eggplant until you apologize to Kana."

Oliver wrinkled his chocolaty forehead. "Why am I apologizing to Kana?"

Adélaïde's smile deflated. "The blizzard? Did you forget? Kana was right. She predicted a blizzard was coming. Don't play dumb. We made a deal, Oliver."

Oliver grumbled and turned to Archer. "The chocolates are ready when you are," he said, and went to wash up.

✦ FACES IN THE CROWD ✦

The night sky was still a miserable gray as the trio helped Mr. DuttonLick with a few last-minute preparations. Adélaïde hung what was left of the blue and red streamers and purple seahorse balloons while Oliver and Mr. DuttonLick roped off the shelves.

"You have no responsibilities during the party, but if you see any sticky fingers trying to steal anything, don't be afraid to shout!"

Adélaïde went to a long table next to the door and arranged cups around Belmont Café's massive hot chocolate machine. Amaury had nearly crushed himself lugging it across the street earlier that day. Now it was churning out what must have been twenty gallons of hot chocolate.

"Wonderful!" Mr. DuttonLick glanced around. "It's beautiful!"

With the decorations up, the sweetshop looked like a beautiful firework had exploded and never faded.

"Now the last thing I'll need are the— Archer? *Archer?* Has anyone seen Archer? I'll grab the tickets!"

Oliver and Adélaïde blinked at each other.

"Have you seen him?" Oliver asked.

"Not since he was sent outside to shovel the sidewalk."

They went to the door and saw a horde of students waiting to push in. Suddenly Archer appeared, clawing his way back to the door. His face was jammed against the glass.

"Let me in!"

Oliver carefully unlocked the door. Archer squeezed through the crack.

"Back!" Oliver shouted, struggling to get it shut again. The students laughed and pushed against it. "Back, you animals!"

Archer and Adélaïde helped Oliver shove the door shut.

"The line goes all the way down Howling Bloom," Archer said, panting, his cheeks flushed.

"We're never volunteering again," Oliver replied, turning the lock.

The shop suddenly filled with music, and Mr. DuttonLick reappeared with a giant reel of tickets. There would be a raffle during the party, and the lucky winner would receive a special card that awarded one free sweet every day for an entire year.

"A ticket for each of you! Now stand back! I'm going to unlock that door. This *could* be dangerous. That's *quite* the crowd."

Archer, Oliver, and Adélaïde fled to the second-floor balcony.

"They're going to demolish him!" Oliver yelled as Mr. DuttonLick unlocked the door.

Excited students gushed in. It had to be the entire Button Factory student body. Or maybe every student in Rosewood. Mr. DuttonLick's arms were a blur, tossing tickets left and right. Alice, Molly, and Charlie got their tickets and, apparently not wanting to fill their own hot chocolates, took three cups from students who already had. Digby spotted the trio at the railing but pretended he hadn't, and joined a clog of bodies fighting to reach a table of sweets. Archer searched the joyous, growing crowd for Benjamin. No one noticed Kana until she was next to them.

"I read about Mr. Bray," she said. "Is it as bad as I feel it is?"

"We think Mr. Mullfort has him locked up somewhere," Oliver explained. Adélaïde nudged him forcefully. "*Oh. Right. I was a rotten eggplant, Kana.*"

Kana's silver streak fell across her forehead. "In a previous life, you mean?" she asked, tucking it behind her ear.

"No. I was never . . . I'm just trying to say I'm sorry for calling you psycho. And Adélaïde told me what you were about to do when we were trapped inside Mr. Birthwhistle's office. Thanks for that."

Kana smiled generously. "I'm just glad you were never an actual rotten eggplant. That would be unpleasant."

"He's here," Archer said.

Benjamin circled up the stairs and shoved his way through students to join them.

"It's like the breakfast stampede at Raven Wood," he said, grinning at Archer. "Is the Doxical Powder ready?"

Oliver tapped his pocket. "Let's do this on the third floor."

The five climbed up one more flight and crammed together on a couch. A huge, rowdy crowd filled in around them. Archer was beginning to think that testing Doxical Powder in such a public setting *might* be a mistake. Everyone seemed to

be staring at them, and it got so loud they had to huddle to hear one another.

"Here are the uniforms," Benjamin said, handing Adélaïde a brown paper bag. "They might not be the best fit, but they'll work. And this is the map."

The Society map was not what Archer had expected. It was very elaborate—like a booklet of maps with layouts of every floor and every room, though Benjamin mentioned he'd found a number of secret passageways and rooms that for some reason weren't on the map.

"If something goes wrong tomorrow and you need my help, you can find me here." Benjamin tapped a room in one of the Society's towers. "That's the Greenhorn Commons. But be careful. Mrs. Malmurna might be there, too."

Archer was still poring over the map when Oliver presented him with three chocolate turtles. Archer gulped when he saw them.

"I spoke to Mr. Spinler at the Society," Benjamin said, watching Oliver hand them to Archer. "A pinch of Doxical Powder will last an hour. It's a small dose and will only affect your most prominent attribute. It'll make a coward brave or a nasty person nice. The more you take, the more of your personality it will affect."

Archer lined the turtles up on his palm and sniffed them. He couldn't smell the Doxical Powder.

"I'd take one," Benjamin advised.

Archer gazed nervously at his friends. All of them were staring, eyes wide, back at him.

"I should apologize now," he said. "In case I become someone miserable. And please don't let me go home or go anywhere I shouldn't. And if I— NO!"

Charlie swooped in and swiped the turtles. Archer jumped to his feet. Alice and Molly, right behind Charlie, giggled with delight.

"You don't want to eat those!" Archer yelled, trying to grab the chocolates. "They're not what you—"

It was too late. Alice, Molly, and Charlie gobbled the turtles and raced to the other side of the room, singing, "Meegflog! Wolpshure! Fishperg! Gloop!" all the way.

✦ THE VERY MERRY THREE ✦

"It's been ten minutes."

"I don't think it's working."

"How long is this supposed to take?"

"Ten minutes."

They were studying the terrible three, unsure what they were expecting to see.

"I was a little worried about this," Benjamin explained. "I think the chocolate might have altered its—"

Charlie's eyebrow twitched. They all saw it. Then it twitched again. Charlie must have noticed it, too, after the third time. He became very quiet. Alice and Molly were still yapping. Charlie's entire eyelid twitched. Then Alice fell silent. She seemed afraid to open her mouth—perhaps afraid something other than a nasty word would come out if she did. It was the opposite for Molly. Her mouth kept opening and closing like a fish. Charlie gazed around as though he'd forgotten where he was. Alice and Molly stared at each other as though hidden deep in the other's face were the secrets of the universe. Then it was over. Like nothing had happened at all.

"Did it work?" Adélaïde asked, sounding disappointed.

No one could tell. Alice, Molly, and Charlie were still among their friends, but they didn't seem to be enjoying the company anymore.

"They're staring at us, Archer," Kana warned. "They're smiling. They're . . . they're coming. . . . Everyone look busy!"

Adélaïde practically dove into the brown paper bag. Kana covered her face with her hair. Archer and Benjamin opened the map. Oliver glanced left and right. He had nothing to do but panic.

"I'm sorry, Archer," Charlie said, poking Archer's shoulder. "I shouldn't have eaten your chocolates. Do you want to— Archer?"

Archer and Benjamin kept their eyes fixed on the map.

Molly pulled Adélaïde's head from the paper bag. "I'm

sorry I tripped you," she said. And she meant it. She actually meant it. "Would you like to—"

"Thanks, Molly, but I'm a little busy with this paper bag," Adélaïde said, leaning away from Molly's creepy grin. She pointed to Oliver. "Why don't you spend time with him? All of you. Oliver's been very lonely lately."

Oliver's incredulity became a strained smile as Alice, Molly, and Charlie surrounded him. For reasons no one could understand, Alice and Molly looked perfectly smitten. It was like Oliver was a precious jewel—with hair that didn't sit flat.

"We want to sing carols!" Alice said, glomming onto one of Oliver arms. Molly took the other. "You have to come with us!"

Oliver flashed his friends a desperate grimace. *Don't let them take me!* But a minute later, he was gone.

"I guess Doxical Powder works," Adélaïde said.

Kana blew the hair from her face. Everyone was laughing.

"We should *probably* keep an eye on them," Benjamin suggested.

"Let's get some chocolates first," Kana said. "Before they're all gone."

Adélaïde and Kana led the way to the chocolate tables. Archer and Benjamin followed, but with the wild crowd, it was like trying to keep your eyes on two buoys while bobbing in waves. The tables on the third floor had been ransacked and were completely empty. So were the second-floor tables. They circled down the stairs to the first floor.

"Well, that's depressing," Adélaïde said when they reached the final table.

All that remained were the dregs, bits of chocolate scattered here and there. They grabbed what they could and found a pocket of space below the balcony where, for a while, they too enjoyed the party. Archer didn't want to talk about tomorrow, and Benjamin never mentioned it either. Everywhere they looked, students were laughing and toasting, and a few were even dancing. A boy shot past them wrapped in purple streamers, followed by a girl with a seahorse balloon taped to her face.

"I think sugar is just as strong as Doxical Powder," Archer said, laughing.

"What's she talking about?" Benjamin asked, nodding to Kana.

It was difficult to hear, but Adélaïde was giggling as Kana acted out a story involving a horse. Or maybe it was a cow? Had Kana been trampled by a cow? Suddenly she stopped her story and pointed to the second-floor balcony.

"Look!"

Oliver was at the railing, surveying the crowd with a kingly air. Alice, Molly, and Charlie were at his sides, serving him chocolates, which Oliver ate with great benevolence. They were also singing what sounded like Good King Wenceslas, but with different words.

Good King Ol-i-ver looked out,
On the feasting party.
Where the sweets lay all around,
Rich and sweet and hearty.

"They *are* treating him like a king," Kana marveled.

"This is going to go straight to his head," Adélaïde said, trying not to laugh.

"If you're right about the time, Benjamin," Archer said. "Oliver has thirty minutes left to enjoy this."

"It might be a rough transition for him," Benjamin replied.

Oliver shouted down to them over the noise of the party.

"These guys are hilarious! They were singing 'Jingle Bells' to Digby—except they changed the words to 'Digby's Swell.' Digby was all confused. He thought they were going to attack him. He's still crouching in a corner. I'm going to cherish this night for the rest of my life!"

Oliver disappeared again for a while, but when it came time for the raffle, he was back at the railing, flanked by his merry companions. The crowd parted for Mr. DuttonLick, who wheeled a large raffle drum to the front of the shop. Everyone quieted, clutching their tickets as Mr. DuttonLick began spinning the drum.

Archer and Benjamin peered over the shoulders of a boy and a girl in front of them.

"You lost it, didn't you?" the girl was saying to the panic-stricken boy, who was desperately emptying his pockets. "I'll bet you ate it by mistake. I told you to keep it safe."

Archer and Benjamin laughed quietly. Tickets bounced all around the raffle drum as Mr. DuttonLick spun it rapidly. He released the handle and reached in.

"And our lucky winner is . . . ticket one hundred and thirty-nine!"

Archer frowned. Not him. Benjamin hadn't won either. Adélaïde and Kana shook their heads.

"I repeat! Ticket one hundred and thirty-nine!"

Everyone was mumbling and looking around. Benjamin nudged Archer and pointed toward Charlie at the balcony. He was trying to swap tickets with Oliver. And though Oliver seemed uncomfortable about it, Charlie triumphed and raised Oliver's hand.

"Good King Oliver has won!"

The crowd cheered and made room for Oliver to get to the main floor.

"Look at him," Adélaïde said, smiling as Oliver received the free-sweet-a-day card from Mr. DuttonLick. "He's going to burst with joy."

Oliver thrust the card into the air. The crowd roared, none

louder than Archer and Adélaïde. But the shop suddenly fell silent when a piercing cry rang out from the balcony.

"Something's wrong!"

"It's over," Benjamin whispered to Archer.

Charlie's eyes were twitching again. Molly and Alice were twitching too. Everyone stepped forward, peering up at them, not sure what to make of it.

"It's the Helmsley Curse!" someone shouted. "My parents warned me about this!"

Archer shrank back, fearing the party might turn on him. Adélaïde, Kana, and Benjamin leaned over him protectively. Up on the balcony, the twitching stopped. The merry three were once again the terrible three, and Charlie's eyes were fixed on the card in Oliver's hand.

"That's mine!" he shouted. "Oliver took my ticket! He *stole* it!"

A girl next to Charlie grabbed

Oliver's former ticket from Charlie's hand.

"Charlie's lying," she said, waving it above her head. "His ticket is right here."

The terrible three left the balcony amid a chorus of boos.

✦ SILENT NIGHT ✦

"I'm not sure it's possible," Benjamin said as Archer walked him to DuttonLick's front door, "but once the Inquiry is over, maybe we could be friends again."

Archer wasn't sure that would be possible either. "Thanks for your help, Benjamin," he said, watching as Benjamin trudged off down Howling Bloom Street.

Archer rejoined Oliver, Adélaïde, and Kana, but his thoughts left the party when Benjamin did. He stared past his laughing friends to the front windows. The Doxical Powder worked. They were sure to get the truck now. His grandparents' fate was in his hands. A few chocolate dregs were also in his hands, but at a sudden flash of color outside, he dropped them all over the floor.

"What's going on?" Oliver asked, picking them up. "Archer? You're scaring people with that look on your face."

Archer stood silent, staring at the windows.

"Did you see something?" Adélaïde asked.

"You look frightened," Kana added.

"I could have sworn I . . . it happened so quickly that I'm not . . . I think he was watching me—watching us."

"Who was watching us?" Oliver asked.

"Mr. Mullfort."

They searched the windows, but there was no sign of Mr. Mullfort. Adélaïde and Kana even went outside and squinted both ways down Howling Bloom Street.

"There's no one out there, Archer," Adélaïde said, shivering as she shut the door.

"Are you sure you're not just *worried* about seeing him?" Kana asked.

Had he imagined it? Mr. Mullfort had appeared and disappeared so quickly.

"Maybe you've just seen too much chocolate," Oliver suggested.

"We've all seen too much chocolate," Adélaïde agreed, glancing around the sweetshop. "This place looks like a crime scene. Let's get out of here before Mr. DuttonLick asks us to clean up."

They grabbed their coats.

"You keep the Greenhorn uniforms," Archer said, handing Adélaïde the bag. "We'll meet at your house first thing in the morning. Here, I'll take the map. I'd like to go over it."

The party was still going strong when they shut the front door and set off for home. There was a break in the clouds overhead, and through it, the moon and the stars glowed brightly in the crisp, cold night. Adélaïde and Kana were laughing about the merry three as they turned onto Foldink Street. Oliver kept pulling his free-sweet-a-day card from his pocket to make sure he hadn't dreamed it. Archer trailed a few steps behind everyone, still unconvinced he'd only imagined Mr. Mullfort.

"Get a good night's sleep," Adélaïde said, turning with Kana on North Willow Street. "We're going to need it."

Archer and Oliver continued home.

"We haven't told anyone about the communications," Oliver said, putting a hand on Archer's shoulder. "Mr. Birthwhistle can't know our plan. I'll be honest, Adélaïde and I were a little worried about Benjamin. We were watching him during the party. Well, I got tied up. But Adélaïde and Kana were. And they're convinced he's not against you."

Archer didn't think so either.

"This might sound strange coming from me," Oliver continued as they turned onto Willow Street. "But I don't think you have anything to worry about. Not until tomorrow. Try to get some sleep."

"Tomorrow," Archer repeated, watching Oliver step through the Glubs' front door.

Archer was hoping to see his grandparents at home, but they were off with Mr. Dalligold again. Mrs. Helmsley cheered when he told her the party had been a success. He climbed the stairs to his room and spent a few hours at his desk, poring over the elaborate Society map. He marked the Archives and Greenhorn Commons to make it a little easier, then clicked off his lamp and crawled into bed.

It must have been close to one in the morning when Archer finally began drifting off to sleep. He wasn't quite there yet. He was in a moment we all experience—that moment where you still have one foot in your bedroom while the other foot steps into a dream. It's a moment where even the slightest sound inside your room can snatch you from entering that dream and sit you straight up in bed. And that's what happened to Archer. But it wasn't a slight noise that snatched him. It was a thunderous noise. It was a terrible noise. And it happened so suddenly that Archer leaped from his bed.

✦ PART THREE ✦

THE STORM

FOURTEEN

✦ Helmsley House Disappears ✦

Archer's eyes dashed around his dark bedroom. Had he dreamed it? It sounded like an explosion. He poked his head into the hall. If it had only been a dream, his mother must have had an identical one. Shouts echoed from his parents' bedroom. The ostrich was bellowing up the stairs.

"What did that dirty thing do now? Did someone see it? Get this lampshade off my head!"

Archer hurried down the stairs, but stopped on the third floor. Cold air was surging from the front of the house, like every window had been left open. He threw on the light.

There wasn't an open window. There was no window at all. The alcove window above the front door—the window that bubbled out and was capped with a copper roof and a leaping goat—was gone. In its place was a massive hole, at least six feet tall and four feet wide, as though an elephant

had escaped Helmsley House. Archer *had* to be dreaming.

Mrs. Helmsley tore down the stairs. Mr. Helmsley hurried after her. Neither said a word. Snow whirled in, forming miniature drifts on the rug. Mr. Helmsley approached the hole. Archer followed.

"Archer!" Mrs. Helmsley demanded. "Come away from there at once!"

Archer and his father stood a few feet from the hole—a few feet from broken glass and splintered floorboards and torn wallpaper and missing chunks of wall. Outside, a truck was stuck halfway up a snowbank on the opposite sidewalk. Four ropes were tied to its bumper. The other ends were tied to columns that had once flanked the front door to support the alcove window. Now those columns and window and bits of wall were scattered across Willow Street. The copper goat had landed on the front steps of the house just opposite them. That house suddenly lit up, and little old widowed Mrs. Darington opened the front door, spotted the goat, shrieked, then slammed the door shut.

This had to be Mr. Mullfort's doing.

Archer sprang from the room, narrowly dodging his mother's arms.

"ARCHER!"

He shot past his grandparents in the hall, who tried to stop him as well.

"What happened, Archer?" Grandma Helmsley shouted, wrapping herself in her robe.

Down in the foyer, Archer jumped into his boots and dashed across the street. The truck bore the Society seal. It was still running, smoke pouring from its hood. He threw open the driver's-side door. The cab was empty.

Archer backed away, looking one way down Willow Street and then the other. Mr. Mullfort was nowhere to be seen. He turned back to his house. The destruction was even more shocking from the outside. It looked as though a torpedo had struck Helmsley House. His parents were staring out at him from the hole, as were his grandparents.

All along Willow Street, houses began lighting up. Front doors opened and gasps and cries echoed across the snow. Even old Mrs. Darington was back on her front steps. Next door, Mr. Glub hurried outside, pulling on his coat.

"*Archer?*" he called, stepping over a splintered post and broken glass as he approached the truck. "What in the—" Mr. Glub stopped dead when he turned and saw the hole in Helmsley House.

"Archer, get inside right this moment!" called Archer's mother.

But Archer stood frozen next to Mr. Glub, trying to take it all in.

Sirens sounded in the distance, and faint flashes of red lit the sky.

"Best do as she says," Mr. Glub advised, ushering him across the street. "I'll let the police know everyone is all right."

When Archer stepped back inside, his father was in the foyer inspecting the damage.

"Listen to your mother, Archer," he said, grabbing his coat. "Do whatever she tells you to do."

Mr. Helmsley joined Mr. Glub outside. Mrs. Helmsley barreled down the stairs with a suitcase in her hand, her eyes blazing like sparklers. She dropped her suitcase next to Archer and put both her hands on his shoulders.

"Go upstairs and pack your things. We're leaving immediately. I'm going to phone a hotel. Hurry."

Archer didn't argue. He dashed to his grandparents' room, but the door was locked and his knocks went unanswered.

"You know this was Mr. Mullfort," the polar bear said as Archer continued to his room.

"Did you see him?" Archer asked.

"I can't see anything. I can only say what you're thinking."

Archer dragged the scarlet trunk from the closet and was throwing a few days' worth of clothes into it when Oliver stepped through the balcony door, his eyes wide as could be.

"What happened?"

"It had to be Mr. Mullfort," Archer said, dropping sweaters into his trunk. "My mother snapped. We're going to a hotel."

"What about the Society? What about the delivery truck?"

Archer wasn't sure how they were going to do anything now. His thoughts were ricocheting around his head.

"Hold on," Oliver said. "Don't leave."

Oliver hurried out and returned a few moments later with the portable radio. "Adélaïde left it in my room. Take it with you. That way, wherever you end up, even if there's no phone, we can communicate. And give me the Doxical Powder."

Archer opened his dresser and reached into the back corner.

"Tell Adélaïde what happened," he said, handing Oliver the jar.

"I will. We'll go to the café as soon as it's open. We'll wait by the radio."

Archer dragged his trunk to his bedroom door and glanced back at Oliver before going downstairs. Mrs. Helmsley was pacing the foyer. She grabbed one side of Archer's trunk and they hauled it outside toward a taxi parked a few feet from Helmsley House.

"Heck of a something," the cabbie said as they approached. "What happened?"

"When your family associates with strange people, strange things happen," Mrs. Helmsley replied, climbing into the taxi.

Archer saw his grandparents, his father, and Mr. Glub standing next to the Society truck with the police. A crowd of neighbors had gathered around them. Everyone was staring at the hole. Archer was desperate to join them.

"Can I say good-bye to Grandma and Grandpa, at least?" he asked his mother, almost pleading as the cabbie struggled to get their luggage into the trunk.

"No. And I told them to stay away from you. Now get in the car, Archer."

Archer craned his neck to see out the back window as the taxi sped off. He didn't turn around again until Helmsley House had disappeared.

◆ Keeping Secrets Secret ◆

A sleepy bellhop greeted Archer and his mother and helped them carry their luggage through the doors of the North Canal Hotel. Despite it being the middle of the night, the lobby was noisy and crowded with odd individuals. Mrs. Helmsley's disapproval was evident as she tried to get the attention of the concierge, who, to Archer's aching eyes, seemed nothing more than a blur as he dashed back and forth across the lobby.

"There's no pipe smoking, thank you!"

"Boots off that sofa! It's just been reupholstered!"

"No, the kitchen is closed. And we don't serve fried grasshoppers!"

"Excuse me. Excuse me!" Mrs. Helmsley grabbed the concierge's arm before he could fly past them a fifth time.

The horror in his eyes diminished as he focused on Archer and his mother—perfectly normal, upstanding Rosewood citizens.

"*Oh*, I *do* apologize," the concierge said, lowering his voice. "This is all overflow from that—that *Society*, or whatever it is they call it. Apparently their place is filled to the gills. And now every hotel in Rosewood is, too!"

"Is that why it was so difficult to find a room?" Mrs. Helmsley asked, glancing around with dismay. "I thought we'd be sleeping in Rosewood Station tonight."

"You were fortunate. A gentleman cut his reservation short two days ago and fled the hotel with a cheesecake." The concierge ushered her to his desk. "You are Mrs. Helmsley, I presume?"

At the name *Helmsley*, the entire lobby fell silent. Everyone was now fixated on Archer's mother.

"I am. *Please hurry.*"

While the concierge searched his disheveled desk for the room key, Archer stayed by the luggage. He nearly shouted when someone tapped his shoulder, but he was delighted to see Mr. Dalligold peering down at him.

"My grandparents need your help," Archer explained. "Someone tore a hole in our house. The police are there."

Archer was still in shock, and it must have shown on his face. Mr. Dalligold placed a comforting hand on his shoulder.

The odd thing was, Archer instantly felt calm.

"Your grandmother phoned me not five minutes ago," Mr. Dalligold said, staring in a way that made Archer think he was reading his thoughts. "Now is not the time for secrets, Archer. You told us about the journal. What *didn't* you tell us?"

There was no hope of getting to the Society now, but Archer had to do something.

"There's proof the iceberg wasn't a hoax," he said. "I'm sure it's hidden at the Society. It's communications of some kind. In the Archives."

Mr. Dalligold sighed heavily.

"I won't ask why you kept such a thing secret, Archer. I'm sure you had a reason. But time is not on our side. The Inquiry is tomorrow evening. I'll have Beatrice Lune and Cornelius begin a search. With any luck, the Inquiry will be over before it—"

"Wait," said Archer. "You need to have someone watching Oliver, Adélaïde, and Kana. He threatened us."

"Who threatened you?" Mr. Dalligold asked.

"*Threaten?*" Mrs. Helmsley repeated, stepping up behind Archer with the room key in her hand. "Are you threatening my son? Who are . . . *You* were at our house!"

Mr. Dalligold straightened. "I was, Helena. And it was very rude of me not to introduce myself. My name is Mr. Dalligold."

"*Dalligold?*" Mrs. Helmsley's eyes widened. "*You're* the carnival crook!"

Mr. Dalligold tilted his head and smiled oddly. "I've been called many things throughout my years, but that's certainly one I've not heard before."

Mrs. Helmsley blushed, as though she knew she'd insulted someone she shouldn't have. "I didn't mean . . . I apologize if I . . . We'll say good night to you now."

Archer peered over his shoulder as he and his mother carried their luggage to the elevator, but Mr. Dalligold was already gone.

Mrs. Helmsley locked the door as soon as they were inside their hotel room. Archer thought she might swallow the key, but she put it into her pocket instead.

"I'm calling your father," she said, picking up a phone from the table between the two beds.

Archer opened a glass door and stepped out onto a stone balcony. The frigid air felt good on his hot cheeks. He leaned against the railing and saw Rosewood Canal, winding in both directions. He wasn't sure where he was exactly, but it had to be somewhere north of Willow Street. To his right was the giant clock tower above Rosewood Station. It was three o'clock in the morning. The Button Factory smokestacks were straight ahead, but a long way off. Archer wished he could see Helmsley House. What was happening now? And more importantly, what was going to happen now?

"Come inside and get some sleep, Archer," Mrs. Helmsley called. "I couldn't get ahold of your father. We'll sort out this mess in the morning."

There wasn't much night left, and though Archer lay down, he couldn't sleep. Mrs. Helmsley never even got into bed. She paced the room until dawn, muttering quietly to herself.

"We never should have moved in. I knew it was a mistake, and we're not going back."

◆ A Room with No View ◆

Archer didn't remember falling asleep, but he had. When he awoke, he kept his glowing eyelids shut. *It was a horrible dream. I ate too much chocolate. It's time to go to the Society.* He regretted opening his eyes when he finally did. Morning light was streaming into the hotel room, and his mother was dozing at the table.

"You need to eat something, Archer," she said, lifting a menu when he got out of bed. "Order whatever you'd like."

"Aren't we going downstairs?" Archer asked.

Mrs. Helmsley shuddered. "We're not eating with *those* people. The dining room must be a three-ring circus. I'll phone the kitchen." She pointed to small door built into the wall. "Breakfast will arrive on the dumbwaiter."

Their breakfast also arrived with a newspaper.

ROSEWOOD CHRONICLE

HELMSLEY HOUSE IS FALLING DOWN

Archer wanted to read it, but Mrs. Helmsley flung it into a trash can and he didn't dare retrieve it.

"Are we staying here until I leave for Raven Wood?" he asked, poking his fork at a pancake.

"You won't be returning to Raven Wood, Archer." Mrs. Helmsley said, gulping her coffee in one go. She hurried to the phone and dialed the kitchen again. "Please send a pot of coffee to room eight zero one. Yes, *an entire pot*, thank you very much."

"Why not?" Archer asked as his mother rejoined him at the table.

"We received a letter from Mr. Churnick three days ago. Raven Wood is shuttered. He was very apologetic about the short notice. Apparently he's now dean of student affairs at Willow Academy. Many of his students will switch schools. And he expressed a keen interest that you do as well."

Archer didn't believe what he was hearing. The dumbwaiter light blinked. Mrs. Helmsley grabbed the pot of coffee.

"For reasons I'm not quite sure of," she continued, pouring herself a fresh cup, "Mrs. Thimbleton lifted your expulsion, with the caveat that should you return, you would be closely monitored."

Archer was afraid to say it but did anyway. "Am I going back to Willow Academy?"

"Your father and I agreed you would," Mrs. Helmsley replied. "But last night changed everything. Someone is after your grandparents. It's not safe anymore. A long time ago, your grandfather told me he thought bad things were going on at that Society. And if *he* thought they were bad, I can't imagine what I would think. Now I have a long phone call to make."

Archer didn't touch his pancakes. Mr. Mullfort had ruined more than Helmsley House last night.

Mrs. Helmsley spent the entire day on the phone, speaking to a real estate agent. Archer could only hear snippets, but none of it sounded good.

"I have another hidden gem! *Very* hidden. A lovely cottage! Deep in the woods—very deep in the woods, indeed! No one, not a single person would ever find you there!"

Archer spent much of the day on the balcony. Off in the distance, he was almost certain he could see the Society's Observatory. Archer would have given his left eye to Cornelius if it meant he'd know what was happening. Mr. Dalligold and Cornelius and Beatrice Lune must be searching the Archives at that very moment. They'd probably searched throughout the night. Had they found the communications?

Lunch arrived via the dumbwaiter. But once again, Archer didn't eat a thing. When dinner arrived, he was starving. All he'd eaten the previous day was chocolate at the holiday party. Mrs. Helmsley dislodged a gigantic turkey with all the trimmings from the dumbwaiter. Archer sat before the roasted bird, thinking it could have plugged the hole in Helmsley House. He ate half of it, and it made him very drowsy. He climbed into his bed and collapsed into a deep sleep—deep, but not peaceful. He tossed back and forth, stuck in a nightmare.

⋆ PLANTING PROOF ⋆

Archer stood alone in darkness. He didn't know where he was. Lights began flickering overhead, and with each flicker, he glimpsed a figure, drawing closer. All at once the lights held steady, shining brightly, and there, towering before him, was Mr. Birthwhistle, his hands covered in dirt. They were alone inside the Grand Hall. Archer tried to run, but he couldn't. The sapphire rug was covered in chocolate. And so were his feet.

"The thing with dirty hands!" Mr. Birthwhistle howled. "The thing with dirty hands!"

"Why do you keep scratching your arm?" Archer asked.

"I brushed up against two things I shouldn't have. And one of those things was *you*."

Mr. Birthwhistle lunged. Archer shouted and sat straight up in bed, dripping cold sweat. He wiped his forehead, fearing he'd awakened his mother, but she was still sound asleep. Archer slid out of bed and grabbed his journal from his trunk, clicked on the desk lamp, and thumbed through the pages till he found his notes from the radio expedition.

Mr. Birthwhistle *had* told Mr. Mullfort he'd brushed up against two things he shouldn't have. He'd said one of those things was Mr. Mullfort. What was the second thing? Mr. Birthwhistle was scratching his arm. Was it a rash?

Archer leaned back in the chair. That night at the Society, in the greenhouse lab with Benjamin, Oliver had brushed against a plant.

"It's not poisonous, is it?"

It wasn't. Benjamin said poisonous plants were kept in Greenhouse Four. Then they had been interrupted.

"I think that's Malmurna. She'll write me up if she finds me here by myself."

They'd continued their conversation atop the Observatory, where Adélaïde had seen Greenhouse Four light up.

"Malmurna knows I love the Greenhouse."

Was it Malmurna?

"My father is coming, Archer. Or maybe he's already here."

Mr. Dalligold was searching in the wrong place. The communications weren't hidden in the Archives. They were buried beneath poisonous plants in Greenhouse Four. That was where no one would look. That was why Mr. Birthwhistle was scratching his arm. He'd brushed against a plant while burying them.

Archer went to the balcony. A sliver of red pierced the clouds. The Rosewood Station clock tower gonged six o'clock in the morning. What was he supposed to do? He had to tell someone. He had to get in touch with Oliver and Adélaïde. He had to escape.

Mrs. Helmsley was still asleep when Archer stepped back into the room. He hurried the radio into the bathroom and turned on the shower to muffle the noise.

• BELMONT CAFÉ •

Oliver and Adélaïde were shivering outside the café.

"Do you think he's still in Rosewood?" Adélaïde asked.

"I hope so," Oliver replied. "There's Amaury."

"*Another* early morning at the radio?" Amaury questioned, moving briskly to the door. "And any news on Archer? I went to see the hole for myself—couldn't believe it."

"We're not sure where his mother took him," Oliver said, shaking his head.

Amaury unlocked the door and they all hurried in. Oliver and Adélaïde sprinted to the radio. Adélaïde clicked it on as Oliver grabbed the headphones.

"Anything?" she asked. Oliver shook his head. "Wait here. I'll get hot chocolates."

Oliver kept the headphones on while trying to remove his coat and nearly tripped over the cord when he heard Archer's voice.

ARCHER: Can anyone hear me? Oliver? Are you there? It's Archer.

OLIVER: I'm here, Archer!

ARCHER: I know everything. I know where the communications are.

OLIVER: It sounds like it's raining on your side. Can you repeat that?

ARCHER: I know where the communications are. It's not the Archives. We have to get to the Society. You have to come get me. I'm at a hotel.

"What's going on?" Adélaïde asked, setting two mugs on the desk.

"It's Archer. He's still in Rosewood. We need to get him. Do you have a map?"

"There's one in the delivery truck." Adélaïde rushed out.

ARCHER: What happened after I left?

OLIVER: The police were questioning your grandparents. Then Mr. Dalligold showed up. I'm not sure what he said, but the police left immediately. There's something odd about him, isn't there? Adélaïde's got the map. What's the name of the hotel?

ARCHER: North Canal Hotel.

OLIVER: You're . . . north of Howling Bloom Street and west of the Society.

ARCHER: When can you come?

ADÉLAÏDE: Archer, this is Adélaïde. The storm is supposed to hit
             at seven. Amaury is closing the café at six to be safe.
             I don't want to give him the Doxical Powder until he
             locks the door. If everything goes well, we can meet you
             by six thirty. Will that work?

ARCHER: Yes. The Inquiry is tonight. We have to get there before it
             ends. I'll wait for you on the south side of the canal. I have
             to figure out how I'm going to escape.

⁕ TICKTOCK, TICKTOCK ⁕

That day could not have passed any slower. After breakfast,
Archer discreetly searched for the room key while his mother
sat at the table, reviewing a list of potential new homes.
The key wasn't anywhere to be found. It must still be in his
mother's pocket.

After lunch, Archer stood on the balcony, craning his neck
to better see the hotel's facade. There was a drainpipe. If he
held on to that and used the stone windowsills, he might be
able to climb down. It wouldn't be easy descending eight
stories, but that's what he'd do.

At that same moment, on Willow Street, Oliver pulled a
fresh batch of raspberry strudels from his mother's oven.
He slipped the jar of Doxical Powder back into his pocket
while waiting for them to cool and then piled the pastries
into a paper bag, keeping the two with Doxical Powder

on top. He'd put a thumbprint on those so as to avoid any mixup.

On North Willow Street, Adélaïde grabbed the Greenhorn uniforms, slipped into her boots, and knocked on Kana's front door.

As dinner neared, Archer heard a great commotion outside. He went to the balcony and watched a massive crowd of Society members leaving the hotel. They got into Society trucks, which lined the street. One by one the trucks set off, rumbling over a bridge to cross the canal. The clock tower above Rosewood Station tolled six o'clock. A snowflake landed on Archer's forehead. He looked to the sky. It was a giant sheet of cold gray steel.

Inside Belmont Café, Amaury stood at the window, also peering up at that sky. The café was as desolate as the streets of Rosewood. Adélaïde, Oliver, and Kana were seated at the bar, ready to do something they didn't want to do.

◆ AMOUR OR LESS AMAURY ◆

"Time to close up," Amaury said, turning from the window. "All of you need to get home safely." His eyes widened when Oliver opened the bag of raspberry strudels.

"Would you like one?"

"I told your father we need to sell these, Adie," Amaury said, taking a huge bite. His second bite was much smaller.

"Did your mother change the recipe? Or was the milk a bit rancid?"

"I don't think so," Oliver said.

It was obvious Amaury didn't like the pastry as much as he had during the Glubs' Christmas party, but he politely finished it, gagging slightly, and then left for the back of the café.

Adélaïde's, Oliver's, and Kana's eyes were glued to the clock while their ears listened to Amaury tidying up. In almost exactly ten minutes, an eerie silence settled, followed by a loud bang and a crash. A very different Amaury returned to the bar. Adélaïde had never been frightened of Amaury before. She was now. His kind eyes had been emptied of all goodness and his considerable mass, which usually made him warm and approachable, had become menacing.

"What are you still doing here?" Amaury demanded, clamping his hands onto the bar and glaring at them with dead eyes. "I told you to leave!"

"We—we were about to," Adélaïde promised, leaning back and wiping a speck of spit from her nose. "But we were wondering if we could—"

"You don't look like you're about to leave, you *liar!* You told me you'd tell your father I needed help. I believed you! But have you said a word to him? No! I'll bet you like watching me drown in this sea of coffee!"

"I'm sorry," Adélaïde said. "I meant to tell him, but I forgot. I've been busy with—"

Amaury's laugh was as cruel as it was cold.

"*Busy?* You've been sitting around ever since that lamppost fell on you!"

Adélaïde looked as though a hot coal had been dropped down her dress. Kana whispered in her ear. "Remember, this is *not* Amaury."

"I don't like secrets!" Amaury insisted.

"It wasn't a secret," Kana explained.

"It looked like a secret."

"Secrets don't look like anything," Oliver said. "They're just words said quietly."

"Then take your quiet words and . . . Actually, you can stay." Amaury ripped his apron off and nearly cracked the counter in two as he slammed it down. "I'm done spending my every waking hour surrounded by your father's coffee." He marched to the door and almost tore it from its hinges.

Oliver spun on his stool. "Wait! Can we use the delivery truck?"

Amaury dug into his pockets and tossed him the keys. "Do me a favor and push it off the Rosewood cliffs. I'm done with deliveries. I'm done with this coffeehouse of horrors." He turned and slammed the door behind him.

They all felt terrible. Especially Adélaïde. And that's exactly how they should've felt. When you turn someone who is very kind into someone terrible, technically you're the terrible one.

"We shouldn't have done that," Oliver said, fiddling with the keys.

"We can't take it back now," Kana replied.

Adélaïde was staring at Amaury's apron, strewn across the counter. She had known he'd be nasty. But she didn't think he'd dig up her past.

Oliver grabbed the pastry bag and handed her a strudel. "That might cheer you up." He gave another to Kana. And took one for himself.

Adélaïde and Kana finished theirs before Oliver had even taken a bite. He stared at the strudel, then, almost in one gulp, swallowed it. "We'd better get ready," he said, crumpling the bag.

Adélaïde slapped his arm. "Why is the bag empty? You put Doxical Powder into *two* pastries! You wanted a backup just in case!"

Considering the situation, Oliver didn't look tremendously surprised. He simply closed his eyes and dropped his forehead onto the bar. Adélaïde and Kana frowned at each other.

✦ THE DUMBWAITER ✦

Archer and his mother finished their dinner.

"Please return the trays," Mrs. Helmsley said, and stepped into the bathroom.

Archer carried them to the dumbwaiter. He was worried about scaling the icy facade of North Canal Hotel, but he didn't have a choice. His friends would be here soon. He clicked the return button. A light came on—both above the dumbwaiter door and inside Archer's head.

Why hadn't he thought of it sooner? He'd been staring at it for two days. He could escape inside the dumbwaiter! It was small and he wasn't sure it would support his weight, but his only other option included a high probability of plummeting. If Archer was going to plummet, he preferred to do so in darkness inside the hotel wall. He set the trays back on the table and dug the Society map out of his trunk.

⬦ For Good Luck and Good Measure ⬦

"I don't get it," Adélaïde said, staring at Kana. "Something should have happened by now. You look fine. I feel fine. And Oliver is . . ."

Oliver hadn't said a word. His head was still resting on the bar. Adélaïde put a hand to his shoulder. "Are you feeling okay, Ollie?"

Oliver peeled his face from the bar. Kana giggled. Adélaïde groaned. Oliver's expression said it all. He was perfectly serene. He hadn't a care in the world.

"I *love* it when you call me Ollie. And to answer your question, yes, I feel *perfect*. Better than perfect, really. I feel perfectly perfect." His words were both delicate and sweet, like a whispered lullaby.

"You ate the wrong pastry," Adélaïde explained.

"*Wrong pastry?*" Oliver smiled and tapped his finger on Adélaïde's forehead. "Don't. Be. Silly. *Silly,*" he said with each tap. "There's no such thing as a wrong pastry."

Adélaïde turned to Kana. "I vote we leave him behind."

"I don't think that's a good idea," Kana said. "He might wander outside and get lost in the blizzard. Or what if he goes home? I don't think his parents should see him like, *well* . . . look at him."

Oliver was spinning his finger in a sugar bowl. "It's like sand—*sugar* sand. I wonder if stars are filled with sugar sand? Maybe stars *are* sugar sand."

"You have a point," Adélaïde said, jumping down from her stool. She grabbed the bag of Greenhorn uniforms and handed Oliver a pair of pants. He immediately slipped them over his arms and began flailing them like tentacles.

"I'm the creature from the abyss! I've come to take you into my lair!"

Adélaïde wasn't amused. "If the creature from the abyss doesn't sit down and put his pants on, he'll be left behind."

The flailing stopped. Oliver placed a pant-leg arm on Adélaïde's shoulder. "I worry about you sometimes. You can be very negative."

"We're going to the Society, Oliver," Adélaïde sighed, sorting through the bag and handing out shirts, sweaters, and ties. "You need to be a little more serious about this. Mr. Mullfort tore a hole in Archer's house, in case you've forgotten."

"Don't you worry about Mr. Mullfort," Oliver said, taking his arms out of the pant legs. "You leave him to me."

✦ STRUGGLING ✦

Archer clicked the dumbwaiter button a third time and put his ear to the door. The gears ground as a cable carried the box up the shaft and to their room. The grinding stopped. The light went out. Archer threw it open and hoisted himself inside. He fit— barely. His face was jammed against his knees and he struggled to reach back out to press the return button. He'd finally managed it . . . when the bathroom door opened.

Mrs. Helmsley saw him wedged inside the dumbwaiter, but it must have taken a moment to register. Archer had just enough time to click the button before she sprang forward.

"Archer! What in name of all that's good and proper do you think you're—"

Archer wrenched the door shut, and the box began its descent.

⋆ To the North Canal Hotel ⋆

Adélaïde unhitched the cargo trailer of the delivery truck and made room for Oliver, who sat not unhappily amid crates of coffee.

"You better get inside, too, Kana," she said. "Archer should be up front."

Kana climbed in, and after shutting the trunk, Adélaïde took her seat behind the wheel. A small round hole was cut into the rear cab, and as soon as she sat down, Oliver shoved his head through it.

"It's like one of those carnival things!" he cheered. "You know, where you stick your head through a piece of wood with a hole in it and your body becomes a lobster or something. What do I look like?"

"You look like a boy who stuck his head through a hole," Adélaïde said.

"*Oh*. That's not very fun, is it?"

Adélaïde stuck the key into the ignition, wishing she'd had a chance to learn how to drive. As the engine idled, she studied the pedals at her feet. She pressed her foot to the gas. The truck moved forward. She put her foot to the brake. It stopped. "Simple enough," she mumbled.

"Lights," Oliver said. "Don't forget the lights."

Adélaïde pressed a button on the dashboard. Windshield wipers squeaked back and forth.

"Those aren't lights."

"Keep quiet!"

Adélaïde pushed a second button and the headlights came on. Kana passed her the Rosewood map. North Canal Hotel was circled in red. Adélaïde set it on the seat next to her and peered into the side-view mirrors. Her eyes widened, not sure if she was seeing things. But Kana saw it too, through the window on the cargo door. Two figures in long black coats were rushing the truck.

"Hurry, Adélaïde!" Kana called. "I think we're being—" Kana shrieked as one of the figures grabbed the cargo-door handle. The other figure was outside Adélaïde's window with one hand on the windshield and the other on her door.

"DRIVE!" Oliver shouted, his head still in the hole. "It's Birthwhistle's people!"

Adélaïde slammed on the gas. The truck flew out onto Howling Bloom Street and, a moment later, was swerving sideways onto Foldink. Adélaïde jammed on the brake. Oliver's head was no longer sticking through the hole.

"Is everyone okay?" Adélaïde asked, leaning out the window and looking back. The two figures had been launched into a snowdrift. Neither was moving.

"I'm fine," Kana said, securing the cargo door.

"I'm fine too," Oliver added. "The coffee boxes broke my fall."

"Did you crush them?"

"It's difficult to . . . it's very dark back . . ."

"He crushed them," Kana confirmed.

Adélaïde winced. Her father wouldn't be happy about that.

"We need to leave," Kana said. "They're standing up."

Adélaïde gripped the wheel, and they were off.

If you were sitting near a window, waiting to see the storm roll in, you'd have found yourself watching a peculiar thing instead. The delivery truck would speed up all at once, then stop, then begin again, slower now, then faster, then too fast! Then stop. But as they made their way up Foldink Street toward North Canal Hotel, Adélaïde was learning how to control the vehicle.

✦ ESCAPE FROM NORTH CANAL HOTEL ✦

Archer was terribly uncomfortable stuffed inside the dumbwaiter box. The gears ground much louder than before. Like his heart, the dumbwaiter struggled to keep a steady pace. His mother would be getting into the hotel elevator at the very same moment. He was sure she'd be fuming. Whatever Mr. Churnick had said to convince her that he was a changed person was now out the window. The dumbwaiter stopped.

The door opened. Archer's eyes were flooded with light, and his ears with a thunderous clanking of pots and pans and hissing water.

"It's a boy!" someone shouted.

Archer popped out of the dumbwaiter like a piece of toast from a toaster.

"What are you doing?" a chef demanded. "That's not a toy! You could've broken it and fallen to your death!"

Archer bolted for the kitchen door, then sprinted down a hallway, shoved through another door, and nearly tumbled face-first into the lobby. The concierge was hunched over a sofa, grumbling and scrubbing a footprint off it. Archer raced for the doors. Behind him, the elevator dinged. He sprang out onto the snow-covered streets and never once looked back.

CHAPTER

FIFTEEN

⋆ INTO A POISONOUS DREAM ⋆

Archer flickered in and out of light as he dashed beneath lampposts that lined a canal bridge. The wind was picking up and snowflakes speckled his forehead. He was breathing heavily when he reached the other side and paused to search the deserted streets.

Archer heard the delivery truck before he saw it. It sounded like a windup toy. A headlight suddenly appeared down a narrow alleyway. The beam swerved left and right as it grew closer. Archer backed up onto a mound of snow and raised his hands over his head. The truck slowed, slid sideways, and stopped.

Adélaïde unrolled the window and tossed him his Greenhorn uniform. "We didn't think we'd ever see you again," she said, smiling.

"It's been a long two days, hasn't it?" Archer replied, hopping into the truck. "How did everything go for you?"

"Mostly fine, but something happened at the café."

"To Amaury?"

"No. Well, *yes*. We turned him into a monster. But there were—"

"Archer!" Oliver shouted as his head popped through the hole. "I'm glad you could make it! This is exciting, isn't it?"

Archer blinked at Adélaïde.

"He's filled with Doxical Powder. And pastry. We thought about leaving him behind."

"But we didn't want him to get lost in the blizzard," Kana called.

"It might be fun to get lost in a blizzard," Oliver mused, and lowered his voice, trying to whisper to Archer. "But Adélaïde has been a bit stuffy since before we left the café."

"I can hear you, Oliver. I'm *right* here."

"See what I mean?" Oliver said, wiggling his eyebrows and disappearing into the back.

"We'll keep an eye on him," Archer whispered.

"*Two* eyes," Adélaïde agreed. "But that's not what I'm talking about either. There were two people outside the café. They tried to stop us."

"We think they were Birthwhistle's thugs," Kana called again. "They must have been following us."

"It could have been Mr. Dalligold's friends," Archer said, scanning the streets. "I told Mr. Dalligold about the

communications and to keep eyes on all of you. What did they say to you?"

Everyone was silent.

"We didn't really give them a chance to say anything," Oliver explained. "We kind of, *well* . . ."

Adélaïde bit her lip. "We almost ran them over."

"You *what?*"

"Don't worry," Kana called. "I saw everything. They were shaken. And covered in snow. But they stood up. They're not dead."

"We've been a little anxious. I'm sure they'll understand," Adélaïde said, putting her foot to the gas.

⋅ THE ROAD SOUTH ⋅

The snow grew thicker as they sped south. Adélaïde turned up the windshield wipers. "How did you figure out where the communications were?" she asked.

"It's a long story," Archer said. "But they're buried in Greenhouse Four. Where the poisonous plants are kept. I had a nightmare about it."

"You figured it out from a nightmare?"

"Mostly after the nightmare."

Through the windshield, they watched the houses give way to warehouses.

"We're in Barrow's Bay," Archer said, reviewing the map.

The snow got heavier as the streets got narrower and the warehouses got taller. Adélaïde sped up the windshield wipers again as they turned onto a bridge to cross the canal. Gusting winds cut across their path, tossing the truck from side to side.

"Hold on back there," Archer called to Oliver and Kana.

On the other side of the canal, they entered the maze. Streetlamps were flickering. Many weren't working at all. The wind swept snow all around the truck. They were glad not to be outside, but inside that tiny truck, they didn't feel much safer. Even Oliver had grown quiet.

"Why did you turn off the windshield wipers?" Archer asked.

"I didn't." Adélaïde twisted the knob back and forth. "I think they froze."

Snow piled on the windshield.

"We're going to hit something," Adélaïde said, hunching over the wheel to see out what little bit of glass was not covered. "I can't see anything."

Archer rolled his window down and stuck his head out. The snow stung his face. "Keep straight. We're fine. There's a gap up ahead. I think it's—There it is!"

The Society was standing tall and glowing brilliantly through the storm. Archer marveled at the sight and guided Adélaïde across the piazza to one of the footbridges. They parked just next to it, and everyone got out. Oliver started to run toward the Society, but Adélaïde snagged him.

"Wait. You don't go anywhere without us," she insisted.

Oliver rolled his eyes at Archer. "She's a wet sock sometimes."

"She's right, Oliver. You have to stay with us."

"Two wet socks."

"We need to get inside," Kana said, gazing up into the storm. "It's about to get worse."

The four locked arms and crossed the footbridge, taking great care not to slip. Archer couldn't tell if it was the wind howling or Oliver as they passed the narwhals with crossing tusks, stumbled up the front steps, and pushed through the door.

⋆ WHAT IS AN ICEBERG? ⋆

"Is anyone home?" Oliver called, his voice echoing around the empty entrance. "Did we get all dressed up for nothing?"

"Is the Inquiry over?" Kana asked.

"It can't be," Archer said, staring at Adélaïde. "That's not possible."

They hurried across the checkered floor and up the staircase. Archer pressed his ear to the doors of the Grand Hall. *Was* it over? He heard a voice inside and opened the door a crack.

The Inquiry was *not* over. The Grand Hall was *packed*. It made DuttonLick's party look like an intimate gathering. Row upon row of chairs stretched before him, all the way up to the stage. There wasn't an empty seat. Members lined the sides of the hall, and still more sat in the windows.

Up on the stage, before a roaring fire, ten Deputies in black robes were seated around Mr. Suplard, who was elevated on a small platform. Archer's grandparents were on one side, with Mr. Dalligold. On the other side was Mr. Birthwhistle, by himself. He was on his feet, addressing the silent hall.

"And what is an iceberg? It's a rogue chunk of ice that breaks from a glacier after deciding it would rather do its own thing. Are the Helmsleys not precisely that—an iceberg to our glacier? No one would deny the contributions they've made to our organization. And I don't doubt there are many here this evening who *still* think highly of them. But we mustn't allow emotion to cloud sound judgment. The Helmsleys were a threat to our work before they vanished and will go on being a threat should they be reinstated!"

The hall erupted. Archer was heartened that there were just as many shouts of disapproval as shouts of agreement. Even so, there was no time to waste. He shut the door and pulled the Society map from beneath his sweater.

"Let's get to the greenhouse."

⋆ STRAIGHTENING CROOKEDNESS ⋆

"It's that way."

"No, you're looking at it upside down."

"This door says TREASURY."

"So it's this way."

"*No*, it's *that* way."

Even with a map, finding their way to the Greenhouse was difficult. The only way they could do it was to match titles above doors to rooms on the map. It was slow going.

"We were never here with Darby," Archer said as they crossed an interior causeway overlooking a room filled with taxidermied animals and the equipment to do it.

"No, but look." Adélaïde pointed to the map. "The elevator should be on the other side."

Kana opened a door, and sure enough, straight ahead was the elevator. Adélaïde rushed to it and clicked the button. Archer, Oliver, and Kana stopped a few feet back.

"We have to be careful," Archer warned them as he folded the map and tucked it under his sweater. "This is the poisonous greenhouse. Benjamin had a plant at Raven Wood that he said was deadly. I'm sure many plants in there are."

"You're afraid of *plants*?" Oliver scoffed. "I'll fight them off if they come at us. I'll pluck their little leaves and send them packing."

"No, Oliver, he's talking about poison," Adélaïde said. "You can't fight poison."

"Watch me."

The elevator arrived. Through the gate, Archer saw a pair of deep-set deep-blue eyes, but before he could say anything, Adélaïde opened it. Suddenly, she was in Mr. Mullfort's arms, dangling like a dead fish—a dead fish with a wooden leg. Archer, Oliver, and Kana froze. No one knew what to do.

"Well, isn't this a surprise!" Mr. Mullfort hissed, his eyes sparkling with a sick delight as he swung Adélaïde back and forth. "Returned for more, have you? And did you enjoy your little party at the sweetshop? Good King Oliver, was it?"

Mr. Mullfort spotted Kana and smiled something nasty.

"So it's true! I was convinced Digby was mistaken. *My*, how you've grown, Kana. Not half the mousy girl you once were!"

Archer and Oliver exchanged a glance.

"Do they not know about you, Kana?" Mr. Mullfort asked. "President Birthwhistle was *certain* you'd told them. And he thought you'd be *just* the person to scare some sense into them with our letter. But he wasn't happy, Kana. President Birthwhistle does *not* like to repeat himself."

"What's he talking about?" Archer asked.

Kana shook her head. "Please don't, Mr. Mullfort."

Mr. Mullfort was overcome with laughter.

"*Oh*, come now, Kana. Were you ashamed? Ashamed to admit you stood a chance to stop the iceberg from happening, but instead, did *nothing*?"

Kana's eyes were wide and filled with guilt.

"Yes, wunderkind. She knew. Before anything happened. The little eavesdropper. Listening to a private conversation in the garden next door? It was *very* sneaky of you, Kana. But I straightened you out, didn't I?"

"I'm sorry, Archer," Kana finally said. "I should have said something. I wanted to. But I was frightened. He said he'd come for me if I didn't keep my mouth shut. I was nine years old."

Archer wasn't angry. Not even a little. He had been nine himself when his grandparents vanished. And nine-year-old Archer had thought penguins had eaten them. Mr. Mullfort had threatened Kana when she was only a *nine-year-old*? What kind of—

"You really *are* a crooked man," he said, glaring at Mr. Mullfort.

"And *you're* a sneaky boy who should know when he's been beaten. Now where are you off to, all dressed up like Greenhorns? Do you know where the communications are?"

Adélaïde squirmed as Mr. Mullfort pressed his crooked ear to hers as if trying to hear her thoughts. Oliver leaned in to whisper to Archer and Kana.

"Kana, you're coming with me. We're going to straighten

him out. Archer, you and Adélaïde keep searching. And I'm sorry for what I'm about to do to you."

Archer didn't have a chance to respond. A sharp pain shot through his stomach. Oliver had slugged him. Archer slumped over, his back to Mr. Mullfort. Oliver whispered loudly, "You're wrong! I'm the fastest!" and shoved his hand up under Archer's sweater. He yanked it out just as quickly and threw it behind his back.

"We have to go now, Mr. Mullfort," Kana said. "I hope things don't end as badly for you as I have a feeling they will."

Oliver and Kana bolted. Mr. Mullfort threw Adélaïde at Archer and shot after them. Oliver and Kana vanished around a corner, Mr. Mullfort hot on their tail.

"That was brilliant," Archer said, rubbing his stomach. "I know you don't like this version of Oliver, but he's impressive."

"I just hope this version has enough caution to not get himself and Kana killed," Adélaïde replied, following him into the elevator. They stared at each other, both thinking about Mr. Mullfort and Kana. "And I thought Amaury was a monster."

"I have a feeling Mr. Mullfort's the real reason for the silver streak in her hair," Archer agreed, and pushed up on the lever.

✦

✦ CHANGE OF PLANTS ✦

Archer and Adélaïde stood at the back of the central greenhouse, squinting through the glass. According to the map, Greenhouse Four was outside next to the canal wall, not even thirty feet away. The trouble was, they couldn't see it. They couldn't see anything. The blizzard was blinding.

"We have to get this right the first time," Archer said. "If we miss Greenhouse Four, we might fall off the edge."

"Let's not do that," Adélaïde agreed.

They joined hands and stepped out into the storm. It was like wandering into a dream. They couldn't see a thing, only a snowy whiteness whirling all around them. Adélaïde's hair swirled every which way as they inched forward with their free hands outstretched.

"Do you feel anything?" Archer asked.

"Nothing."

Another step. Nothing. Another step.

"Do you think we missed it?" Adélaïde asked.

"Let's go a little farther."

Another step. Their hands were frozen. Another step. Cold metal.

"That's it!" Archer said.

They moved faster now, feeling along the greenhouse wall. Adélaïde found the door, and they pushed through into utter darkness. Archer felt for the light switch and bumped

it with the back of his hand.
Greenhouse Four lit up.

"I'm glad Oliver's not here,"
Adélaïde said, her eyes wide.

The plants encircling them were
sinister. Some resembled hands that would
grab them if they got too close, while others
lured them with beautiful colors. Even the air smelled toxic.

"Don't let anything touch you," Archer warned, grabbing
a small shovel and handing a second one to Adélaïde. "I'm
guessing that the communications must be buried inside
a box. Push the shovel straight into the dirt and see if it
hits something."

"That's going to take a while," Adélaïde replied, staring at
the long metal troughs encircling the greenhouse.

"Do you have a better idea?" Archer asked.

Adélaïde shook her head. "I'll start on this side," she said.
"You start over there, and we'll work
our way back."

The search commenced,
but avoiding the plants wasn't
easy. It was as if they wanted
Archer and Adélaïde to bump
into them. Six pendant lights,
hanging overhead, lit their paths,

while outside the storm raged, beating and howling against the glass. They jabbed their shovels into the soil, pulled them out, and moved down the troughs.

Adélaïde stopped.

"Did you find something?" Archer asked, glancing over his shoulder.

"No. Keep moving."

Archer was getting worried. They'd searched the troughs along the sides of the greenhouse and were now nearing each other, searching the troughs at the back. He jabbed with greater frequency, fearing he might miss something.

"Nothing?" he called.

"Not yet."

But it had to be here. Archer jabbed his shovel into the dirt, pulled it out, and bumped into Adélaïde. They froze. Before them, in the dirt, was a hole. And in that hole, a dirty, empty, tin.

"I don't understand," Archer said, reaching in and pulling out the opened tin. "Why would they be gone? Why did he dig them up?"

He turned to Adélaïde, but she wasn't there. She was on the ground.

"Adélaïde!" Archer crouched next to her. "What happened?"

"There was a potted plant beneath the trough. I didn't see it. It pricked me. I can't feel my leg."

Archer leaned over her and carefully plucked a gigantic

thorn from her leg. He stared at it, then searched the potted plants along the floor. There *was* a *Paria glavra*, just like the plant Benjamin had. Its long, spiraling stems were now covered in the biggest thorns Archer had ever seen.

"We have to hurry," he said.

Archer wasn't sure what to do, but he knew who would. He hooked his arms under Adélaïde's and dragged her across the greenhouse floor.

"You're heavier than you look," he said, pushing through the door.

"Or maybe you're only as strong as you look."

Archer kept glancing over his shoulder as he dragged Adélaïde through the blizzard. But he wasn't afraid of missing the main greenhouse. It was huge. And when he finally bumped it, he felt for the door. He left Adélaïde on a stool in the lab and went to find Benjamin.

✦ A Cinder Block and Thorn ✦

Archer reached the Greenhorn Commons and opened the door only enough to get his head through, wary of being spotted by Mrs. Malmurna. Inside, most of the Greenhorns were seated along comfortable couches, speaking quietly to one another. Benjamin was alone in a window seat. Archer waved to get his attention, and he did. Unfortunately, he also got the attention of the cinder block named Fledger.

Fledger opened his mouth, ready to shout, but Darby rushed up behind him. She cupped her hands over his mouth and wouldn't let go. The two of them struggled as Benjamin crept to the door.

"What's going on?" he whispered.

"I need your help. It's Adélaïde. *A Paria glavra* pricked her."

Benjamin glanced at the opposite side of the room. Mrs. Malmurna was seated at a desk, lost in a book. Benjamin slipped out. Archer waved to Darby and she smiled, hands still clamped around Fledger's mouth.

"What were you doing in Greenhouse Four?" Benjamin asked as they hurried along.

"We were searching for proof."

"Did you find it?"

"No."

Adélaïde was still on the stool when they rushed in. Benjamin crouched before her leg and inspected the puncture wound. "You can't feel your legs, can you?" he asked.

Adélaïde giggled, though it didn't seem like the time for that. "It's only half bad. I only have one leg to lose feeling in."

"I don't want you to panic," Benjamin said calmly. "But if we're not quick, you might lose your other leg too."

Adélaïde remained calm. Archer didn't. "Lose the other one! That's impossible! How can I help?"

"You can't," Benjamin said, opening a cabinet. "It'll be

fine. I just need to mix a few things and suck out the poison."

"Archer, you need to go," Adélaïde whispered.

"I have no idea where to look now," Archer whispered back. "I was sure they'd be in the greenhouse. Maybe Mr. Mullfort has them. Maybe that's why he was in the elevator."

"He wouldn't have chased Oliver and Kana if he had them."

Archer glanced at Benjamin, who was lining up bottles and jars on the counter. He paused, and the two locked eyes. Neither said a word. Then Benjamin resumed his work, and Archer turned back to Adélaïde.

"I'll find you as soon as this is over," he promised, and left the Greenhouse.

Benjamin knelt before Adélaïde, suctioned out the thick, yellowish poison with a blunt syringe, and grabbed the mixture he'd made. "This might sting a bit. You'll feel your leg soon."

Adélaïde studied Benjamin as he bent and straightened her leg. "What will you do if Archer finds something that proves your father was responsible for the iceberg?"

Benjamin slowed. "Archer won't find proof. It doesn't exist. Now, try to stand up."

⬩ PRESIDENT BIRTHWHISTLE ⬩

Archer walked down the hallway, feeling something like a yo-yo. Where was he going to look now? He turned a corner and wondered where Oliver and Kana might be.

Why *was* Mr. Mullfort searching for the communications? And why was Mr. Birthwhistle hiding them from him? Did they not trust each other? Was that why Mr. Birthwhistle had dug them up? Had Mr. Mullfort guessed that they were buried in the poisonous greenhouse? If that was the case, they now had to be somewhere Mr. Mullfort wouldn't think to look.

Archer stared at the map. Would they be in a place Mr. Mullfort had *already* searched? A place he wouldn't likely check again?

"How would you know they were in my office unless you were also in my office?"

Archer was off again and didn't stop until he spotted the door to Mr. Birthwhistle's office. He slipped inside, hurried past a dying fire and the mantel of piranhas, and threw open the top drawer of Mr. Birthwhistle's desk. Inside was something wrapped in fabric. Archer set it atop the desk, his fingers shaking, and unwrapped the fabric, revealing a stack of telegrams.

TELEGRAM ONE: As you've requested, Captain Dorn has gotten sick. I spoke with Captain Lemurn. He's on board, but he wants more money.

TELEGRAM TWO: The money was transferred. You don't have to remind me of our terms. Lemurn knows nothing of your involvement. No one knows. I've just returned from Rosewood Port. The Helmsleys have departed.

TELEGRAM THREE: Everything went smoothly. The Helmsleys got onto an iceberg during the voyage south to observe penguins. Lemurn used that as his opportunity. Once they were on the iceberg, he reversed the engines.

TELEGRAM FOUR: Your last message was rather testy. The iceberg was perfect. Lemurn didn't have to cover his tracks. There were no tracks. Apparently Ralph and Rachel were shouting and begging for him to return. Even I would have paid money to see that.

TELEGRAM FIVE: I see your point. I don't think they retrieved the dinghy the Helmsleys used to get onto the iceberg. Don't worry. The dinghy won't let them get very far. I'm on my way to the Society to place bets.

TELEGRAM SIX: Lemurn returned to port. I took him and his crew to Suplard. He didn't suspect any foul play. Lemurn and his crew were wonderfully distraught.

TELEGRAM SEVEN: I saw the story in the Doldrums Press. Other papers are picking it up. It's a real circus.

TELEGRAM EIGHT: You won't believe who came into Strait of Magellan today. It was the grandson. He had two friends with him. He said he was heading to Antarctica to find his grandparents. This is not an update. I just thought it would give you as good a laugh as it did me.

TELEGRAM NINE: How is it possible? It's been two years!

TELEGRAM TEN: Why aren't you responding? I'm going to Helmsley House now. I've heard rumors they're back. I shouldn't have to ask, but you've destroyed this correspondence, haven't you? I've destroyed yours as per our agreement.

Archer shuffled through the telegrams again and again, his heart sinking. Mr. Birthwhistle's name wasn't anywhere.

These only proved Mr. Mullfort was guilty. That was why Mr. Birthwhistle had kept them. And that was why Mr. Mullfort wanted them.

But they'd been inside Mr. Birthwhistle's desk. Wasn't that proof enough that Mr. Birthwhistle was involved? Should Archer put them back and run to get Mr. Suplard so he could see for himself? But what if Mr. Birthwhistle sent someone to get them before Archer returned with Mr. Suplard? He was holding proof that his grandparents didn't *want* to vanish—proof that the iceberg *wasn't* a hoax. He couldn't let it out of his sight. He couldn't risk losing it just to prove Mr. Birthwhistle was guilty. He wrapped the letters back into the fabric, grabbed the bundle, and left the office.

Archer broke into a sprint, running as fast as he could. When the door to the Grand Hall came into sight, he closed his eyes, tucked his shoulder, and plowed in.

⁜ A Grand Entrance ⁜

Whatever had been happening inside the Grand Hall came to an abrupt halt. Archer's entrance sent a thundering echo through the room. Before him were rows of seats stretching up to the stage, and every single occupant of those seats had turned around, all staring at him in perfect silence. If you've ever stood before a large crowd of strangers, all gawking at you, then you'll know exactly how Archer felt.

"These Greenhorns are out of control!" someone shouted. "What's Malmurna been doing to them?"

"Is he a Greenhorn? I didn't recognize the other two, and I don't recognize that one either."

The other two? Had Oliver and Kana already been here?

Archer looked at his grandparents, who were seated as far away as it was possible to be.

"I recognize this one. He's the grandson."

"Whose grandson?"

"*My* grandson!" Grandpa Helmsley rose to his feet. Grandma Helmsley did, too.

"But what is he doing here, Ralph?" Mr. Suplard demanded, squinting at Archer from the podium. "And why is he impersonating a Greenhorn?"

Only Archer could answer that question, but he stuttered. "I'm . . . well . . . I—"

"Speak up, boy!" Mr. Suplard insisted.

Archer swallowed. This was his moment. But now that he was in it, he was struggling.

"He's a lunatic like Ralph and Rachel!"

"Order!" Mr. Suplard shouted. He banged his gavel on the podium and then pointed it at Archer. "Attendants, escort that boy out *immediately.*"

Archer peered over his shoulder as two attendants pushed off the wall.

"Don't you lay a hand on my grandson!" Grandma Helmsley warned.

"Not even a *finger!*" Grandpa Helmsley added.

The attendants paused.

Archer's head was spinning. He wasn't sure if anyone would believe he'd found the telegrams in Birthwhistle's desk, but what would happen to Benjamin if they did? *Why* did it have to be Benjamin's father? He wished Mr. Mullfort had acted alone. But he hadn't. Mr. Birthwhistle had orchestrated everything. That was the truth. Archer held the telegrams above his head.

"Proof," he said. "I have proof."

"What's that?" Mr. Suplard asked, looking to his Deputies. "Did anyone catch what he said?"

"I think he said he has proof."

"Proof of what? What's in your hands?"

Archer hesitated again.

"For heaven's sake, boy," Mr. Suplard cried. "Either state your purpose for being here or *get out.*"

"It wasn't a hoax," Archer said, much louder now. "The iceberg wasn't a hoax. My grandparents aren't crazy. Mr. Birthwhistle is lying. These telegrams prove it. They were hidden inside Mr. Birthwhistle's desk!"

The hall fell deathly silent. The only sound to be heard was that of a cane tapping the floor as Mr. Dalligold slowly made his way to Archer.

"Come forward, Master Helmsley," Mr. Dalligold said with his regal air.

The hall remained silent as Archer stepped before Mr. Dalligold and presented the telegrams. Mr. Dalligold secured his glasses and carefully unwrapped the fabric. He lifted the telegrams one by one, and Archer watched his lips moving as he silently read them all.

"Well, Dalligold? What *are* those?"

Mr. Dalligold removed his glasses. His eyes, twinkling at Archer, seemed to shout, *You've done it, Archer! You've done it!* But all Mr. Dalligold did was wink and clear his throat.

"What I have here is . . . Mr. Suplard, a brief recess, in light of *new* evidence. Every member must read these telegrams before *any* vote is to take place."

Mr. Suplard raised his gavel. Mr. Birthwhistle sat perfectly still. He'd shown no emotion during any of this, and he wasn't showing any now.

"Keep to my side, Archer," Mr. Dalligold whispered. "We're about to be swarmed."

"I will consent to a recess," Mr. Suplard announced, and crashed his gavel on the podium.

✦ A Long Journey Home ✦

Ten telegrams were set on a heavy oak table in the Elk Horn Room. Archer stood in the corner with Mr. Dalligold, watching an unending line of Society members cycle past them and waiting to see his friends. He still hadn't had a chance to speak with his grandparents. When Mr. Suplard crashed the gavel to suspend the meeting, he and Mr. Dalligold were immediately surrounded. But Mr. Dalligold never left Archer's side.

Beatrice Lune approached the table. Her nose crinkled as she smiled at Archer. A moment later, Oliver and Kana rushed in, laughing and looking like the best of friends.

"You made it!" Archer said.

"We didn't think Mr. Mullfort would," Oliver replied, with quite a spring in his step. "We thought he might have a heart attack."

"He's *really* out of shape," Kana agreed. "But he did keep up all the way to the Grand Hall."

"*You* were in the Grand Hall?"

"On the stage, actually," Oliver said. "It was a bit awkward. Mr. Suplard certainly wasn't happy. We didn't realize the door led to the stage until we were already through it. Mr. Mullfort shot in after us."

"And you'll never guess who was on the stand, Archer," Kana said. "It was Mr. Bray! He was testifying about the journal. Then Mr. Mullfort pulled a new journal from his pocket and held it up."

"But I thought Mr. Mullfort took Mr. Bray."

"*We* took Mr. Bray," Mr. Dalligold said. Archer had forgotten he was there. "Once the news of the forged journal leaked, we had to keep him safe. Mr. Mullfort showed up that same evening, broke into the shop, and pocketed another journal. It was our mistake. But now that you're in good hands, Archer, I must see to a few things before this Inquiry is brought to a close." He smiled at them in an odd way. "I must also check in on two friends who were nearly run over earlier this evening."

They all went bright red.

"We can explain," Archer said.

"I look forward to it," Mr. Dalligold replied, still smiling as he made for the door.

"Where's Adélaïde?" Kana asked.

"There she is." Oliver waved furiously.

Adélaïde limped past the table, staring at the telegrams. Oliver gave her a hug, then looked embarrassed about it.

"Did something happen to your other leg?" he asked casually.

"It's a long story," she replied, eyeing him. "But I'm glad to see you're still alive, too, *Ollie*." Oliver soured. Adélaïde smiled. "Not feeling the Doxical Powder anymore?"

The Doxical Powder had indeed worn off during the chase, but if Oliver said that, he might not be able to explain the hug.

"Where did you find them, Archer?" Adélaïde continued.

"In Mr. Birthwhistle's office. The place Mr. Mullfort had already checked and wouldn't check again."

"Speak of the devil," Oliver said.

Mr. Birthwhistle strolled into the Elk Horn Room as though he hadn't a care in the world, waving and shaking hands as he made his way to Archer.

"On behalf of the Society, Archer," Mr. Birthwhistle said with a serene smile, "I would like to thank you for preventing us from making a terrible mistake."

"Why are you *thanking* him?" Oliver asked. "He just proved you're guilty."

Mr. Birthwhistle seemed genuinely surprised. "You mean he proved *Mr. Mullfort* is guilty?" he asked, rubbing his beard.

"Both of you," Kana said, pointing to the telegrams.

"If I'm not mistaken," Mr. Birthwhistle replied, glancing at the table, "*my* name isn't anywhere on those."

Oliver, Adélaïde, and Kana turned to Archer, but he wasn't going to explain it now.

"Of course it's clear Mr. Mullfort was working with *someone*," Mr. Birthwhistle continued.

"We know it was *you*," Archer said. "You buried them in Greenhouse Four and then moved them to your desk."

Mr. Birthwhistle held out his hands as though expecting them to put him in cuffs. "Do you see any dirt? They look perfectly clean to me."

"They're only clean thanks to Mr. Mullfort," Archer said. "You *used* him."

Mr. Birthwhistle's face froze.

"*My dear boy*, as the former Director of Transport, I can assure you there are *many* items one *uses* to ensure a successful expedition. Take a life raft as an example. Your grandparents survived the iceberg thanks, in part, to a life raft. I'm told *you* once survived a pack of tigers thanks to a life raft. If I'm not mistaken, you bought that very life raft from Mr. Mullfort. I find that rather amusing. I've always thought Mr. Mullfort *himself* would make a *fine* life raft."

Mr. Birthwhistle smoothed his vest and straightened his already perfect tie.

"Now that's *quite* enough for this evening. Tomorrow is a new day and with it, new opportunities. I hope you will join us. The Society will greatly benefit from having a Greenhorn as *clever* as you."

"Clever, yes," Mr. Suplard said, waddling over with papers and folders. "But we mustn't tell *lies*, Master Helmsley." He turned to Mr. Birthwhistle. "One of my Deputies received an anonymous tip. Mr. Mullfort hid the communications in Greenhouse Four. We found the hole and the tin."

"Do we know *why* he did it?" Mr. Birthwhistle asked, placing a concerned hand on Mr. Suplard's shoulder.

"*Money.* And this is *precisely* why I've said that the betting on vanished members *must* end. We have no leads on the accomplice, but my department has already begun investigating." Mr. Suplard's gaze sharpened. "And I don't believe I'm out of line when I say, in the future, you are *not* to speak to *any* newspaper until my department has all the facts. The Society is of many minds, but when our president speaks, it *must* reflect the whole."

Mr. Birthwhistle bowed slightly. "I do apologize, Mr. Suplard. But you know it was never my ambition to become the Society's president. I've devoted much of my life to the Order of Magellan."

"It's a relief to hear you say that." Mr. Suplard sighed. "I was afraid I'd have to suggest it myself. Had you not been so public about everything . . . Regardless, yes, your decision must be announced."

Mr. Birthwhistle frowned. Archer saw it. They all saw it. Mr. Birthwhistle actually frowned.

"What decision?"

"Your resignation, of course," Mr. Suplard said, moving to the door. Mr. Birthwhistle hurried after him. "Your lack of discretion was troubling, but this decision reflects well on you. I will notify our members when the Inquiry is brought to a close."

Adélaïde, Kana, and Oliver smiled at one another. Archer didn't. Neither did Benjamin, who'd followed his father into the room and now stood before him. Benjamin pushed his leafy hair out of his eyes.

"Why is everyone saying you claimed to find those telegrams inside my father's desk?" he asked, breathing heavily.

"That's where they were, Benjamin," Archer said.

"You're lying!" Benjamin nearly shouted. "They were found in the hole in Greenhouse Four. It was all Mr. Mullfort's doing, and you told me you didn't find anything. Why are you trying to blame my father?"

Archer didn't know what to say.

"My father was right," Benjamin said, shaking his head. "You *are* like your grandparents."

"Mr. Mullfort was only doing what your father told him to do," Archer tried. "He met with your father before the forgery was discovered. You must see the connection."

"Mr. Mullfort was getting the business records for Strait of Magellan. My father doesn't even like him. He kicked Mr. Mullfort out of his order. And even though my father had no reason to feel guilty, he gave Strait of Magellan to Mr. Mullfort. That's who my father is, Archer. He's generous. He's not a murderer."

"That's not true, Benjamin. He—"

But Archer fell silent. He wasn't sure what it was exactly, but he suddenly saw a resemblance between Benjamin and his father. Yet as cold as Benjamin's eyes had become, colder still were his final two words.

"Prove it."

Benjamin stormed out of the Elk Horn Room. Archer wanted to chase after him, but there was nothing he could say. If he were in Benjamin's shoes, he'd think he was lying too. He turned to his friends. No one had anything to say.

Archer's spirits lifted when his grandparents entered the room. He hadn't seen either smile so wide since the day they'd arrived home. Grandma Helmsley crouched before him and licked her finger to clean a bit of greenhouse dirt from his forehead.

"Words are never enough," she said. "But for now, I want you *all* to know you have our deepest gratitude."

Grandpa Helmsley's pale green eyes sparkled with pride as he sized up Archer's baggy Greenhorn uniform. "I believe we have two options, Archer. We'll either have to grow you as quickly as we can, or find you one that's a better fit."

"That's for another day," Grandma Helmsley said, rubbing Archer's shoulders gratefully. "For now, we must get you all home. Your parents must be worried sick."

Archer had completely forgotten about his mother. "She's going to . . . when I escaped in the dumbwaiter . . . her face."

"*Dumbwaiter!*" Grandpa Helmsley roared. "Now *there's* a story I'm looking forward to hearing!"

"We're ready to go," Cornelius said, suddenly appearing, covered in snow and grease. "I've loaded the delivery truck into mine."

"Thank you, Cornelius," Grandma Helmsley replied. "And do be careful out there. Take it *slow*. Get them home safely. And Archer, we'll be home as soon as the dirt settles."

⋆ Cornelius Takes It Slow ⋆

Archer, Adélaïde, Oliver, and Kana peered up at the Society from the backseat of Cornelius's truck. Snow was still falling, but less so.

"Will they turn Mr. Mullfort over to the authorities?" Adélaïde asked.

"That's not how we handle things," Cornelius explained. "We have our Code. A prison cell is unusually cruel for an explorer—even a shoddy explorer. But don't you worry about

Mr. Mullfort. He'll have plenty of time to think on what he's done. Might even turn him straight in the end."

"I can't believe Mr. Birthwhistle got away with it," Oliver sighed.

"Got away with it?" Cornelius repeated. "What did that pelican get away with? Whispers say he's stepping down from the presidency. Of course he didn't get caught. But that doesn't mean there aren't other consequences."

"What other consequences?" Kana asked.

"Birthwhistle has surrounded himself with a shady flock. He didn't care two sticks about Mr. Mullfort, and the reverse was true, too. Can you imagine that? Having no friends you cared about more than yourself? I can't think of a worse punishment."

"I can," Oliver grumbled. "And it would be a lot more satisfying."

Cornelius laughed heartily. "You only say that because you have what I'm talking about. You stick your necks out for one another."

The truck rumbled over a bridge.

"That's my opinion anyway. I still can't believe you four braved this storm in that jalopy. I don't mean that insultingly, of course. My ship's a jalopy, too. You'll have to come down to Rosewood Port. I'll take you for a ride around the coast. We'll go to Amber Hollow lighthouse. It's a small island. Very peaceful. I'll bring sandwiches. We'll make a day of it. Though

I should warn you about my ship. It has a tendency to . . ."

Cornelius went on talking as they drove off into the waning storm. Archer had never heard him speak so much. He liked it. He liked Cornelius. And though he tried his best to pay attention, the trouble was that, unlike the delivery truck, the Society vehicle was very warm and very comfortable and for the first time in a long time, Archer felt perfectly safe. Oliver, Adélaïde, and Kana must have felt the same way. They were already asleep. Archer fought it, but eventually he too closed his eyes.

◆ AMAURY THE REGRETTABLE ◆

When Archer opened his eyes again, they were parked outside Belmont Café. The delivery truck had been unloaded, and Adélaïde was standing in the snow before a desperately confused Amaury.

"I don't know why I let you . . . I know I'm overworked, but . . ." Amaury scratched his forehead. "I'm sorry, Adie. I don't what got into me."

"I do," Adélaïde replied, unable to look at him. "And I'm the one who must apologize."

The two stepped inside the café.

"We'll bring Amaury a box of pastries tomorrow," Oliver said, staring droopy eyed over Archer's shoulder. "*Normal* pastries."

"What was it like?" Archer asked. "Doxical Powder. Adélaïde said you ate it by mistake?"

Oliver glanced at Kana to make sure she was still asleep. "I knew I'd eaten it," he explained. "I planned it. Kana was right. I thought I'd be more help if I didn't worry so much. But it was strange—like my normal self was stuck inside, watching my opposite self."

"What you did with Mr. Mullfort was brilliant."

Oliver grinned. "I still can't believe I did that."

"I'm not sure Adélaïde liked your opposite."

Oliver's grin widened. "Is *that* why she almost drove the delivery truck into the canal? I thought it might be the wind, but it looked intentional."

Archer gently nudged Kana when they reached her house. Kana's eyes flickered open and she sat up, yawning.

"I'm glad my wish is finally over," she said, tucking her hair behind her ear. "The whole thing was beginning to feel like a curse. And I'm sorry, Archer."

Archer didn't have to say anything. Kana understood.

"I'll see you at school," Oliver said. "Well, you'll probably see me first."

Kana giggled and was gone.

The truck roared to Willow Street. Oliver thanked Cornelius and jumped down. Cornelius inspected Archer before letting him leave. "I haven't gotten any grease on you, have I? Good. Don't want your mother screaming again. That was a heck of an entrance, by the way, Archer. In the Grand Hall, I mean. Beatrice Lune and I were quietly cheering you. And I meant it before. Come to Rosewood Port. I'll teach you how to sail."

"I'd like that, Cornelius," Archer replied. "And thank you."

Cornelius sped off.

"Maybe you should slip your mother a little Doxical Powder," Oliver suggested, staring at the plywood now covering the hole in the front of Helmsley House. "It might make things a little easier."

After parting ways, Archer waited for Oliver to step inside the Glubs' house before he entered his. The phone rang as he was taking his boots off, and he peeked around the corner. His parents were in the sitting room. His father answered the phone, his mother hovering nearby. She was covered in snow. Had she gotten lost in the blizzard searching for him?

"It's the Glubs," Mr. Helmsley said. "Oliver just showed up."

"What about Archer? Is he there, too?"

Archer took a breath and stepped into the room, braced for lots of shouting. And while Mrs. Helmsley did look ready to shout lots of things, to Archer's surprise, she hugged him instead.

"Now into the kitchen, Archer. We both need a hot drink." She eyed his baggy Greenhorn uniform. "And a long talk."

"We *all* need a talk," Mr. Helmsley agreed, and followed them in.

✦ Digging Out of the Storm ✦

The final days of the winter holiday were a whirlwind. Once Rosewood dug itself out from the storm, the restoration of Helmsley House began. Oliver and Adélaïde sat on Archer's bed, amid the noise of drills and hammers, staring glumly at his scarlet trunk.

"Do you know where you're moving?" Adélaïde asked.

"Hopefully it won't be too far away," Oliver sighed.

Archer let their disappointment swell before a smile betrayed him.

It had taken Mr. Helmsley multiple cups of coffee and many hours to coax Archer's mother into the idea of remaining at Helmsley House. And while she was by no means thrilled, after hearing that the man behind the Helmsley Curse had been caught, she'd finally relented, consoled by the fact that Archer would return to the Button Factory and remain under Mr. Churnick's guidance.

"It's a shame," Mrs. Helmsley had mumbled, tossing a paper listing home options into the trash. "That small island sounded promising."

Archer and his father exchanged a glance. Neither smiled. But they wanted to.

Now Oliver and Adélaïde's glum expressions evaporated when Archer lifted the lid of his scarlet trunk and showed them that it was empty. They punched his arms and laughed as he explained.

"We have to celebrate!" Oliver said, pulling his free-sweet-a-day card from his pocket.

"I'll join you later," Adélaïde replied, following them to the bedroom door. "I'm helping Amaury train three new waiters. They're hopeless with espresso machines. What time is your grandparents' reinstatement?"

"Cornelius is picking us up at six."

"Did you hear about the *Chronicle*?" Oliver asked as they went downstairs. "My father thinks they might collapse. But he's been flooded with new subscribers. Hopefully this means we can fix my radiator."

The *Rosewood Chronicle* had been rather understated and unreliable about the whole situation.

ROSEWOOD CHRONICLE
SIZING UP AN ICEBERG IS DIFFICULT

Mr. Glub had been far less subtle.

THE DOLDRUMS PRESS
EXPLORERS VINDICATED!

⋆ SECRETS ⋆

That evening, on the other side of Rosewood, hidden deep in the warehouses of Barrow's Bay, there was much hullabaloo going on at the Society. To the chagrin of every Rosewood hotel concierge, all of the Society members were still in the city.

The Grand Hall was overflowing during Archer's grandparents' reinstatement. Cheers rang from the Order of Orion, but not many from anywhere else. The Order of Magellan was especially silent. Mr. Mullfort had shouted that he'd been paid to do Mr. Birthwhistle's bidding, but everyone thought he was trying to dodge the blame. Even Captain Lemurn and his crew of five said they knew nothing of Mr. Birthwhistle's involvement. They confessed to being paid and led by one single man: crooked Eustace Mullfort. All seven were roughly escorted from the hall. Mr. Birthwhistle was nowhere to be seen during the proceedings. And while no one knew who the next president would be, Archer heard one name whispered more frequently than any other.

"If we do become Greenhorns," Oliver said, poking a broiled elk tongue, "I'm going to talk to someone about this spread. My mother should be in charge of this."

Mr. Dalligold cleared his throat. The trio hadn't noticed he was also scanning the banquet table. "Oh, fried grasshoppers!" He filled his plate and offered one to Oliver. Oliver politely declined.

Mr. Dalligold stood beside them, crunching on grasshoppers and gazing around the hall.

"I want to thank you three," he said. "You've done more for our Society than you even realize. But tell me, Archer. Why do you keep staring at Benjamin?"

Archer was silent a moment, his eyes fixed on his former roommate, who was seated with the other Greenhorns. "I don't know what to do," he finally said. "Benjamin thinks I lied. He won't even look at me now."

Mr. Dalligold nodded thoughtfully, crunching away.

"I'm sorry to say that, for the time being, there's nothing you can do, Archer. Losing a friend is never easy. But it might help if you try to see Mr. Birthwhistle the same way Benjamin does. It's only natural that Benjamin should trust his *father*. That's not so difficult to understand, is it?"

"But Mr. Birthwhistle *did* try to kill Archer's grandparents," Oliver said.

"*We* know that," Mr. Dalligold replied. "All Benjamin knows is that you tried to frame his father. It's a difficult situation. But I don't believe Benjamin is your enemy, Archer. And while things *do* have a tendency to get worse before they get better, I hope you'll remember that."

Archer rubbed his thumb against his palm and looked up at Mr. Dalligold. "My grandfather said Mr. Birthwhistle is keeping many secrets from the Society. Why? What does he want?"

"Mr. Birthwhistle is a meticulous man. And a *gifted* explorer. He's fond of the natural world because the natural world is just that—*meticulous*. People, on the other hand, are messy. Often times, irrational. Mr. Birthwhistle has never liked that. I can't tell you what I don't fully understand, Archer, but I suspect Mr. Birthwhistle would like to see our Society become something it must never be—a single-minded force, united under him, all members working for the Order of Magellan. Mr. Spinler's work could've helped with that. I'm told you three had an interesting experience with Doxical Powder?"

Oliver smiled. Adélaïde didn't. "I turned someone into a monster," she explained.

Mr. Dalligold's eyebrows went up. "*Yes*. Mr. Spinler's work is powerful. Had Archer's grandfather not revealed it, Mr. Birthwhistle could have manipulated any of us without anyone guessing what was happening."

"Is Mr. Spinler out there?" Oliver asked.

Mr. Dalligold pointed to a funny little man, quite rotund and jolly, with a face like a cherry, perhaps from having drunk one pint too many.

"He doesn't look dangerous," Oliver said.

"That was the problem. Mr. Spinler wouldn't step on an ant. You'll see that for yourselves when you become Greenhorns. He'll teach you fascinating things. I'm not sure how Mr. Birthwhistle convinced him to keep his work secret, but I imagine, being a man who wouldn't step on an ant, Mr. Spinler didn't think it would ever be used for harm."

"He must be the most famous Society member," Adélaïde said, watching as Mr. Spinler, laughing loudly, nearly fell off his chair.

Mr. Dalligold smiled in his odd way. "Wigstan Spinler is *one* member. The Society has *many* explorers and *many* wonders that are still unknown to the world. It's not every day one receives an iceberg in the post, is it, Archer? It's a funny thing about ice. It has a tendency to melt. Even in winter. And now that Mr. Birthwhistle's attempt to banish your grandparents has failed, I suspect Rosewood's *peculiar* snow accumulation will soon dissipate as well."

Mr. Dalligold turned to refill his plate. Archer, Oliver, and Adélaïde stared at one another, certain that couldn't mean what it sounded like it meant.

"Welcome home, Mr. Dalligold!" Darby called, rushing over and grabbing Archer's arm. "My parents are *thrilled* you're back. And if they're right, you won't be *Mr.* Dalligold for much longer."

Mr. Dalligold's smile grew very warm. "It's lovely to see you again, Darby. But would you mind taking charge of Archer and his friends? Show them a good time. Tonight's a celebration. And they haven't done much celebrating."

"Come sit with the Greenhorns! All of you! We'll flick fried grasshoppers at Fledger!" Darby pointed to Adélaïde's leg. "And remember, it was a *crocodile*."

✦ LITTLE TIME TO LOAF ✦

Archer, Oliver, and Adélaïde followed Grandma and Grandpa Helmsley up the steps to Helmsley House. His grandparents still hadn't said anything about Archer becoming a Greenhorn, but he knew it was only a matter of time. He'd spotted his grandfather grinning and whistling while sneaking three trunks with Greenhorn emblems into the house. He'd also eavesdropped on a conversation, certain his grandparents stood no chance of convincing his mother, but there'd been a fifth voice in the discussion. A regal voice. And even Mrs. Helmsley respected Mr. Dalligold.

"What happens now?" Archer asked as they hung coats on the caribou's antlers.

"You're at the end of your beginning, Archer," Grandpa Helmsley said. "Your grandmother and I are at the beginning of our end."

Grandma Helmsley smiled and put a hand on his grandfather's shoulder. "Nearly twelve years ago, your grandfather and I realized our final adventure had begun. And while we're not sure what it is just yet, we can say it has a nice ring to it."

"A very nice ring to it," Grandpa Helmsley added.

Oliver whispered in Archer's ear. "Did you understand that?"

Archer did, but didn't say so. His grandparents thanked him once again with their eyes and stepped down the hall.

"Let's make a fire," Archer said.

He led Oliver and Adélaïde to the rooftop, where a fire was already crackling. And next to it sat Kana. She waved as Oliver and Adélaïde joined her. Archer went to the chimney and grabbed two gifts he'd hidden behind it.

"I've had some loafing time," Archer explained, handing them to Oliver and Adélaïde. "I know Christmas is over, but I wanted to thank you. For everything."

Archer sat down beside Kana. She smiled and stuck her hand into her pocket. Tucked inside was the gift she'd already received from Archer—a jade elephant house that had once belonged to him.

Oliver wasted no time tearing open his gift. It was a book.

Relvina Rummroll's
THE ART OF
Making Chocolate

"I promise it's not secretly a vacuum cleaner," Archer said.

"I'm going to make my first batch tonight!" Oliver cracked the spine. "Thank you!"

"I'm not the guinea pig," Adélaïde said.

"You were trickier," Archer explained as she tore the wrappings off hers. "Kana and I went to every shop on Howling Bloom Street. We saw this in Trumm and Drumm."

"We had a good feeling about it," Kana added.

Chest of
GAGS & PRANKS

"I'm not sure I understand," Adélaïde said, peeking inside the wooden chest.

Archer and Kana bobbed their heads at Oliver. *Torture him.* A smile stretched across Adélaïde's face. This was not lost on Oliver. He set aside his book and grabbed a mound of snow.

"This will soon be a snowball," he explained with a grin. "I suggest all of you make one as well."

"No faces," Adélaïde warned, scooping up snow herself.

Archer and Kana quickly did the same.

With snowballs ready, the four stood up, waiting to see who would strike first. And in the flickering firelight, no one noticed Adélaïde concealing both hands behind her. Archer and Oliver ducked when she let a snowball fly. It whizzed over their heads. They took their eyes off her to smile at each other. Kana saw their mistake. Adélaïde had a secret. And it was no longer behind her back.

NICHOLAS GANNON

studied art and design and held a number of odd jobs before becoming a full-time author and illustrator. He has lived in Tennessee, Minnesota, and upstate New York. He now resides in Brooklyn, and he can sometimes be found eavesdropping on curious conversations at the Explorers Club.

www.nicholasjgannon.com

FOLLOW NICHOLAS GANNON ON

Explore these books by
NICHOLAS GANNON

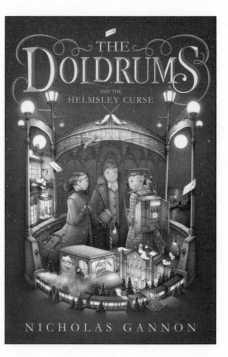

Greenwillow Books
An Imprint of HarperCollinsPublishers

www.harpercollinschildrens.com